"Grab the crystal. Let's go!"

Annja was happy to see that Orta was already picking up the manuscript sheets and replacing them in their protective case. Grabbing her backpack, Annja quickly shoved her gear into it and pulled it on. Orta looked at her. "There are more of these men?"

"Yes." Annja pulled the ear-throat mic into place and clipped the walkie-talkie to the ammo belt. A deep, controlled voice spoke at the other end, demanding that Fox Six reply. She ignored the command and nodded to Orta. "You know the campus layout. Which is the quickest way out?"

"Follow me." Orta headed to the back door.

Krauzer had the crystal wrapped in one arm like an oversize football and was reaching for the other machine pistol lying on the floor.

Taking a quick step, Annja kicked the weapon under the table and out of Krauzer's reach.

He whirled on her, his features taut with rage and fear. "What are you doing?"

"Trying to keep Orta and me alive," Annja said. "You're a movie director, not a commando."

"And you think you're some kind of action hero?"

Annja glanced at the two unconscious attackers. "I've got experience with this sort of thing."

Titles in this series:

ROGUE Angel

Alex Archer

MYSTIC WARRIOR

A GOLD EAGLE BOOK FROM

WORLDWIDE®

TORONTO • NEW YORK • LONDON
AMSTERDAM • PARIS • SYDNEY • HAMBURG
STOCKHOLM • ATHENS • TOKYO • MILAN
MADRID • WARSAW • BUDAPEST • AUCKLAND

Recycling programs
for this product may
not exist in your area.

First edition November 2015

ISBN-13: 978-0-373-62177-4

Mystic Warrior

Special thanks and acknowledgment to
Mel Odom for his contribution to this work.

Printed in U.S.A.

THE
LEGEND

...THE ENGLISH COMMANDER TOOK
JOAN'S SWORD AND RAISED IT HIGH.

The broadsword, plain and unadorned,
gleamed in the firelight. He put the tip against
the ground and his foot at the center of the blade.
The broadsword shattered, fragments falling
into the mud. The crowd surged forward,
peasant and soldier, and snatched the shards
from the trampled mud. The commander tossed
the hilt deep into the crowd.
Smoke almost obscured Joan, but she continued
praying till the end, until finally the flames climbed
her body and she sagged against the restraints.

Joan of Arc died that fateful day in France,
but her legend and sword are reborn...

PROLOGUE

Bourthes, Nord-Pas-de-Calais
Kingdom of the Franks
752 AD

Pepin the Younger, also called the Short behind his back, sat at the head of the large wooden table under the wheel of lighted candles and struggled to contain his anger at his "guest."

Childeric III sat sulking at the other end of the table. Like all of the Merovingian royal family, Childeric wore his bright red hair in long, flowing locks. People often whispered that the hair contained the power of the Merovingians.

This night, Childeric didn't look powerful. Any mystical might perhaps contained in his hair was not working to salvage his fate. Pepin had already sealed that.

The events of the past few weeks, and the knowledge of what was to become of him, had worn heavily on Childeric. In the beginning he had been hopeful, certain that he would remain king. Now those hopes had dwindled.

Like a truculent child, he sat at the table and refused to eat.

Pepin gestured with his knife. "Come, Childeric, you must eat. The road to Saint Bertin is long and wearying. You must keep up your strength."

"Must I?" Childeric braced both his hands on the table and made as though to rise. "I am still king, and you presume to tell me what to do like I was some idiot?"

To the king's left, his son, Theuderic, placed a restraining hand on the older man's shoulder. "Father, do not engage him," Theuderic whispered. "He seeks only to antagonize you."

Pepin toyed with his knife and smiled. Death would have been easier and was probably preferable to what Pepin intended for his two prisoners.

"I will not sup with a betrayer," Childeric said hoarsely.

"You have eaten with me on plenty of occasions before this. *My lord.*" Pepin waved the protest away. "We are still two men who seek to break our fast. I thought you would enjoy eating indoors for a change after the meals we have suffered upon the road. This inn is a pleasant change from the days of hard winter travel we've endured."

"I am your lord! I am your king and your master. God will punish you for what you do."

"Might I remind you that God does not favor *you* overmuch these days?" Pepin gestured to the papal representatives sent by Pope Zachary who were seated on the other side of the long table.

"Sacrilege. You have bought off the Greek scoundrel who pretends to listen to holy words! You cannot buy off God, you wretched creature, and you doom your eternal soul to play at such games."

Lifting his wine goblet, Pepin drank to give himself a moment to control his anger. He focused on enjoying the power he wielded. Carefully, he replaced the goblet on the table. "For eleven years, I have toiled as mayor of the palace, caring for your household and running your kingdom while you took no note of the business affairs and trade agreements that kept our country running. You were nothing more than a figurehead, as was your father before you.

"The time has come for the true power to step forward from the shadows. I shall be crowned king, and I will rule as I have always done. Only now I shall be recognized."

Pepin glared at the man. "There is only one thing that I require from you."

"I will give you nothing. I will fight you until my dying breath."

Pepin shrugged. "I can ensure that release from this mortal coil is a long time in coming, with plenty of pain before."

Theuderic spoke before his father could, and the younger man's words cracked with fear. "What could you possibly still want from us, you monster? You have already taken all that we have."

Childeric placed a hand against his son's chest, perhaps afraid of the wrath Pepin would visit on him.

"In all the years I have managed your affairs, I have never found the hidden treasure of the Merovingian kings." Pepin swirled the contents of his wine goblet.

Theuderic looked to his father in confusion. Childeric sat back in his seat and his eyes shone.

"I have listened to legends and rumors about this treasure." Pepin wanted to remain silent, but he found he could not still his tongue. "Before me, my father, may God rest his soul, gave his life in service to your family. During all that time, he heard bits and rumors about the mysterious object, an unholy and unwholesome thing of dark magic hammered on a forge in hell, that protected the Merovingian kings from their enemies."

"You think I will tell you?" Childeric smiled slightly.

Pepin paused to sip more wine. "I do not think such a treasure exists. Do you know what saved the Merovingian kings from the bloodthirsty Saxons? From the caliphate's men at the Battle of Tours?" He paused, and when there was no answer forthcoming, he slapped his hand against the table. "My father did that. And he bent Frisia, Alemannia and Bavaria to his will." He banged his fist against the table once more. "*My* father. Not some demon-spawned thing your family has claimed to hold captive."

The innkeeper, a short, thin man with a long face and deep-set eyes, stepped into the dining hall. Other men stood behind the innkeeper. The scuff of their boots announced them, and the rattle of their armor and weapons gave them away.

Pepin sat for a moment, frozen in surprise that there would be any who would dare such aggression against him.

"I am sorry, my lord." The innkeeper wrung his hands, then lurched forward as a blade burst through his chest. Blood spilled down his quivering lips as he struggled to stand. Then the soldier behind the dead man kicked the corpse forward, freeing his blade.

A dozen armored men swarmed into the dining hall. Their drawn blades flashed in the firelight.

Pepin heaved himself from his seat and freed his sword from the scabbard beside the table. He was not a gifted fighting man, but his father had trained him in the way of the sword.

Steel shrieked and bit, and the screams of dying men filled the dining hall. In mere moments, blood covered the stone floor and made footing treacherous. The attackers fought with skill and fury, but Pepin had chosen some of his best warriors to accompany him on his journey with the deposed king and the prince.

With his back nearly to the wall, Pepin blocked another swing, then reached to his waist for the long knife he carried there. He fisted it and turned aside another blow, then slid beneath the bigger man's right arm as the heavy sword cut the air over his head. Before the man could turn, Pepin thrust his knife between the man's ribs in the chain mail opening under his arm.

Even though the man was already dying, Pepin shoved

the knife into the man's throat and robbed him of the last few seconds of his life. Breathing hard, Pepin studied the room. Though his men had been surprised, they had recovered quickly. Corpses now littered the dining hall, and only a few of them were his soldiers.

Childeric knelt on the floor and bled profusely from his nose while two soldiers with drawn blades flanked him. The soon-to-be-deposed king swayed unsteadily and looked disoriented. Theuderic lay on the floor nearby with a sword to his throat, his eyes round with fear.

"Do you see?" Childeric gazed balefully at Pepin. "My people will never accept you as their king. They will fight for me. This night or some day later, they will kill you."

"These men?" Pepin spit on the corpse nearest him. "These are not warriors who sought to aid you. These men were brigands hoping only to loot who they presumed to be only wealthy travelers, not soldiers. You cling to false hopes, Childeric, and it does not become you."

"Liar!"

Pepin strode over to Childeric. The king struggled to get to his feet, but the soldiers beside him held him in check.

Pepin sheathed his sword and the clang of metal against metal suddenly filled the hall. "I grow weary of your lack of acceptance of reality." He held the bloody knife before his prisoner. Pepin knotted a fist in Childeric's hair. "Tell me what I want to know and I will suffer you to live."

Childeric glared up at him. "Never. You will live in fear of the Merovingian power coming back to strike you down."

"Father!" Theuderic tried to push away the sword holding him in place. Instead, the blade bit into his unprotected chest and he lay there helplessly.

"I will not live in fear. And I will have your secrets. If they exist."

Childeric locked his eyes on Pepin's. "For everything,

runt, there is a time. God made this so. You will regret everything you have done."

For just a moment as he looked into the other man's gaze, Pepin felt the cold breath of fear.

1

Present day

Annja Creed sat braced in the passenger seat of the burnt-orange Lamborghini and tried to divide her attention between the GPS screen on the dashboard and the late-afternoon traffic in West Los Angeles as they peeled around yet another corner. Traffic flashed by, though the number of cars was sparser than she had thought it would be. Los Angeles gridlocked a lot, and the streets were often choked with stalled vehicles.

Of course, their luck could end around the next corner, which was coming up much too quickly. She pulled her chestnut hair back and tied it in a ponytail. Dressed in charcoal pants, a dark green pullover and a short-waisted jacket, Annja had been prepared to spend the day at the Hollywood lot where she was currently consulting on a movie.

Riding kamikaze through LA traffic hadn't been on her itinerary.

The voice streaming from the GPS was a steamy contralto Annja hadn't heard before, but it sounded familiar and comforting.

"Steven, you need to make a right turn in one hundred feet."

The voice had to be a custom package. That was something Steven Krauzer would want as a member of Hollywood's elite director-producers.

"Turn now, Steven." The car slung around the corner and the tires shrieked and slipped wildly before grabbing traction again. Annja's seat belt tightened around her. She was safe, for the moment, but certainly not comfortable. Especially with an insane person behind the wheel.

On his best days, Steven Krauzer was believed to be not quite in touch with the real world. This wasn't a good day at all.

Several more car horns blared in protest as the Lamborghini powered through the turn, holding contact with the street through what had to be the thinnest layer of rubber. A cab loomed before them, growing larger as they approached. For a moment Annja saw the Lamborghini's volatile color reflected in the shiny chrome bumper, but Krauzer yanked the wheel to the right, went up on the cracked sidewalk momentarily, then pressed harder on the accelerator. "Did anyone ever tell you that I trained to race at NASCAR?" Krauzer sat grinning confidently in the driver's seat, belted in by a five-point system.

"No." Annja caught herself lifting her foot for a brake pedal that wasn't there. With effort, she put her foot back on the floor.

In his early thirties, and one of Hollywood's wunderkinder as a child of famous parents—his father a powerful producer of movies and his mother an international film star—Steven Krauzer never really had time for anyone else in his life. He was lean and muscular, and he trained in a gym with near-fanatical devotion. He wore Chrome Hearts Kufannaw II sunglasses over dark eyes, and his black chinstrap beard matched his short-cropped hair. His jeans were custom-made and full of holes, and the tailored beige Carhartt men's work shirt gave him that everyman look he cultivated. He was egocentric, prideful and a prima donna, but he tried to put himself out there as just one of the guys. Krauzer's image was as much a production as any movie he'd ever directed.

"In one hundred twenty feet, turn left onto West Pico Boulevard, Steven."

Krauzer was already sailing through the intersection. He missed colliding with a city bus by inches. "You know," Annja said, "there's really no rush to find Melanie."

For a moment, the cool, cocky composure Krauzer displayed evaporated. He curled his left hand into a fist and banged it on the steering wheel.

"Melanie Harp *stole* from me! She took that scrying crystal because she knew I was going to need it for the scenes today. She's trying to destroy my film."

"She probably doesn't even know the theft has been discovered." The realization that the scrying crystal was missing had occurred only a little over twenty minutes ago. Since Annja had been hired as an expert on the authenticity of the props, Krauzer had demanded she come with him to find the woman he believed had taken the scrying crystal.

"Ha!" Krauzer reached down and flicked the gearshift, skidding through another corner and nearly locking bumpers with a delivery truck that pulled hastily to the side. "That just goes to show that you might know a lot about anthropology, but you don't know squat about Hollywood."

Archaeology.

But she didn't press the issue, because it would only serve to distract the director. Since she'd been in LA serving as a consultant on his movie, Krauzer hadn't paid attention to her anyway.

Krauzer hadn't even known about her show, *Chasing History's Monsters*. She'd been requested as a consultant on the film by one of the producers. When Krauzer had discovered she was something of a celebrity herself, he hadn't been happy. He'd warned her about becoming a distraction to the filming. What he had meant was she shouldn't steal any of the the director's thunder.

Chasing History's Monsters had a large international fan base, and Annja enjoyed doing the show. She strove for actual historical authenticity and audiences responded well to her stories. An elf witch's scrying stone, however, was off the beaten path for an archaeologist.

"If you check social media," Krauzer went on, "I'm sure someone has posted about the theft of the elf witch's scrying crystal. Five minutes after Melanie Harp took that thing, you can bet the whole *world* knew. No. We're going to be lucky if she hasn't left town and gone back to wherever it is she's from." He looked at Annja. "Do you know where she's from?"

"No."

Krauzer returned his attention to the streets. "I thought you might have known."

"Why would I know?"

Krauzer shrugged. "She's a girl. You're a girl. Girls talk."

Annja struggled not to take offense at the offhand summation, but it was difficult. She took out her smartphone, entered the security code and studied the viewscreen when it opened up the websites she'd been inspecting.

"What are you doing?" he demanded.

"When we found out the scrying crystal was missing, I programmed in some online movie memorabilia sites to see if the prop showed up there. In case Melanie is trying to sell it."

"The *prop*? Seriously? Just yesterday you were telling me that we might have a real artifact on our hands. You were begging me for a chance to examine it. Now the elf witch's scrying crystal is a *prop*?"

Begging was a strong word. After seeing the crystal briefly in one of the scenes Krauzer had shot the previous day, Annja had been curious about the piece. She wasn't all that invested in the crystal. She'd wanted to see it, but Krauzer had refused, insisting that the crystal had to be locked up when the filming had finally finished. She'd known the director was deliberately throwing his weight around.

Annja hadn't lost any sleep over not getting to see the crystal—even if that seriously hampered the job she'd been paid to come here and do!—but the possibility that it might be authentic kept scratching at her mind. Los Angeles—California in general—was a melting pot of the world's history.

Annja had planned on taking advantage of the movie deal to pursue research into Juan Rodriguez Cabrillo, the Portuguese explorer who had sailed under a Spanish flag to explore the West Coast of North America. Annja had turned up some rumors on the alt.history and alt.archaeology sites she'd wanted to check out while she was in town. And Doug Morrell, her producer on the television show, had wanted her to investigate sightings of "ghost pirates" he'd heard about on some late-night radio show.

The research she'd done on Cabrillo had actually led to her interest in Krauzer's so-called prop, but she hadn't told him that.

And now the scrying crystal had been stolen and might disappear before she got to find out.

"If Melanie took the scrying crystal—" Annja began.

"Which she did!"

"—then she might think of selling it on one of those sites. How much do you think it's worth?"

Krauzer cursed. "Fans are idiots! Do you remember when that comic-book artist, the guy who drew Spider-Man or something, paid over $3 million for a baseball?"

"That was Mark McGwire's seventieth home run in the 1998 season."

"You're a baseball fan?"

Annja shrugged. "I live in Brooklyn."

"Baseball. Bunch of guys standing around waiting for stuff to happen." Krauzer blew a raspberry. "My point is, this comic-book-sketch guy blew the prices for collectible baseballs for a long time. And they're *baseballs*! They sell those *everywhere*. You can write *anybody's* name on them.

But that scrying crystal? That's one of a kind. I made sure of that."

Annja believed it was one of a kind, too. She needed to study it. "If she was smart, she'd sell the crystal back to you."

"Me?"

"You'd pay for it if you had to, and you'd pay a lot. You've got it insured, right?"

"Of course I've got it insured. Do you think I'm some kind of idiot?" Annja ignored the question, certain Krauzer really didn't want to hear her answer.

"Insurance companies routinely pay off on buyback situations."

"This is something you know about?"

"Yes."

"How?" Behind the sunglasses, Krauzer's features knotted up in suspicion.

"Insurance companies have sometimes hired me to verify a certificate of authenticity on objects that were stolen and bought back. Sometimes thieves have created copies of the stolen items and attempt to sell those to insurance companies, doubling down on the original theft."

"That *cannot* happen. I *cannot* shoot this movie with a counterfeit. Do you know what would happen to my reputation if I did something like that? When fans go to see a Steven Krauzer picture, they see a genuine Steven Krauzer picture. There's nothing fake about it!"

Krauzer slammed on the brake hard enough that the seat belt cut into Annja as it held her to the seat. The tortured shriek of shredding rubber echoed through the neighborhood, and the Lamborghini came to a stop half on the street and half on the sidewalk.

Leaning over, Krauzer popped open the glove compartment and took out a nickel-plated revolver with a six-inch barrel. "Let's go."

He opened the car door and got out.

2

Shocked at the sight of the gun and the director's apparent willingness to use it, Annja was a step behind Krauzer as he strode toward the building. She caught up to him as he slid the big pistol in his waistband at his back and covered it up with his shirttail.

"A gun?" Annja asked. "Seriously?"

"Having a gun makes people listen to you."

"Do you even know how to use it?"

"Of course I do." Krauzer shook his head. "I cut my teeth on guns-and-ammo movies. Action stuff. Science fiction. I had to know how to use guns so I could film actors using them. You wouldn't believe how many times directors get it wrong because they don't know how to use a gun and the actors don't know, either. Big case of the blind leading the blind."

"This isn't 'Grand Theft Auto.'"

"That woman stole my scrying crystal and she's delaying my film! She's not smart enough to do that on her own. She has partners. Trust me."

Annja was beginning to think Steven Krauzer lived inside a movie in his head. "Melanie Harp is not a master criminal."

"Exactly my point. She couldn't have thought of this on her own. She had help."

"I don't think she knows any master criminals, either."

"Do you know that for a fact? Because I don't."

Annja didn't bother to argue, because she knew she wouldn't win. She just hoped no one got hurt.

A green awning covered the double-door entrance, which

had seen better days. Gold lettering on the door announced The Wickersham Apartments. The red carpet leading up to the doors was thin and worn.

There was no guard on the door, but another sign promised Security.

An older woman wearing a sundress, a floppy hat and big sunglasses and holding a small dog came through the doors. She wrapped her arms protectively around her pet as Krauzer barreled toward her.

"Don't shut that door," Krauzer barked.

The woman blocked the closing door with her sandaled foot.

Krauzer caught the door, pulled it wide and entered the apartment building.

"Thank you," Annja told the woman.

The woman looked at her conspiratorially and leaned in to whisper, "Is he somebody?"

"He likes to think he is," Annja replied.

Shaking her head, the woman said, "So many people in this town think that. They do one cat-food commercial and they think they're stars." She waved dismissively and continued her walk.

She smiled at the woman, then hurried after Krauzer.

Annja reached the landing with Krauzer and went up the next flight. "Do you know which floor Melanie lives on?"

Krauzer checked his smartphone. "Fourth floor. Apartment F."

"Okay, and if she's there, you're not going to shoot first and ask questions later?"

"I'm not going to shoot unless I have to. I don't want to hurt that crystal."

"THIS COULD ALL be some kind of mistake," Annja said as they stepped into the fourth-floor hallway from the stairwell. The hallway was narrow and poorly lit. Evidently, Melanie

Harp's career had been skidding farther over the edge than the entertainment shows had reported.

"You're saying Melanie *accidentally* stole my scrying crystal?" Krauzer demanded.

"She got cut from the picture—"

"She got cut because she drinks and snorts so much she can't get to work on time. Thankfully, she's not in many of the scenes I've shot so far, so I can just get another actress in. The only reason I hired her in the first place was for the extra publicity having her working for us would bring. You know, entertainment media cruising around to see if Melanie Harp was going to have another meltdown." Krauzer cursed. "I just really didn't expect this. Her agent promised me. The schmuck is definitely gonna hear from me."

"Taking the scrying crystal could be a cry for help."

Krauzer growled irritably and shook his head. "Figures you'd stick up for her."

"I'm *not* sticking up for her."

"Sounds like it to me. You're a girl. She's a girl."

For a moment, Annja thought about drop-kicking Krauzer in a way that would remind him he was *not* a girl. She blew out a calming breath and reminded herself that there was a lot of research she was looking forward to this evening.

And she would definitely get to look at the scrying crystal and satisfy her curiosity about the piece if Melanie had it and was still home.

Krauzer stopped in front of the door to apartment 4F, took the pistol from his waistband and gripped it in his fist. He stood there for a moment, ran his free hand through his hair, let out a quick breath and shook himself. Then he knocked on the door.

There was no answer.

For a moment, Krauzer stood there. Then he looked at Annja. "Why isn't she opening the door?"

"I don't read minds."

He shrugged. "So what would you guess?"

"Maybe she's not home. Maybe she's on her way back to the studio with the scrying crystal and feeling really guilty."

Krauzer thought about that for just a second. "Or maybe she's taking a clever forgery back there to pass off as the real thing."

Annja regretted mentioning anything about insurance companies and counterfeit items.

His attention back on the door, Krauzer banged on the door with his fist. "Melanie! It's Steven Krauzer. I know you're in there! You can't hide from me. Open up. I want my scrying crystal back!"

They could hear movement sounding inside. There were at least two pairs of footfalls.

"See?" Krauzer said, frowning at the door. "Told you she wasn't alone. The mastermind of this whole thing is in there with her."

Krauzer stepped forward and banged on the door again, harder and faster this time. "Melanie! Get out here in the next minute and I'll keep you off the entertainment shows. I'll have the PR people whip up a story that the reason you're no longer in the movie is that you had something else come up. You know how this town works. You start putting a story out there, even if it's a lie, pretty soon everybody has heard about it. Then somebody, if you play your cards right, will actually offer you something."

"I have been offered something, you self-absorbed little Hitler," Melanie called back through the door.

Krauzer gazed at Annja in disbelief. "Did she just call me 'little'?"

Annja ignored the question. "Melanie, it's Annja Creed."

"What are you doing here?"

"We need the scrying crystal."

There was a short pause. "It's not here."

Krauzer kicked the door. "What do you mean it's not here?"

They heard a quick flurry of whispering.

"I mean it's not here unless you pay me for it," Melanie replied.

"I'm not going to pay you for something you stole from me!" Krauzer howled.

"If you want it back, you are."

Krauzer stepped back and kicked the door. The frame splintered as the lock tore free. In the room, Melanie Harp stood next to a beefy bald guy wearing a biker jacket and dirty jeans.

The actress's arms were crossed in front of her defiantly. Her blond hair was piled on her head in a twist that was coming undone and looked as though a surge of electricity had shocked it free. She was underweight, something the makeup people had struggled to deal with, and bags bulged beneath her red eyes, one of which was brown and the other an exotic lavender. Evidently, she'd lost one of her contacts.

"You can't just break into my home," Melanie protested.

Krauzer looked around in disdain. "This dump?"

"Hey," the big bruiser rumbled. He sounded like a cement mixer coming to life. He was in his forties and had scars on his head and cheeks that Annja could see through the graying beard that hung to his chest. He wasn't wearing a shirt under the biker jacket. His jeans were tucked into motorcycle boots. "Don't disrespect the lady."

Krauzer turned to the biker. "Did you help steal my scrying crystal?"

The biker stepped forward. "Hey, man, you stole Melanie's job. I'm just helping her even the score."

"I *gave* her that job, you idiot! I took it back because she can't handle it. She's the one who prefers squalor and nose candy over working. And her taste in boyfriends isn't so great either, evidently."

The biker closed his fists and took another step forward. "Now you're gonna get beat."

Krauzer pointed the pistol at the biker's face. "Keep coming, you big ape."

Melanie closed her brown eye and squinted the lavender one at Krauzer. "Oh my God, Barney! He's got a gun!"

Barney the biker? If Krauzer hadn't been waving the big pistol around, Annja wouldn't have been able to keep from laughing.

Eyes popping, Barney stepped back. "Hey, man. No fair."

Annja knew Krauzer was already in danger of getting arrested for threatening Melanie and her guy, and maybe she was, too, at this point. Getting arrested for felonious assault with a deadly weapon would not sit well with Doug. She also knew that if Krauzer accidentally shot someone, things would get even worse in a hurry.

She moved automatically, trapping Krauzer's gun hand, pinching a nerve in the back of his hand that caused him to release the pistol and catching the weapon before it hit the carpeted floor. She popped the cylinder open, dumped the bullets into her cupped palm and walked over to the window at the back of the living room.

Below the room, a half-filled garbage bin sat open. Annja opened the window, wiped the gun and the bullets clean on the curtain, and dropped them all into the trash. The gun and the rounds disappeared into the discarded debris.

She turned to face the three other people in the room, who stared at her in disbelief.

Krauzer peered out the window and looked apoplectic. "Did you just throw my gun away?"

"Yes," Annja replied. "Way too many things could have happened with you waving it around."

"Well, did you happen to think of the things that could happen since I *don't* have it to wave around?" Krauzer looked back at Barney the biker, who had pulled a ten-inch hunting knife from behind his back.

"I'm gonna cut you, loudmouth." Barney waved the knife as if it was a weaving cobra waiting to strike. "Then you're gonna get that money you owe Melanie."

3

Krauzer cowered back and nearly fell through the open window. Annja caught the director and moved him over in front of the wall and put herself between him and the biker.

"Move," Barney ordered, waving his arm in a serpentine motion.

"I just saved your life when I took the gun away," Annja pointed out.

He scowled at her and maybe there was a little hurt pride in his slit eyes. "If I have to, I'll cut through you to get to him." He continued moving the knife in the air.

Annja grabbed the big man's wrist with one hand and popped him in the throat with the open Y of her other hand. When he stepped back, gagging, she nerve-pinched his hand and let the knife fall to the floor, where it stood embedded upside down.

Barney yanked his hand back. She stood between him and the knife.

Shaking his head, Barney sucked in a breath, then said, "You're gonna be sorry you did that." He'd clearly meant the statement to be intimidating, but his words came out in a high-pitched squeak. He rushed at her, intending to use his size and weight against her.

Annja swept his lead foot as it came down, putting it in front of the other foot so that he tripped himself. At the same time, she grabbed his jacket lapels, twisted tightly to accelerate and direct his fall, and pulled him face-first into the wall hard enough to break the plasterboard.

Without a sound, Barney dropped to the floor unconscious.

Melanie held her open hands to either side of her face. "Did you kill him?"

"No." Annja knelt to unlace one of Barney's boots, intending to use the string to tie him up. She didn't need him waking while she was trying to deal with the other two in the room.

Seeing how the tide had turned, Krauzer started to reach for the knife.

"Don't," Annja warned as she looped the lace around the unconscious biker's wrists.

"You don't get to tell me what to do," Krauzer replied, even as he pulled his hand back from the knife.

"I'm going to do exactly that for the moment." Annja finished tying the biker's hands behind his back and rose.

In the hallway, neighbors stood in slack-jawed amazement. Several of them were talking into their cell phones. And some of them were taking pictures and video.

Great. Nothing's ever private these days. Annja sighed and turned her attention to Krauzer and Melanie. "The police are going to be here in minutes, so this is how this is going to go down." She looked at Melanie. "You're going to tell me where the scrying crystal is."

For a moment, Melanie acted as if she was going to refuse. Then she collapsed onto a nearby sofa and started to cry. "It's in the bedroom closet."

Annja turned to Krauzer, not trusting him to be in the room alone with Melanie. "Go get the crystal."

Krauzer frowned, but he went to the adjacent bedroom, rattled around and came back with a boot box. "Found it. And it doesn't look counterfeit at all." He smiled in relief and satisfaction, then glanced at Melanie. "Wow, you and Barney boy are into some kinky stuff."

"And you," Annja said, ignoring the comment, "are going to let me examine that scrying crystal."

Krauzer wrapped his arms around the box protectively. "This is mine. I risked my life to get this. I'm never letting it out of my sight again."

On the floor, Barney snuffled, waking, then struggled and tried to get up.

Annja plucked the knife from the floor and looked at Krauzer. "I risked my life to help you, and I'm still going to have to deal with the police for hours because of you, so I'm going to get to study that crystal. Otherwise, I'm going to cut Barney free. I figure you guys have time for a rematch before the police arrive. Do you like your chances?"

Krauzer gritted his teeth. "All right, but we should go, not hang around for the cops."

Pointing at the people at the door, Annja said, "This is probably going out live on television right now."

Outside, sirens filled the street and grew louder as they neared the building.

"And we're all out of time for running."

"THEY WERE READY to kill each other over this?" LAPD sergeant Will Cranmer looked at the scrying crystal Annja was studying. He was in his early fifties; his hair and mustache were gray and neatly clipped, and he wore aviator sunglasses against the dimming sun.

The spherical crystal appeared to have been cast of yellowish glass and was as big as both her fists put together. Each of its four flat spots were about as large as Annja's thumb.

Annja leaned against Krauzer's Lamborghini. "I think *kill* may be a bit strong."

She'd had confrontations with police all over the world. They all wanted people to admit to things so court cases would go more easily. She wasn't going to confirm anything that would possibly bring on more trouble. "The discussion did get heated."

"There is the broken door—"

"That door is very flimsy," Annja said. "I'm sure you noticed that."

"—and the knife—"

"Which belongs to Barney."

"—who also doesn't look so good." Cranmer nodded toward the big biker in the back of a nearby patrol car.

Handcuffs had replaced the bootlace Annja had used to bind the man. Dried blood covered his upper lip and beard.

"That was me," Annja said. "Barney didn't want to give up on the knife after I took it away from him."

"*You* did that?" Cranmer looked impressed.

"Yeah."

"Krauzer is telling the detectives that he did it." The police officer thrust his chin toward the front of the apartment building.

The director stood between two detectives and was enjoying the attention he was getting from members of the local news media, who were held back by yellow tape.

Annja smiled. "He loves telling stories, so we'll let him have his glory as long as he can hang on to it." She had responded only, "No comment," every time a reporter thrust a microphone into her face and they'd quickly gravitated to Krauzer. "But in case Melanie Harp or Barney tell you later it was me, it was me."

"Good to know. I'll clue the detectives in."

Nobody was getting Barney's side of the story. Or Melanie Harp's. The actress had tried to get access to the media, but she'd been locked in the back of another patrol car. "So what makes this glass bowling ball so important?" Cranmer asked.

"It's a prop in Krauzer's new movie," Annja said. "It's the scrying crystal of an elf witch."

"What's the movie?"

"A Diversion of Dragons."

Cranmer crossed his arms and leaned against the car beside Annja. "Fantasy?"

"Yes."

"Can't wait to tell the chief."

"Why?"

Cranmer grinned. "Krauzer kind of mentioned he had a part in the new movie the chief might be great for."

"So Krauzer thinks a part in a movie is a get-out-of-jail-free card?"

Cranmer nodded.

"Is it?"

"Yep."

"That doesn't sound fair, does it?"

Cranmer grinned. "You still believe in fair?"

"That does sound kind of funny, doesn't it?"

"Everybody wants to be in front of the camera."

"How about you?"

"I was a bit player in a lot of cop shows when I was younger. I got over it," Cranmer said. "So tell me about the crystal ball."

"Scrying crystal."

Cranmer shrugged. "I've arrested fortune-telling con artists with bigger balls."

Annja raised her eyebrows.

"I'm a fan of your show," Cranmer said after a moment's hesitation. "I was a history major at college before I spent time in the military and became a police officer." He nodded at the scrying crystal. "I noticed you weren't just looking at that like it was a prop."

Annja turned it in her hands, feeling the heft of it and the irregularities along the surface. When she'd first glimpsed the object, she'd gotten a sense of antiquity. After handling it, she was pretty sure that initial impression had been correct.

"I don't think it is."

"So what do you suppose it is?"

"Serendipity. Sometimes when you're looking for one thing, you discover another by accident. You've heard of Juan Cabrillo?"

Cranmer nodded "Sailed with the conquistadores, with Hernán Cortés, and later explored the West Coast while searching for a trade route to China."

"And his last voyage?"

"In 1542 he sailed most of the West Coast and ended up on what we call Santa Catalina Island, intending to stay the winter. Some of his men got attacked by Tongva warriors around Christmas Eve. Cabrillo stepped off the ship and splintered his shin, ended up getting gangrene and dying there. He never made it back to Europe. On San Miguel Island, somebody found a headstone that might have been his."

"Now I'm impressed."

"I've got four kids. My wife helped them with math and science. I helped them with history and English... They like *Chasing History's Monsters*, too. I think my older two boys like it for the other host, but my daughter wants to be you when she grows up. When I tell her I met you today, she's going to freak."

He pulled his smartphone from his shirt pocket.

"Do you mind...?"

"Sure." Annja stood beside Cranmer and he got the phone ready. "Wait!" She reached up and took her hair down and ran her fingers through it. "Okay." She smiled, Cranmer smiled, and he took the selfie. Twice.

"Thanks." Cranmer put the phone back in his pocket.

"How does Juan Cabrillo fit in with the elf witch's scrying crystal?"

"Cabrillo's logbook of the voyage along the West Coast was never found," Annja said. "There's only a concise summation made by Andrés de Urdaneta, a Spanish navigator who also worked on finding a way to sail around the world after Magellan's crew managed."

"Another ship's captain who didn't finish a voyage."

"Exactly. Anyway, one of the local professors of history at Cal State has some old journal pages that one of his students said had been in the hands of his maternal grandmother's family for years. They were an heirloom of some sort, saved in a safe-deposit box that ended up bequeathed to the student in a will. He asked Dr. Orta to have a look at it. Dr. Orta had read I was in LA working with Krauzer, so he called me."

"He's a fan of the show?"

"Claims to be, but he's more interested in history. The papers Dr. Orta showed me claim to be from one of the mates aboard the *San Salvador*, a man named Julio Gris. Gris was a treasure hunter and in the papers he states that he found a lead to a lost treasure."

"But this could be a hoax."

Annja held up the scrying crystal. "It could be, except the papers describe this perfectly."

4

The papers Dr. Vincent Orta possessed had a sketch of the scrying crystal. The drawing was on the fourth page of Julio Gris's manuscript. The parchment was old and weathered, unevenly burned along one side, and had turned the amber hue of honey. All twelve sheets were hermetically sealed in individual plastic protectors.

Some of the ink had faded, but Orta had brought the lines back to clarity with a chemical treatment. Annja just hoped that the work hadn't erased the hidden message she thought might be there.

She sat on a high stool at an architect's desk in the university classroom Orta had opened for their use that night. He'd also taken the liberty of sending out to a Mongolian restaurant and had ordered enough so that Krauzer could join them for dinner.

Orta had been polite about the unexpected company, but he wasn't overly friendly to Krauzer, who continued to be loud and obnoxious. The director didn't notice the snub on Orta's part, though.

"So that's my scrying crystal?" Krauzer leaned over Annja's shoulder to look at the page.

"I believe so." Once she'd carried the crystal in, Orta had become as excited as she was, and he was just as certain it was the artifact described in Gris's papers. Krauzer shook his head. "Nah. Doesn't look anything like my crystal."

Annja shot him a look. "It's round. It's glass. It has four flat spots on it. That," she said, pointing the chopsticks at the glass ball, then at the drawing, "is this."

"I don't see it." Thankfully, Krauzer's phone rang and he turned away to answer it.

Orta shook his head. "That man's an idiot."

"I heard that," Krauzer said.

"Good. I don't have to repeat myself." Orta heaved a sigh.

"So we're in agreement?" Annja asked.

"Definitely. I can't believe you found this."

"I wouldn't have if you hadn't shown me these papers. Sometimes it's like that. There are places all over the world where artifacts have sat in plain sight for years and no one knew what they were until they started investigating."

"Do you know where Krauzer got it?" Orta asked.

"Not yet."

Orta studied Krauzer. "He didn't tell you?"

"He doesn't know. He got it from a set designer. She's out of town on a shopping spree somewhere in South America. I've sent emails, so hopefully, when she gets somewhere with internet access, she'll have more information."

"There's not a bill of sale or something? No means of tracing this?" He shook his head in disbelief.

"Set designers collect from everywhere and often the objects sit in warehouses—or their homes—until they can find a movie to sell it to. They're given a budget and, more or less, told to spend it. I've also discovered that sometimes the bills of sale are as fictitious as Hollywood. Tracking down where things actually came from can be difficult. Besides, we're more interested in where this is going to take us. If we find out for sure what this is, we'll figure out where it's been."

A rueful frown pulled at the corners of Orta's mouth. "Where it takes *you*, perhaps. One of us still has classes to teach."

That was true. Annja felt bad for him. She couldn't imagine being trapped on a schedule without recourse to follow up on an artifact. "I appreciate you calling me in on this. And I appreciate dinner."

"It's the least I could do. I haven't forgotten you agreed to take a lecture for me at some point." Orta grinned. "That's got me in pretty solid with the dean."

"Well, let's see if we can decipher what Julio Gris was protecting."

"ARE YOU GOING to get me out of here?" Melanie Harp pulled at the oversize orange jumpsuit as she sat at the visitation window in the LAPD jail. "This place is horrible, Ligier. They're treating me like I'm a criminal."

She spoke in French because using the language made her feel special and because she didn't want the guards and prisoners around her to listen in.

She ran her fingers through her hair and tightened her grip on the phone that connected her to the man on the other side of the bulletproof glass that separated them.

"I'll get you out as soon as I can, baby," Ligier de Cerceau replied calmly. He was always calm. That somber solidness was one of the things about him that had first attracted Melanie. When he was in LA, he was her rock.

He looked as if he was carved out of rock, too. He was six and a half feet tall and broad shouldered. His blond curls hung in disarray around his bronzed face, making his bright blue eyes appear startling. Amber stubble covered his square chin.

For the jail visit, he'd claimed to be her lawyer and had dressed the part: Italian suit, nice loafers, a high-end watch and a leather briefcase. Instead of softening him up, the suit made him look even scarier.

"Why can't you get me out of here now?" Melanie thought she was going to start crying again. Getting fired from the movie was bad. Getting locked up was bad. But there was nothing like coming down cold from an addiction. She was already covered in sweat and she was freezing. She felt as if her insides were about to explode.

"Because they haven't charged you. Once they charge you, I can get you out."

"Promise?"

"Sure, baby."

De Cerceau blew Melanie a kiss and she felt a little better.

"Now tell me about this glass ball you had."

"I already sent you pictures of it." Melanie didn't know what he wanted out of the prop. She wouldn't even have stolen the stupid thing if he hadn't told her to. It had been his idea for her to take it after she'd gotten released from the picture. He'd even flown back in from…*wherever* he'd been before he got back to LA. He didn't always tell her his business, and she liked that he could be so mysterious. Just ride into town and sweep her off her feet. He'd told her he'd seen her in *Fifty Hues of Indigo* and had fallen in love with her. That had been so romantic.

"I got the pictures, baby, but I'd like to know a little more about the ball."

"Why?"

He grinned at her the way he did that drove her crazy, and then he leaned close to the window. "Because I thought I'd steal it back for you, have it for you by the time you get out tomorrow, and we could make the studio pay to have it returned. That way you still get severance and a nest egg until you get a serious role."

Melanie hesitated even though he always knew just what to say to her. "That's what we were going to do the first time. That didn't work out so well."

"If I'd been here, things would have gone better—you know that—but I couldn't be here until now. I came as soon as I could." De Cerceau shrugged. "Besides, this time I'm going to take that director, too. Make the studio pay to get them both back. That way your nest egg will be even bigger."

A bit of hope and excitement dawned in Melanie, curbing some of the monster that was struggling to get free inside her. De Cerceau was so good at providing for her. She was lucky she'd met him and he loved her so much. "That sounds awesome."

"Where can I find Krauzer?"

"He's probably with that woman. Annja." Melanie struggled to think, but it was hard to do while she was sitting there sweating and freezing. "She's a consultant Krauzer brought in. But she's tricky, too. She knocked out Barney and made it look easy."

De Cerceau smiled at her. "I'm not Barney."

"I know." Melanie smiled at him. "I just want you to be prepared."

"Do you know what hotel she's staying at?"

Melanie shook her head, but the motion only made her head ache. "No." She thought some more because de Cerceau looked disappointed in her. "Wait. I know where she might be. She made Krauzer promise to let her examine the scrying crystal."

"Why did she want to do that?"

"I overheard her talking about the crystal to some professor at SoCal." Melanie dug for the name. It had sounded like some kind of whale... "Orta. He's a professor of history or something. While we were waiting for the police to get there, she talked to him and asked if they could swing by tonight."

"They're going to the university?"

"Yeah."

A frown crinkled de Cerceau's eyes.

"Is something wrong?" Melanie asked.

The frown went away and he shook his head. "Nothing, baby. You don't worry about anything. I have to be going, but I'll see you in the morning. Just remember, don't say anything to anyone until you hear from me." He hung up the phone and blew her a kiss.

She mimed catching the kiss and smiled at him.

When he was gone, she felt completely empty.

She got up and followed the guard back to her cell.

OUTSIDE THE JAIL, Ligier de Cerceau walked toward the waiting dark blue Mercedes-Benz sedan. The driver got out, opened the back door and allowed de Cerceau inside.

"Thank you, Gerard."

"Of course, Colonel." Stocky and well dressed, Gerard Malouel was, like his employer, former Brigade des Forces Spéciales Terre.

As such, they'd served in the French army's special forces unit. Both had undertaken missions in Operation Heracles in Afghanistan. That was where de Cerceau had discovered how much money could be made finding and selling relics. He and the core of his team—then and now, after they'd gone into business for themselves—had stumbled across a group of relic hunters, killed them and found out what the items they were smuggling out of the country were worth.

That discovery had been life changing. These days de Cerceau still did mercenary work, but he made a lot of money dealing in artifacts, as well. He didn't care anything for antiquities, but he liked the money collectors of those things would pay for pieces they coveted.

Gerard slid behind the steering wheel. "Where to, Colonel?"

"The University of Southern California."

Gerard pressed buttons on the GPS as he pulled out of the parking area and onto North Los Angeles Street. "Did everything go well with the woman?"

"She's going to keep her mouth shut for a while, but she's suffering from drug withdrawal."

Gerard considered that for a moment. Then he shifted in his seat. "That doesn't make her sound very trustworthy."

"She's not." De Cerceau checked his email on his phone and discovered a new text from SEEKER4318. He didn't know who was behind the name, but the man paid well and on time. He was new to de Cerceau, but he'd been vouched for by a past buyer.

SEEKER4318: Retrieve the object and I will happily pay you the amount we discussed.

De Cerceau responded, I will have it in my hands soon.

"Do you know anyone who can arrange something for Melanie?" de Cerceau asked.

"The women's section of the jail can be a little harder to set up than the men's, but I'm sure I can find someone. There are plenty of violent women in jail, and some of them are more cold-blooded than their male counterparts."

De Cerceau agreed. In his business, he'd dealt with many dangerous women. "Get it done as soon as you can. I don't want her talking to anyone and complicating this."

Gerard nodded and pulled out his smartphone.

De Cerceau occupied himself with organizing a team for the USC part of the operation. He also wondered who Seeker was. The man had responded immediately when Melanie had posted pictures of the scrying crystal on the internet.

Glancing outside the tinted window, de Cerceau watched downtown LA speed by him, waiting for the call to be picked up at the other end.

WITH THE HARD-DRIVING sound of the Sex Pistols reverberating off the walls in the next room, SEEKER4318 stared at the young woman lying bound and gagged on the motel bed. Excitement thrilled through him as it always did when he had a woman helpless before him.

This one was in her mid- to late twenties and was trim and athletic, strong enough and quick enough to make kidnapping her in the parking lot of her apartment building difficult. But he'd watched her for weeks, and he'd known her schedule. All he'd had to do was lie in wait with a stun gun and grab her when she fell. He hunted regularly, but after finding out about the glass ball made by Julio Gris, he'd accelerated his schedule.

He needed a kill to calm himself.

The panicked woman struggled on the king-size bed. Usually a victim's attempts to escape would have excited him even more.

But his anticipation was blunted. The news from de Cerceau gave reason to be hopeful that Julio Gris's Key of Shadows would soon be in his hands. Everything else paled by comparison.

He sat beside the woman on the bed but didn't try to touch her. Even still, she managed to push herself away a few inches.

"Don't worry," he told her and smiled. "I'm not going to defile you. I'm not interested in that. Do you know what heruspicy is?" he asked.

She didn't say anything, due to the gag, but he liked the sound of his own voice.

"Do you believe in fortune-telling? Ever read your horoscope and tried to see if the day was going to go as it predicted? Surely you've done that."

Cautiously, the woman nodded. Tears tracked down her face, and he knew she was trying to please him. He didn't like when they did that. He wanted hopeful fighters, women who denied their own mortality even when it stared them in the face.

"Ah, you have read your horoscope?"

She nodded but didn't try to talk through the gag.

"Sometimes they come true, you know."

Shaking, she nodded again.

"Well, heruspicy is a lot like that. It's a way to foretell the future. The Romans practiced it. But you still don't know what it is, do you?"

She shook her head.

"It's the practice of slitting open a sacrificial creature and reading its entrails. You do know what entrails are, right?"

The woman knew.

Frantic, she struggled against her bonds again but only ended up exhausted. SEEKER4318 allowed her to fight because she would tire herself out and that would make her easier to deal with in the end.

Finally, drained, panting for breath, the woman lay in a quivering mass on the bed. Nobody had heard the noise she'd made while struggling over the blaring punk music in the next unit.

Anxious to see what the future held, SEEKER4318 plunged his dagger into the woman's stomach and ripped up through her breastbone. Blood poured onto the bed in a pulsing waterfall. Placing the knife to one side, SEEKER4318 pulled apart the wound he'd created and took out two handfuls of the woman's insides for inspection.

He felt even more optimistic.

The Key of Shadows and the treasure of the Merovingian kings would be his soon enough.

All the signs pointed to a good resolution of his present problem.

5

"What are you doing now?" Krauzer clicked off his smartphone and walked over to Annja, who'd placed the scrying crystal on a camera tripod a short distance from the wall where pages of Julio Gris's manuscript hung.

"Checking for a hidden message." Annja took the high-powered miniflashlight from her backpack and shone it through the crystal, concentrating on one of the flat spots.

"Inside the scrying crystal?" Krauzer scoffed.

"The manuscript Julio Gris left indicates that the message is concealed somewhere inside." Annja moved the flashlight and the crystal at the same time.

The diffused beam of light shone through the crystal and onto the first manuscript page.

"You need to be careful with that," Krauzer warned. "That's one of a kind. I can't replace that crystal in the movie. I've shot too many core scenes with it."

"If you got a 3-D modeler, you could make one of these on a 3-D printer," Orta told him.

"Movie audiences can tell when something's real these days. They like real stuff in their movies."

Annja looked at him. "This is supposed to belong to an elf witch."

"Hey, viewers want to believe in elf witches and hobbits and dragons. I'm not going to argue with them. I'm going to give them what they want. In fact, I'll give them bigger dragons than they've ever seen before."

Ignoring the director, Annja continued to shine the light across the pages. She wasn't frustrated yet, but her options were limited. And she was constantly aware of Krauzer growing more and more impatient.

"Did Julio Gris tell you to shine a flashlight through the crystal?" Krauzer asked smugly. "Because that right there would tell you that manuscript is a fake. They didn't have flashlights back when Juan Cabrillo sailed to California, right?"

Annja ignored the question.

"Right?"

Knowing Krauzer wasn't going to let up until he was answered, Annja said, "Right."

"So we're all done here? I've saved you from wasting more time. I can take my scrying crystal and get back to the studio, and you and the professor can look at old crap to your hearts' delight."

"Gris suggested using natural light or a candle flame to reveal the message," Orta said. "We're using a flashlight because it's more accurate and it's not daylight outside."

Krauzer folded his arms. "Shining a light through a crystal sounds really stupid, if you ask me."

"Have you ever heard of a magic lantern?" The frustration in Orta's voice turned his words ragged.

"Of course I have. 'Ali Baba and the Forty Thieves.' Aladdin's lamp. Even Uncle Scrooge McDuck went looking for a magic lamp. That stuff's all old."

"A magic lantern," Orta said in a louder voice, "was an early precursor to filmmaking."

"So were hand puppets."

Orta sighed. "I'm just saying that there was a basis for this use of the scrying ball."

"Okay, but I've got to take that crystal and scoot. We've got an early shoot planned tomorrow. Morning sunlight doesn't last forever." Krauzer tapped his watch, then answered his ringing phone again.

Annja was thankful. The man was too accustomed to

being in control. She rotated the crystal and shone the light through the other flat spots onto the pages.

Her back ached from the combination of constant bending and anticipation. Something had to be here. Unless the scrying crystal was *not* the one mentioned in the manuscript.

Or if the manuscript was a hoax.

Krauzer punched his phone off and returned to observe. "Well, that was good news."

Neither Annja nor Orta bothered to ask what the good news was.

"That was Rita, my personal assistant. She had to wait until the cops left, but she got my gun back."

Annja straightened and reconsidered the problem.

"So, you're satisfied there aren't any secret messages in the crystal?" Krauzer asked. "I can get back to the studio?"

The director's words turned the possibilities around in Annja's mind. She glanced at Orta. "I think we've been going at this wrong."

"What do you mean?" Orta asked.

"Maybe the message is *inside* the crystal." Annja pressed the flashlight onto one of the object's flat areas. The light caused the crystal to glow softly as the illumination diffused through the twists and turns of the sparkling latticework contained within the thing.

"There's nothing inside that crystal." Krauzer shook his head and looked grumpy. "You're wasting my time."

Annja continued her search, but she became quickly discouraged when nothing turned up. The light caught various facets and reflected through the glass ovoid, squirming through to another side in some places and stopping in others. Occasionally, the light snaked back on itself and became looped.

Nothing made sense.

Pausing again, Annja glanced at the manuscript pages. They have to be part of this, she reasoned.

Krauzer sifted through the food cartons and muttered in displeasure. At least he was being somewhat quiet about his irritation.

A new thought struck Annja and she glanced up at Orta. "Let's get the pages over here."

Orta picked up the first page. "Shine the light through the pages?"

"That's the only thing we haven't tried."

"The plastic protectors might interfere." In spite of his misgivings, Orta held the first page against one of the flat spots on the crystal.

Annja placed the flashlight lens against the laminated paper and slowly guided the manuscript page along so that every square inch was covered. After covering nearly the whole page, her hopes steadily sinking while Krauzer continued to stew, Annja blinked to clear her vision when she spotted writing in the lower right corner.

She lowered the flashlight and raised the page to examine the surface with her naked eye. Even holding the manuscript up to the overhead lights didn't show anything. The striations within the crystal somehow translated the image, probably through various degrees of refraction.

"Did you find something?" Orta stood at her side, his chest resting slightly against her shoulder.

"Yes," Annja answered. Her voice sounded quiet in her own ears, but her excitement thrummed like a live thing inside her.

"You're imagining things," Krauzer insisted. "You're tired and you want something to be there." Still, he came to stand on her other side and peered at the crystal. "See? Nothing's there."

"Look inside it." Annja replaced the page over the flat spot and shone the flashlight against the page so the beam shone into the crystal.

Inside the crystal, the neat handwriting stood revealed,

almost too small to read. The penmanship was delicate, ornate and so small. Each space between words was carefully designed.

"I don't see anything," Krauzer challenged.

Annja nodded to Orta. "Hold these."

Silently, enraptured by what he was seeing, Orta held the flashlight and the page. He experimented by pulling the flashlight lens back from the paper. "I can get the writing a little larger, but pulling the light source reflects back too much and throws off the focus, causing it to disappear."

Annja opened her backpack and took out her tablet PC and a small digital camera. She slipped on an equally small macro lens. "If someone had read the manuscript pages in that crystal all those years ago, they couldn't have put a candle flame up against the paper."

"Someone built this crystal to hide the message inside the manuscript pages." Orta shook his head. "But the crystal looks so real."

"The crystal is real. This is old, probably grown over time. I'd like to find out who created it, as well." Annja left the tablet PC on one of the tables and brought the camera to the crystal. She experimented with angles and found the one that best revealed the message within the depths of the crystalline latticework. She snapped images.

"I see it." Krauzer bent so low and so close that his breath temporarily fogged the crystal. Looking embarrassed, he leaned back. "You know, that's pretty cool. I could use something like this in *A Diversion of Dragons*."

Orta blew out an impatient breath. "Seriously? You see this—a secret message in a crystal that has to be *at least* hundreds of years old, the crystal itself even older than that—and the first thing you think of is using it in a movie? You don't even wonder what the message is?"

"Don't go all professor on me, Doc." Krauzer held up his hands defensively. "I'm a movie guy. I'm one of *the* movie guys in this town. People talk about me the same way they talk about Spielberg and Coppola."

"You're an imbecile!"

Krauzer held out a warning finger. "It wouldn't be smart to make this personal."

"Smart? You're not intelligent enough to know when you're not invited to something."

"Are you talking about the food?" Krauzer hooked a thumb over his shoulder at the takeout cartons sitting on the table. "I can pay for that. In fact, I'll pay for it all." He pulled out a black American Express card. "You take plastic?"

Frozen by the sudden outbreak of tempers, Annja couldn't believe what was taking place. Male testosterone was so easily misplaced. "Guys? Maybe we could focus."

Orta blushed a deep red. "I cannot believe the crystal ended up in your hands."

Krauzer glared at his rival. "Yeah, well, it's mine. Whatever secret message is in there is mine, too, so if there's treasure, it's mine."

"The message isn't in the crystal, you idiot. It's on these pages. Which *I* have."

"Yeah, well, I own the decoder ring. Try to figure out your secret message without that." Krauzer shrugged. "I don't need the secret message. It's probably 'Juan Cabrillo was here.' Or maybe 'Today the chef's mystery meat was particularly horrible.' You think Twitter and Facebook invented boring self-indulgence? Try reading some of those *classics* college professors cram down your throat."

"Have you even wondered why anyone would go to the trouble of putting a secret message in these pages and that crystal?"

"I don't care. I'll just take my crystal and be going. I'm making a movie. I don't have time for this crap." Krauzer started to reach for the scrying crystal, then stopped when Annja narrowed her eyes.

"Not yet," she told him.

"It's mine."

"Not until I'm done with it," Annja said. "We agreed."

Glaring at her, Krauzer backed away. "Hurry."

Annja nodded to Orta. "Ready?"

Breathing out slowly, Orta picked up the flashlight and manuscript page to return to their joint task. It took him only a moment to find the hidden writing.

Peering intently at the handwriting, Annja said, "Looks like calligraphy that was made with some kind of tool."

"Probably jeweler's instruments," Orta replied. "The Portuguese were constantly looking for treasures. Gold, silver and gems. For the message to be rendered so small, I'd say the writer used a jeweler's loupe, too, though I'm not certain those had been invented at the time this was made. Some type of magnifying glass at the very least."

Adjusting the magnification of the image on her camera viewscreen, Annja tilted it toward Orta. "This looks like Latin."

He peered more closely. "Yes, it is. But see the name?"

"Julio Gris."

"Yes."

"And unless I'm mistaken, this says it is the last will and testament of Gris."

"Let's see what's on the next page."

IN LESS THAN an hour, Annja and Orta had the hidden messages from the manuscript pages shot and mostly decoded. She loaded the images onto her tablet PC and enlarged them. She'd shot them so they could be enhanced. Compiling the images into a single file she could flip through with the touch of a button took only a few minutes.

The person who had written the message had a fine hand at calligraphy. The whorls and loops looked as though a machine had punched them out.

"Well?" Krauzer sat on a stool on the other side of the large table. His arms were folded across his chest and his lips were pursed into a petulant frown.

"What?" Annja asked.

"Isn't somebody going to read the message?"

"I thought you weren't interested."

Krauzer shook his head in irritation. "You know, you might want to borrow my crystal again at some point."

That was true. Annja focused on the message. "'This is the last will and testament of Julio Gris, second mate of the good ship *San Salvador*. 1542.

"'In my life, I have been many things before I took my post on Captain Juan Cabrillo's ship, may God rest his unfortunate soul. If I had been caught for many of the things I did, I would have been shot by jealous husbands or hanged for thievery or murder.

"'Captain Cabrillo only knew me as a mate aboard his ship, and I worked hard for him because I have always loved the sea. Even more than I loved the sea, though, I have loved the idea of treasure.

"'God knows of the larceny in my darkest thoughts, and He has taken pains to see that I am properly punished, for it seems I may never claim this prize. I heard the story about the lost treasure of the Merovingian kings from a man who knew György Dózsa, a warrior from the Kingdom of Hungary. According to the man who gave me the story, Dózsa read the pages from the Bibliotheca Corviniana himself.'"

"Wait." Krauzer held his hands up. "Just hold on. You're throwing too much information out too fast. Who are the Merovingian kings?"

Before Annja could answer, the room's main door opened and two armed men strode inside. They wore black clothing with abbreviated Kevlar armor and carried H&K MP5 machine pistols with thick sound suppressors. Dark eyed, the men looked related, but one of them was easily ten years older than the other. He was clean shaven with a well-kept mustache, while the other man had deliberate scruff. Both moved economically, spacing themselves out so they commanded the room.

"Put your hands in the air," the older man commanded. His accent echoed faintly of French.

Not having any options, Annja did as she was told.

6

"Fox Leader, this is Fox Six."

Moving quickly through the dim college hallways, Ligier de Cerceau carried his machine pistol in both hands. Adrenaline surged through him as he waited for his companion to unlock the classroom door they stood in front of.

"You have Fox Leader."

"I have the packages in sight."

De Cerceau stepped into the empty classroom, flicked on the bright light attached to the machine pistol and surveyed the space. Only tables and chairs occupied the space other than a lectern at the front of the room.

"Are the packages in good shape?" De Cerceau pulled back out into the hallway and took his smartphone from inside his jacket. The Kevlar body armor made the task more difficult, but he managed. He pressed the friend app and watched as the red pins popped up onto the screen to mark the locations of his men.

Twelve of his men roamed through the college of history, and all of them were dangerous, hard men. He'd handpicked each man for his core unit.

"The packages are in excellent shape," Georges Dipre answered.

"Keep them that way." De Cerceau gestured to the man beside him to proceed. "I'm on my way to your location now."

He followed the other man, both of them as quiet as shadows as they drifted through the silent halls.

STANDING BESIDE ORTA, Annja watched the two men who were holding them prisoner. Their movements were precise and methodical. Professional soldiers, she realized.

"What do they want?" Krauzer whispered.

"The crystal," Orta answered. Either he spoke French, too, or his native language was close enough that he had no problem following the rapid-fire conversations between the men and the person they were talking to at the other end of their communication units.

Annja had already discerned their interest and hated her helplessness.

"You can't have the crystal!" Krauzer took a step toward the men. "I need that in my movie."

"Stay back," the older man commanded. He squeezed a quick burst from his machine pistol and, while the thick suppressor on the end of the weapon kept the noise quieted, the bullets ripped into the wall at the other end of the room, tearing divots and smashing through framed pictures.

"Okay, *okay*!" Krauzer dropped to his knees on the floor and held his hands up in surrender.

"Deal with that idiot," the older man said in French.

The younger man put a knee in Krauzer's back, pushing the movie director forward as he pulled a zip tie from a thigh pocket.

For a moment, the older man's attention was diverted as he watched his companion and talked to other members of his group. Partially blocked from the man's sight and standing to the right of the man handling Krauzer, Annja reached for the thick ceramic plates Orta had brought for their dinner. She wrapped her fingers around the edge of the top plate and hurled it in a discus throw, spinning and getting her weight into the effort.

The older gunman brought his weapon to bear and fired a short burst that sliced through the air above Annja's head as she ducked. Spinning, the heavy plate struck the gunman in the throat and knocked him backward.

Shifting his attention from Krauzer to Annja, the second gunman tried to spin to cover her. Balanced on both hands and one foot, Annja shot her other foot out and caught the gunman in the chest and arm, driving him back toward the table. His head struck the table's edge with a hollow thump and his eyes slid up so that only the whites showed as he toppled to the floor.

Still in motion, aware that the older gunman had been only momentarily put off, Annja stood and reached for the second plate. She held the plate at the end of her arm like a tennis racket and swung it into the surviving gunman's face in a backhand swing as she spun.

The plate shattered across the man's grizzled features and shards exploded in all directions. Blood streamed from the man's broken nose and a deep cut on one of his cheeks. Unconscious, certainly concussed, the man sank to the floor.

Annja knelt over the man and quickly went through his pockets but found nothing that identified him. A demanding voice spoke over the walkie-talkie the man wore over his shoulder.

She looked at Krauzer and Orta, both of whom stared at her in shock. "There are more coming," she told them.

"For my crystal?" Krauzer sounded amazed.

"Get it and get moving," Annja ordered as she took the man's machine pistol and recognized it as one she was familiar with. She dumped the partially expended magazine and shoved in a fresh one taken from the man's tactical gear.

Krauzer stood slowly, moving as if he was in a daze. He started at the blood pooling around the gunman's head. "Is he dead?"

"No." Annja stood and slung the machine pistol over her shoulder. She listened for footsteps out in the corridor.

She didn't hear anything, but she'd noticed the thick soles on the gunmen's boots. The team would be moving quietly.

"This is stupid crazy," Krauzer announced. He wiped his face.

Annja shoved him into motion. "Grab the crystal. Let's go." She was happy to see that Orta was already putting the manuscript sheets back in their protective case. Grabbing her backpack, Annja quickly packed her gear into it and pulled it on. She tried to think of how much time had passed and knew that she had no clue.

Orta looked at her. "There are more of these men?"

"Yes." Annja pulled the ear-throat mic into place and clipped the walkie-talkie to the ammo belt. A deep, controlled voice spoke at the other end, demanding that Fox Six reply. She ignored the command and nodded to Orta. "You know the campus layout. Which way is the quickest way out?"

"Follow me." Orta headed to the back door.

Krauzer had the crystal wrapped in one arm like an oversize football and was reaching for the other machine pistol lying on the floor.

Taking a quick step, Annja kicked the weapon under the table and out of Krauzer's reach.

He whirled on her, his features taut with rage and fear. "What are you doing?"

"Trying to keep us alive," Annja said. "You're a director, not a commando."

"And you think you're some kind of action hero?"

Annja glanced at the two unconscious attackers. "I've got experience with this sort of thing."

"I can shoot! Two guns are better than one."

"Are you coming?" Annja asked as she jogged toward Orta at the back door.

Krauzer started to go around the table, but another gunman slid into place out in the hallway.

The radio came to life in Annja's ear. "Fox Leader, Fox Six is down. The woman has a weapon."

"Kill them," the deep voice ordered. "Do not harm the crystal."

Annja lifted the machine pistol and aimed. Then she fired off three short bursts. Bullets hammered the door frame, throwing splinters out into the hallway, and they struck the gunman, knocking him down. Annja didn't know where the man was hit and knew she didn't have time to confirm his condition.

After fumbling with the back door, Orta opened it and stuck his head outside. Then he yelped and pulled back inside the room just ahead of a salvo of bullets that ripped into the doorway and outside wall.

Grabbing the man's arm, Annja pulled him back from the door, squatted and snaked around the door frame. Two men held the hallway, one positioned on either side, with their machine pistols at the ready. As Annja leaned out, one of the gunmen broke cover and rushed toward them.

Annja brought up the machine pistol and fired at almost point-blank range. The gunman managed to get off another burst that burned the air beside her. Her bullets stitched the man from his chest to his face.

She forced herself not to think about what she'd just done. She didn't have time. She stepped into the guy and gripped his bloodstained tactical vest with her free hand.

Leaning into him, guiding his slow fall by partially supporting his weight as he went down, Annja aimed at the other gunman in the hallway and fired a burst that scored the wall above his head. She corrected her aim as the dead man sagged on her, careful not to let his weight trap her.

The other gunman fired his weapon, either knowing his partner was dead from the blood pooling on the floor or not caring if the other man survived. Bullets thudded into the corpse, some of them burrowing into the tactical armor and some biting into flesh.

Ignoring the vibration of the bullets' impacts and the grisly weight of the dead man, Annja fired again, emptying her weapon in two short bursts. Tossing the weapon away, she scrambled from beneath the falling dead man, slipped in his blood and recovered as she stripped his weapon from his hand.

Landing on her knees, Annja brought up the new weapon and hoped that the dead gunman hadn't emptied it during his charge. As she centered the machine pistol on the surviving attacker, the gunman collapsed to the floor. She was on her feet immediately.

When she paused over the second man, Annja dumped the magazine in her weapon and grabbed a fresh one from his gear. She glanced back at Orta and waved him on.

"Fox Nine," the deep voice called over the radio. "Report. *Report!*"

The tinny echoes of tactical gear jangling in the hallway reached Annja's ears and her pulse accelerated. Orta reached her, looking pale.

"Where?" Annja asked as she stood.

Behind the professor, Krauzer spoke rapidly on a cell phone.

"Two corridors ahead, there's a door that will let us out of the building," Orta said.

"We can't leave the building," Annja replied. "Not yet. Whoever's after us, you can bet they have someone watching the exterior of the building." From the professionalism of the gunmen, she suspected there would be snipers.

What was it about the crystal that had drawn attention like this? She had no clue. Yet.

"We need somewhere we can hide," Annja said, focusing on Orta. "Somewhere safe."

"Sure, sure." Orta nodded. He glanced at the elevator farther down the hallway. "The elevator's there." He pointed.

"Stairs," Annja said.

"Next to the elevator."

Annja took the lead, sprinting down the hallway and reaching the doorway. She paused long enough to peer through the safety glass and saw no one in the dark stairwell. As soon as she stepped through, the lights came on. She pulled the machine pistol into position and stared up the steps.

"It's automatic," Orta said. "They're on timers to conserve electricity."

The lack of lighting until now also meant that no one was in the stairwell. Annja felt a little safer because of that and led the way up the stairs. At the landing, pausing to make certain the way was clear, she checked on her charges and saw Krauzer putting away his phone.

"Did you get hold of the police?" Annja asked.

"Better than that," the director said. "I've got a package plan with Sabre Race."

"What's that?"

"Not *what*. *Who*. He's the best protection guy there is in Hollywood. And I've got him on speed dial. He'll be here in minutes."

Anger rushed through Annja. Calling in an outsider was only going to complicate things.

The doorway on the floor below was just starting to open. Setting aside her feelings, she leveled the machine pistol and waited as she waved Orta and Krauzer forward.

7

"You have beautiful hands, Sabre. Strong hands. With so much history in them." The woman clung possessively to Sabre Race's hand, pulling it close to her breast.

She was five feet nine inches tall, six inches shorter than Sabre, with coal-black hair cut in a bob that hung to her sharply defined jawline. Her bangs hung over her plucked eyebrows and shadowed her violet eyes. The black dress left her toned shoulders bare, showing off her dark brown skin and a hint of cleavage.

"You simply must let me tell your fortune one day." Her voice carried the spice of the Caribbean in her words. Seated at a private table inside the club, she drew the attention of every male in the room and a good number of the females.

"I would love to," Sabre said, "but tonight is not the night. I have to leave."

She released his hand and drew back with a pouty smile. Her name was Tessanne Evora and she was reputed to be one of the best fortune-tellers in LA.

"Are you playing hard to get?" she asked him with hooded eyes.

Enjoying the game, Sabre gave her a small smile that he knew was charming because he'd worked on it. He was fit and in his early thirties. He worked hard on his look. Everyone in LA did. It was all part of the package, and presentation was everything. "Another time," Sabre promised, "and I would be all yours."

"Who is claiming your attention this evening?"

"A client in Santa Barbara. But I will definitely see you

again." He palmed a business card from his jacket sleeve, held up his empty hand and flicked the card into view with a flourish. "Soon."

Tessanne smiled in delight as she took the proffered card. "You do magic, as well."

"Small things. I lack the skills that you have." Sabre's smartphone rang. Only important calls came through to that phone, so he took it out of his jacket pocket and glanced at the screen.

STEVEN KRAUZER CODE RED
I'M OUT FRONT

"Is there a problem?" Tessanne asked.

"A pressing matter," he replied as he put the phone back inside his jacket. He stood and tapped the business card she was still holding. It held only his name and his private cell. "Not everyone has that number. Call me."

"I will."

Sabre nodded and headed for the door, sweeping effortlessly between the club clientele and the servers.

Out on the street, Lajos Meszoly sat at the wheel of a black Mercedes G-Class SUV. Sabre sprinted through the valet lines, dodging new arrivals, departing guests and parking attendants. When he reached the vehicle, he slid into the passenger seat. Meszoly punched the accelerator and sped through the traffic.

"What have we got?" Sabre shucked off his suit and tossed the clothes into the back, where two other armed men sat. He pulled on the combat suit that hung at the ready in the vehicle. Tucking the black pants inside calf-high military boots, he tugged a fitted black sweatshirt over his head. He straped on the Molle tactical gear.

"Krauzer says he's trapped inside USC campus," Meszoly replied calmly as he blared his horn and rolled through an intersection on a red light. Traffic on both sides of the intersection halted and honked back at him.

"College?"

"Yeah." Meszoly was a thickset man in his early thirties. He and Sabre had been together for the past six years, both of them having been contractors in Afghanistan before starting up the protection business in Hollywood. Meszoly's head was shaved and he kept his face clean, as well. Except for his size, he was instantly forgettable, and he knew how to dress that down, too. That skill made him valuable in close-cover situations. This night he was outfitted with body armor and weaponry.

"Wouldn't have figured Krauzer for college," Sabre said. "Is he shooting there?"

"He didn't say. What he did say was that guys with guns were chasing him down. Him and his elf-witch crystal."

Sabre shoved an FN Five-seveN pistol into the holster at his hip. "Elf-witch crystal?"

Meszoly shrugged and said, "Hold on," right before he performed a rubber-shredding left turn. "I don't think he's being chased by elf witches."

"Good, because I forgot my fairy dust." Sabre glanced at the GPS screen at the center of the console. "Did he mention who was chasing him?"

"Says he doesn't know."

"Krauzer is there alone?"

"He has two people with him. A professor and a woman named Creed."

"Should I know her?" Sabre made an effort to keep up with rising stars in the city, but that was difficult.

"She does cable television."

"How many people are on-site?"

"The way Krauzer tells it, a small army."

"Right."

"Krauzer had a run-in with a biker earlier in the day," Dyson spoke up from the back.

Sabre glanced into the mirror on the back of the sun visor in front of him. Dyson was one of the young guys, a Marine veteran of Afghanistan.

"The guys hunting Krauzer are bikers?"

"I don't know. I caught the story on the internet. Krauzer didn't call, so I didn't follow up. He usually only has us out when he's got a new release."

"And this is over an elf-witch crystal." Sabre shook his head.

"Krauzer also mentioned something about Merovingian kings," Meszoly said, "but that got garbled up in gunfire, so maybe I'm wrong about that."

The mention of the Merovingians sent a jolt of electricity through Sabre. All of the old stories his father had told him came pouring out of his memory, the stories that had been handed down for generations.

Bottling his excitement with the professionalism he'd learned over the years, Sabre looked at the GPS screen again and the red line to USC that had gotten drastically shorter. "How far out are we?"

"Two minutes."

"Other teams are en route?"

"Two other cars. Eight more guys. If we pull any more, we'll be leaning out other ops. Want me to do that?"

"No. Twelve of us *are* a small army." Sabre reached to the back of the vehicle and Dyson slid an M4A1 into his hands.

How could Krauzer have gotten involved in the Merovingian legends?

8

"Give me an update." Ligier de Cerceau skidded to a stop at the doorway to the stairwell his quarry had entered. One of his men lay across the doorway threshold, holding the door partially open. Bullet holes showed in the glass viewing section and shards lay scattered in the hallway, telling him at once the bullets had come from within.

"We don't have access to the security cameras, Colonel," Gerard Malouel said. He'd remained with the vehicle out in the parking lot so he could monitor the insertion and capture. "I've got two helicopters in the air."

As he leaned against the wall near the stairwell doorway, de Cerceau heard the drumbeat of one of the helicopters' rotors overhead.

"They're searching the building, lighting it up with spotlights," Gerard went on. "One of them is switching over to thermographic systems. We should know more in another minute or two."

"Have the police been alerted?" De Cerceau hadn't detected any alarms that had been set off inside the building, but there could be a silent warning system.

"Affirmative. They're en route."

De Cerceau cursed, knowing they were running out of time. "If we're not done here soon, we'll need to slow them down."

"We're already preparing for that. This is going to get messy." Gerard's tone remained neutral, but he was unhappy. He wouldn't have mentioned the potential problem if he hadn't been disconcerted.

De Cerceau gazed down at the dead man in the doorway. "It's already gotten messy. We've got four dead and one wounded. Almost half the team down." Because of one lone woman. That was something he couldn't believe. The first man might have been careless in approaching the people they were after, and perhaps even the second man. But there was no way this many would have been lost through carelessness. Reading the combat situations they'd been engaged in, de Cerceau knew that someone with Krauzer was used to military operations. He cursed.

"Yes, sir."

Two men closed on de Cerceau's position, stepped into position against the wall and waited for his orders. The remaining three gunmen held the other end of the building and were advancing up the stairwell there.

Holding the machine pistol tight against his shoulder and aiming it up the stairs, de Cerceau stepped across the dead man and into the stairwell. The enclosed space trapped the stench of death and cordite. He held his position and listened.

Farther up the stairwell, footsteps and quiet voices echoed for just a moment. Then a closing door shut them away. De Cerceau headed up the stairs with the machine pistol leading the way. The dead man behind him had been caught unaware. De Cerceau didn't intend for that to happen to him. He took the stairs two at a time, his forefinger resting on his weapon's trigger.

As SOON AS he stepped through the stairwell doorway, Krauzer took off down the hallway to the left. The lights came on just behind him as the automatic systems cut in, making him look as if he was leading the charge against the darkness.

Annja kept pace with Orta. "What rooms are this way?" She slid a fresh magazine into the machine pistol.

"Classrooms." Orta sounded out of breath. He was in good shape, but adrenaline had to be wreaking havoc on him. "Alcoves for the graduate assistants. A research archive. The graduate dean's office."

"The research archive sounds big enough to hide in." She matched Orta stride for stride as they followed Krauzer down the hallway. Glancing at the windows, she realized that the lights reflected from the large windows along the hallway made seeing outside difficult.

Still, she was able to spot the helicopter's red running lights as it dropped to hover just outside the building. Shoving a leg out, Annja tripped Orta and grabbed his shirtsleeve, pulling him to the ground hard and falling on top of him. As they skidded along the marble tiles, a burst of heavy machine-gun fire chewed through the windows in a ragged line.

Annja threw her arm over her head to protect herself. The helicopter's whirling rotor noise suddenly rose to a deafening roar inside the hallway.

"Stay down," she told Orta as she slithered along the hallway through the spray of broken glass. Once she was past the line of destruction, she rose to her knees, pointed the machine pistol at the helicopter's nose and pulled the trigger.

Bullets tore through the window, blowing shards outside the building. The light made it impossible for her to see where the rounds struck the helicopter, but she thought she saw a jagged line stitched along the pilot's door.

The helicopter fell away, dodging to put distance between itself and the building. The machine gunner in the cargo area fired, trying to vector in on Annja's position, but the helicopter's sudden movement jerked the gunman's aim off and tracers stabbed into the night.

Shaking the broken glass from her clothes as best as she could, Annja rose to a crouched position and returned to Orta's side. "Let's go."

He pushed himself up on trembling arms and looked at her.

"The archives," Annja reminded him. "Let's go there."

Numbly, Orta nodded, pointed down the hallway and stumbled in that direction.

Annja followed him and only then realized she'd lost track of Krauzer. She struggled to make sense of the sheer magnitude of the assault made by their attackers and what they thought they had to gain by their efforts. She had no answers.

SABRE STARED UP at the two helicopters circling the USC campus like buzzards eyeing roadkill. "Are those birds ours?"

"Negative." Gerard pulled on the wheel and guided them over the low curb separating the parking area from the street. The Mercedes's large wheels climbed the curb easily and the high-tuned suspension smoothed out the bump.

Green machine-gun tracers flitted from the helicopter closest to the building while the second craft circled at a wider radius.

"Who are these people?" Sabre asked.

"Professionals." Gerard scowled through the windshield. "*Messy* professionals. This isn't how you contain a situation. Law enforcement agencies are going to be all over this. The clock's working against us now."

Sabre silently agreed but knew that was both a positive and a negative. Police were doubtless on their way now, which took away time from whoever was after Krauzer, but that knowledge was going to make those men tracking Krauzer take even bigger risks.

"Police." Dyson leaned forward and pointed to the right. "On our two o'clock."

Glancing to the right, Sabre watched as a black-and-white patrol car, light bar flashing red and blue, pulled into the campus parking area. While it was still in motion, a rocket streaked across seventy yards and impacted against the patrol car's grille.

The warhead exploded and knocked the patrol car's front end up like a boxer taking an uppercut to the chin. The engine hood sprang open and a ball of fire engulfed the vehicle, spreading quickly.

Sabre doubted the driver had survived the immediate detonation, and when the flames leaped into the patrol car's interior and the officer didn't try to escape, he was certain of it.

Meszoly cursed and launched into evasive action, yanking on the steering wheel, almost avoiding the second rocket that sped toward them. Instead of catching the SUV dead center as the shooter had intended, the warhead slammed into the Mercedes's right rear quarter panel.

Flames wreathed the rear of the SUV and the force knocked the vehicle over onto its left side. Heat filled the interior at once as Sabre jerked helplessly in the five-contact seat belt harness. The air bag blew out and slammed into his chest like a giant fist. The stench of cordite filled the air, and the detonation rang against his ears and stole part of his hearing. He tasted blood in his mouth.

"This is Black Legion One," Sabre called over his headset. "We need assistance. Our vehicle has been disabled." He slipped a combat knife from his vest, flicked the blade open and sawed through the seat belt. "Does anyone copy?"

"Copy, Black Legion One. Ten is on your six."

Through the cracked windshield, Sabre watched as another SUV pulled in front of the one he was in, providing partial cover. The men in that vehicle deployed in two two-man groups and laid down suppressive fire.

Sabre gave up on trying to open his door. He drew his pistol and slammed the butt into the window, shattering the safety glass so he could pull it out. "Do you see the shooters?"

The radio crackled in response. "We have the shooters, One. Two of them at eleven o'clock. One of them is down. The other is running."

"Get me some ID on these people if you can."

"Roger."

"These people are in heavier than expected." Sabre pulled himself through the window and crouched, leathering his weapon and then extending his hand down to Meszoly. "Watch yourselves."

"Copy that."

Meszoly grabbed Sabre's hand and allowed himself to be helped as he clambered up from the overturned vehicle. "This can't be about Krauzer," he said, then wiped blood from his split lips with the back of his hand. "That man is more self-indulgent than important. This is about something else."

The Merovingian kings, Sabre thought. That's what this is about. Still, so many years had passed since those days and the time of Matthias Corvinus. Something that had been lost for so long couldn't just reappear. And who would be so interested in finding it?

Dyson broke through the rear passenger window as the heat of the burning vehicle swirled over them. Blood ran from two cuts on the side of his face and dripped from his chin. Still, he seemed steady enough as he reached back inside the SUV and hauled out the man he'd been seated with. Sabre helped Dyson because the other man was unconscious. Together, they hauled the man's deadweight from the stricken vehicle just before the gas tank exploded and knocked them to the ground.

Rising again, Sabre told Dyson to stay with the unconscious man. Then he and Meszoly headed toward the target building, taking cover where they could. One of the men who'd wielded a rocket launcher lay bleeding on the ground and managed to pull his sidearm. Sabre shot the man in the face and leaped over the corpse. Behind him, two other police cars pulled into the parking lot, sirens howling. They rolled to a stop on either side of the burning patrol car.

"Black Legion Nine." Sabre reached the next clearing and

peered across the open area separating him from the next building. The helicopters continued circling above, but their attention was split between their mission goal and the arrival of Sabre's people and the police. "This is Black Legion One."

"Go, One. Nine copies." Saadiya Bhattacharjee's British accent sounded unflappable. She'd been born to a Sikh family in Telangana, India, and had finished her education in crisis communication at Oxford. Sabre had hired her immediately when their paths crossed three years ago, headhunting her from other corporations by promising her a more exciting career than patching political careers and spin-doctoring bad products put out by corporations.

"I need you to interface with the local police," Sabre said. "Let them know we're on the job."

"Copy that."

"And don't get shot."

Saadiya laughed, then said, "Ta."

Taking his smartphone from his tactical vest, Sabre pulled up the GPS locator he had that connected him to Krauzer's position inside the building. All of his clients were programmed into his locator systems. He and Meszoly were only 179 meters out and closing fast. He broke into a run with Meszoly following behind and to the right so they'd both have established fields of fire.

ANNJA HEARD KRAUZER before she saw him. Orta followed in her wake, crouched as she was. When she reached the door, she stood and peered through the small window beside the closed entrance. Inside, the soft glow of a cell phone revealed where Krauzer was.

The director knelt under a computer desk in a dark room and spoke in a hoarse whisper that carried. "Sabre! Where are you? I'm in trouble!"

Annja tried the door but it was locked.

"Allow me." Orta stepped forward. "Most of the classrooms on this floor open with the same key to facilitate matters."

She stepped back and allowed the professor access to the door. He took a set of keys from his pocket and started sorting through them.

Keeping calm in spite of the tension that filled her, Annja divided her focus between the hallway and the shattered wall of windows. She'd noted the second helicopter circling the building, as well, and kept expecting one or the other to sweep in. She still didn't know what the explosions outside the building had been about.

After succeeding in unlocking the door, Orta opened it and entered. The yellow rectangle of the hallway lights fell into the dark room. He started to reach for the lights but caught himself before Annja pointed out that wouldn't be a good idea.

"What are you doing?" Krauzer glared up at them. "Get out of here! This is my hiding spot!"

"Don't be ridiculous." Orta turned away from him and faced Annja.

"They're after me." Holding the crystal between his knees, Krauzer waved his free hand at Orta, keeping him away. "You're leading them right to me."

"They're after all of us."

"Really? *Really?* You're here every day, so these guys just happen to show up tonight to get you and I'm unlucky enough to get caught in the middle of that? Do you even hear yourself?"

"They're totally happy to kill all of us," Orta stated. "They want the crystal."

Krauzer wrapped his free arm around the crystal and turned his attention to the phone. "You need to get here. *Now!*"

"You know, if they get him, maybe they'll leave us alone," Orta said.

"Wait." Krauzer wasted no time thinking about that. He grabbed hold of the desk and partially scuttled out from hiding. "You can't just desert me. We need to stick together."

Shaking his head, Orta looked back at Annja.

She slipped her miniflashlight from her backpack, switched it on and swept the high-intensity beam around the classroom. It was larger than she'd initially thought, actually built like a small auditorium with stadium seating. The only other door out of the room was on the same side of the wall.

Voices echoed outside in the hallway, and she knew they were out of running room.

9

"Get down." Annja switched off the miniflashlight as she closed the door softly and locked it behind her. The barrier was too flimsy to put up much resistance, but maybe the men looking for them would hurry on by. On the other side of the door, police sirens screamed and the *whop-whop-whop* of the helicopter rotors was somewhat muted.

"Up there." She pointed Orta to the highest seat. "Stay away from the windows and hide in the corner—otherwise you'll be skylined against the outside lights."

Clutching the manuscript case to his chest, Orta sprinted up the long steps and hunkered down behind the curved row of tables. He disappeared in the inky pools of shadows, and Annja hoped that he would be safe during the coming confrontation.

Sliding back under the desk, Krauzer drew his legs farther into the darkness, but the phone's light illuminated his face.

"Turn off the phone." Annja slid the machine pistol out of the backpack and readied it.

Reluctantly, with a last whispered command to whoever was listening, Krauzer broke the connection and pocketed the phone. He held on to the crystal with both arms, and Annja didn't know if he was trying to protect the object or hide behind it.

Quietly, breathing evenly, Annja put her back to the front wall, where both doors were, staying away from the gleaming whiteboard behind her so she wouldn't be easily seen. She waited, willing herself to be calm.

Out in the hallway, the voices quieted. Annja didn't know if the men looking for them had passed or if they were listening on the other side of the locked doors. A moment later, the door handle on her right twisted with a soft metallic click.

The gunman pushed the door open with a foot, letting the light from the hallway into the room. His dark shadow shifted slightly.

Annja waited, resisting the impulse to shoot the man in the foot, even though he was dressed like the other men they'd encountered. Wounding the man while they were trapped in the room wouldn't help. A wounded man could call out for reinforcements, and if he was the only man, once she put him down, they might be able to get free.

The other door opened more, letting Annja know the attack was going to come from two fronts by an unknown number of attackers. She kept calm, knowing everything was going to come down to split-second reaction time.

A whispered conversation she couldn't make out took place in the hall. Then the first man shouldered his way into the room with his weapon tucked in close to his shoulder. The noise outside became louder immediately.

As soon as the gunman breached the entrance, Annja opened fire, aiming for the man's shoulder and letting the machine pistol rise until the rounds hammered the man in the neck and the side of his head.

Dead, dying or unconscious, the man dropped as the second door exploded open.

Annja whirled, trying to cover the second entrance and knowing the gunman there had seen her muzzle flashes reflected in the dark windows on the other side of the room. He would know where she was standing. She whirled, but the man was already firing. At least one of his bullets struck her machine pistol and tore it from her hands, while the others dug into the wall behind her with jackhammer impacts.

Deserting her position against the wall, Annja slid and

dropped behind the desk at the front of the room. As she came up again, she reached into the Otherwhere for the sword and instantly felt the hilt, sure and steady in her hand.

The sword looked plain and simple, three feet of double-edged steel forged in a simple cross pattern. The weapon was a warrior's instrument, designed to kill and maim, meant to be carried onto a battlefield.

Annja rose on the other side of the desk while the gunman searched for her. His eyes hadn't gotten used to the gloom trapped in the classroom, and he fired again, missing her by inches as she raced at him. The heat of the bullets burned across her cheek and the muzzle flashes lit up his hard face, hiding him in the sudden intense illumination.

Holding the leather-bound sword hilt in both hands, Annja slashed at the machine pistol as the gunman tried to correct his aim. The blade sliced through the weapon, cutting the suppressor and barrel from the machine pistol and knocking what was left from the man's hand. He reached for the pistol at his hip but didn't get to it before she put the sword's point through his throat.

Bleeding, frantic, the man fell back into the hallway and tried to stem the wound in his neck.

"Annja, look out!" Orta called from the back of the room.

She'd already caught a peripheral glimpse of the third man coming through the door the first man had, and she took shelter in the door frame. Bullets drummed a lethal beat on the door, tearing through the wood.

The gunman, in a Kevlar mask and body armor, fired a couple bursts toward the back of the room. The windows there shattered and Orta cried out in pain. More of the outside pandemonium poured into the building.

"Get up, Krauzer!" The gunman kept his weapon pointed in Annja's direction as he spoke to the director under the desk at the side of the room. Annja thought she detected a French accent, but her hearing was cottony from the noise in the room. "You can carry that crystal or I can take it out of your dead hands!"

"I'm coming! I'm coming!" Krauzer climbed out from under the desk on one hand and his knees. He carried the crystal in the other hand.

Annja glanced at the back of the room but she couldn't see Orta. Frustrated, she watched as Krauzer joined the gunman in the hallway. She thought briefly of trying to reach the doorway but knew that she would be cut down by gunfire before she got to the man.

The gunman yanked Krauzer to one side. The director followed his captor's snarled directions as they pulled back out of the room. Lifting the weapon in front of him, the gunman fired at the second door, driving Annja from her hiding place and back into the room.

Sliding into place beside the door, availing herself of the scant cover, Annja watched helplessly as the gunman pulled Krauzer farther down the hallway. Trusting that the director was safe for the moment, she turned her attention to Orta. The illumination from the open doors revealed where the machine pistol had landed after being ripped from her hands. She scooped up the weapon on her way back to the professor.

As Annja approached, Orta tried to raise himself from the floor, but his hand slipped in the blood that had gushed from the wound in his abdomen. His lips trembled and his eyes were wide with fear. He held his free hand to the wound.

"Lie back." Placing the machine pistol to one side and letting the sword return to the Otherwhere, Annja put her hands on his shoulders and pressed him back against the carpeted floor.

"They shot me." Orta pulled his hand from his wound and tried to examine it, but blood soaked his shirt.

"It'll be okay." Annja ripped his shirt open, searching for the wound. She slipped her miniflashlight from her pocket and switched it on, then clamped it between her teeth as she angled the beam on the gunshot. "You're going to be okay. Do you hear me?"

"Yeah." Orta nodded, but he was shaking and his eyes unfocused and refocused as he fought the onset of shock.

"We're going to stop this bleeding and the paramedics will be here soon." The warm blood gushed over Annja's fingers as she shrugged off her short-waisted jacket and the green pullover she was wearing. The jacket material was too coarse, but the pullover was soft enough to work as a compress.

"Sounds good." He seemed to be on the verge of sleep.

"Stay with me, Vincent."

"I will. I'm just going to close my eyes."

"No. You need to stay awake. I'm going to roll you over for just a moment."

"Sure."

Putting her free arm under the man, Annja rolled him onto his unwounded side briefly. His back was whole, letting her know the bullet was still inside him. Having only one wound to control was better, but there was no way to know if the bullet had bounced around inside and torn through other blood vessels.

She hoped help arrived soon. Concentrating on her patient, she kept the compress in place and reached for her sat phone.

ON THE TOP FLOOR of the building, Sabre sprinted as fast as he dared, aware that a gunman could be around the next corner. So far, though, the only men he'd seen were dead. Someone with Krauzer knew how to shoot.

According to the GPS signal on Sabre's phone, he was only forty-three meters from Krauzer, but that didn't indicate which floor he was on. Sabre had followed the trail of violence to his current position.

At least two men lay sprawled in the hallway ahead of

him, coming out of both doors. One man's feet lay in the way of the door. Another man had fallen out into the hallway, visible from his head to his knees. He lay on his back and the slash in his throat no longer fountained blood, indicating that his heart had stopped pumping. Both of them were in the same uniforms and armor that the other men had been wearing.

"Watch out!" Meszoly's hand fell heavily onto Sabre's shoulder and drove him down.

They hit the ground just as a helicopter outside the building opened fire. Heavy 7.62 mm rounds chopped through the glass and left fist-size holes in the wall and tore the display cases to pieces, spilling books and artifacts across the tiles.

Rolling onto his side, Sabre brought up the machine pistol and aimed at the helicopter's gunner, centering on the muzzle flashes spewing from the weapon. The machine gun fell silent almost immediately and Sabre pushed himself to his feet, his ears ringing.

Looking through the empty space where the window had been, boots crunching on shards, Sabre dropped the empty magazine from his weapon and reloaded. He knew without looking that Meszoly had his back. Holding the machine pistol steady, Sabre fired bursts into the pilot, watching the glass around the man flare out around him.

The helicopter went out of control, diving and listing, coming around in a slow semicircle into one of the buildings.

"Get down!" Sabre turned from the window an instant before the rotors struck the building.

Meszoly threw himself down and rolled toward the outer hallway wall, seeking shelter. When the rotors struck the building, they turned into a screaming cloud of shrapnel that peppered everything around them. The helicopter exploded in an orange-and-black fireball that cast wavering light into the hallway.

Getting to his feet, Sabre checked the doorways in the

hallway and saw no new movement. He checked the GPS and saw that the distance separating him from Krauzer hadn't changed. The movie director was either down or he was in the stairwell.

Not wanting to leave anything to chance, Sabre ran to the darkened room and halted at the wall beside the dead man. He flicked on the miniflashlight clipped to the side of the machine pistol's barrel and scanned the room. He stopped on the half-naked woman pointing a machine pistol at him while on her knees in front of a man lying in the corner of the room.

The woman didn't flinch and Sabre respected that about her. She held his gaze easily and looked capable.

"I've got a wounded man here who needs medical attention." She spoke calmly without taking her eyes from Sabre.

For a moment, Sabre thought she was talking to him. Then he spotted the phone glowing on the floor beside her.

"He's been shot in the stomach and is going into shock." The woman described where she was.

"Are you in danger at the moment?" a man asked over the phone's speaker.

The woman waited, staring at Sabre.

He lifted the machine pistol and held his other hand up, as well. "I'm looking for Krauzer."

The woman shook her head. "He's not here. If you're not here to kill us and you have someone with medical experience, we need help."

"I'm not your guy." Sabre took a step back. "I'm looking for Krauzer."

"I need *help*." For the first time, the calm cracked and she sounded rattled.

"I'm sending someone. Saadiya, do you copy?"

"Affirmative."

"I need a med team up here now."

"Understood."

Sabre pointed to the fallen man with his chin. "A team will be here soon. Don't shoot them."

"Tell them to let me know who they are."

Grinning, Sabre tossed the woman a quick salute and whipped around the side of the doorway. He checked the GPS again and ran full tilt with Meszoly at his heels.

10

Trotting down the stairwell, de Cerceau cursed Krauzer for his slowness and he cursed whoever had shown up to interfere in the ongoing operation. The man who had hired him had mentioned nothing about the possibility of another team being involved. Especially not one that came so well equipped.

When he reached the first-floor door leading back into the building, de Cerceau yanked the entrance open and propelled Krauzer ahead of him in case anyone was lying in wait. When no shots were fired, he followed the man into the hallway.

Krauzer stood like a lemming, frozen in the hallway with his arms wrapped around the crystal. He was breathing hard and looked pale, as if he might pass out at any moment.

De Cerceau shoved Krauzer into motion again, driving him toward the nearest exit.

When de Cerceau reached the door, he tried the knob and discovered it was locked. He leveled the machine pistol and fired. Sparks jumped as the bullets shredded the locking mechanism. He pushed Krauzer through the doors and followed him, urging the man into a run while scanning the surroundings.

To the south, the debris of one of the helicopters lay scattered between buildings. Small fires clung to some of the pieces, and the main body lay canted to one side. Trapped in his seat harness, the dead pilot lay halfway out of the aircraft.

"Gerard." De Cerceau spoke loudly, hoping his voice would be heard over the commotion.

"I'm here." Gerard's response was tense.

"Are you free?"

"Yes, but if we don't get out of here now, we're not going to escape the police."

The police were the least of de Cerceau's worries. The rival team concerned him more.

"I am outside the building now. I will meet you at the northeast corner."

"I will be there." A flurry of gunfire ripped into life at Gerard's end of the conversation.

Staying to the shadows as much as he was able, de Cerceau herded his prisoner in the direction they needed to go.

As de Cerceau and Krauzer cleared the last building and headed toward the street, Gerard's car glided around the corner and slid to a stop. Behind them, de Cerceau spotted the men running from the building they'd just quit. Trusting that the men would not shoot for fear of hitting Krauzer, trusting that they wanted the man alive, de Cerceau swiveled and unleashed a burst that drove the two men on his heels into cover.

Beside him, the director yelped in fear, dropped the crystal he'd been carrying and ran toward the nearest oak tree.

Cursing the men behind him and Krauzer's cowardice, de Cerceau grabbed the crystal from the ground as bullets tore into the landscaped bushes around him.

Having no choice, de Cerceau sprinted for all he was worth, heading for Gerard. Just before he reached the car, a salvo of bullets ripped into a tree as he ducked behind it.

Gerard pushed the passenger door open. De Cerceau tossed the crystal into the back of the vehicle and slid into the passenger seat. Gerard floored it and de Cerceau allowed the acceleration to slam the door shut while he scanned the college grounds.

The two men had reached Krauzer and were half-masked in shadows. Before Gerard cleared the area, one of the men dropped his machine pistol and drew his sidearm. De Cerceau sat comfortably behind the bullet-resistant glass and tried to recognize the man.

In the next instant, armor piercing bullets holed the window and the car.

Gerard swore and pulled through the parking lot of a nearby restaurant, one of the many such places that ringed the campus. Panicked college students ducked out of the way as Gerard skidded for a moment before regaining traction on the side street.

Then they were rolling, gaining speed as they drove away from the college.

"CAN YOU HEAR ME, Vincent?" Annja kept the pressure on Orta's wound, wondering if he'd lost too much blood, knowing he'd lost a lot because it was soaked into the carpet and the knees of her pants.

"Yeah…yeah. I'm still here." Orta's voice was faint, barely heard above the wind shear that entered the building through the shattered windows.

"Good. You just stay with me, okay?"

"I'm here." He blinked, and from the way his eyes moved and his pupils dilated, she knew that he couldn't focus his vision.

Annja remained calm through sheer force of will. She'd been in dangerous situations before, and she'd lost people she'd known. That was always the hard part: losing people whom she felt she should be able to save.

She didn't want Vincent Orta to die. He was innocent in this. Whatever this turned out to be.

A light flashed from the doorway.

Startled, Annja reached for the machine pistol but didn't bring it up.

"Ms. Creed, are you still there?" That was the 911 dispatch operator, as collected and as efficient as ever. The phone lay on the ground beside her on speaker mode.

"I am."

"A team of EMTs are en route to your position. The police are holding them up until they make sure everyone is safe."

Annja stared into the bright light in the doorway. Whoever was out there was not with the police. "They need to hurry."

"I understand that, but we want to make certain everyone is safe."

"I know."

"Ms. Creed." The voice from the doorway was calm and deep and had an accent that sounded Caribbean. "My name is Eric Magloire. My employer sent me to help your friend."

Annja relaxed, but only a little. Once inside, the man could kill them both. She reached for the sword and felt it in the Otherwhere. "Hurry."

The man stepped through the doorway dressed in Kevlar and carrying a white case with red crosses on it. He moved quickly and dropped to his knees beside Annja and Orta. "What do we have?" His words held calm reassurance, not threat.

"Bullet wound. Looks like a 9 mm. Entry point only. No exit."

"Very good." Magloire pressed gloved fingertips to the side of Orta's neck. "He's lost a lot of blood."

"I know."

Magloire opened his case and started taking out supplies. "You're no stranger to bullet wounds?"

"No."

"Good. You've probably saved his life. I'm going to put a compress on the wound, start him on some plasma to replace the blood loss and get him stabilized for the EMTs to move him."

"Thank you."

"That's what I'm here for. If I need assistance, you can help?"

"Of course."

Magloire smiled. "Good. I'm very good at what I do, Ms. Creed. I will take care of your friend and he will be fine."

That reassurance lifted a huge weight off Annja's shoulders. "Do you know if Krauzer is all right?" She wanted to ask about the crystal, but she felt too guilty to do that.

"He's been recovered. He is fine."

"What about the people who did this?"

Magloire shook his head as he worked with deft movements, bandaging Orta and starting an IV. "I don't know. Perhaps you could talk to your friend and keep him with us?"

"Of course." Annja focused on Orta and leaned down to speak into the man's ear.

LAPD DETECTIVE PERRY BISHOP was a no-nonsense kind of guy. He was totally focused when he listened, and when he spoke, he was succinct and to the point.

He sat primly on the other side of the table in the interview room and took notes in addition to recording their session. "These men were after Steven Krauzer, but you don't know why. Is that correct, Ms. Creed?"

Annja sat in the uncomfortable chair in an orange jail jumpsuit. The detectives had claimed her clothing as evidence. She wrapped her hands around the hot mug of tea that Bishop's partner had brought to her. "Yes."

She kept her answer simple and direct. Bishop's soft approach and his partner's willingness to sit and be silent let Annja know she was in the hands of professionals who weighed every movement and facial tic.

Detective Leslie Connolly was about Annja's age but was as controlled and as professional as her partner. Both of the detectives had clip-on holsters that had been left, with their weapons, locked in their desks.

"You can ask me the same questions over and over again or find new ways to ask them, but that's all I know." Annja sipped her tea and hoped they believed her. "May I ask questions?"

Bishop shrugged. "Sure."

"Who were the men who attacked us?"

Bishop shook his head. "We don't know for certain yet. Two of the men have turned up in international files. They were mercenaries. Why would mercenaries be hunting you, Ms. Creed?"

"If you've checked any of the stories and references I've given you in the past three hours, you'll understand that my path has often crossed those of men who traffic in stolen goods."

"Artifacts."

"Yes."

"That you were looking for because of your television show, *Chasing History's Monsters*."

Annja sighed. "Not always."

"Not always?" Bishop cocked his head slightly.

"Things get complicated."

"Maybe you could help me understand these complications."

"In addition to the television show, I also work as an archaeologist and help with certification of authenticity on different objects."

"But that isn't what you were doing in Los Angeles."

"No. I'm consulting on a movie."

"A movie that Mr. Krauzer is directing."

"Yes."

"In particular, you were consulting on the crystal Mr. Krauzer lost."

The news that Krauzer had lost the piece shocked Annja, as she knew Bishop intended it to. She knotted her hands and leaned a little farther forward in her chair before she caught herself. "He lost the crystal?"

"Yes."

Annja had already asked if Krauzer was okay and if he was safe. Bishop had told her that the man was, which had made her feel better. Vincent Orta was still in surgery and under police guard.

"The crystal was only one of the pieces that I was brought in to consult on," Annja said.

"And now it's missing?" Bishop cocked an eyebrow.

"The last time I saw it, Krauzer had it."

"Who wants the crystal?" Bishop asked.

"Tonight? I don't know. You know more about these mercenaries than I do."

Bishop refolded his hands. "We know a few names, but we also know there was an altercation yesterday morning involving this selfsame crystal between you, Mr. Krauzer and Bernard Molk."

"Bernard Molk?" Annja thought for a moment. "You mean Barney? The biker who was with Melanie Harp? She stole the crystal off the movie set. He was there when Krauzer went to Melanie's apartment to get his property back." She made sure her story got recorded in case there was any blowback from the home invasion.

"Why would Ms. Harp take the crystal?"

"She and Barney were planning on ransoming it back to Krauzer."

Bishop looked at his partner, who made a note on the pad she kept. "How well do you know Mr. Molk and Ms. Harp?"

Annja shook her head. "I don't. Including yesterday morning, I've met Melanie Harp twice. She didn't show up at the set, which was why she was let go. I only met Barney the one time."

Bishop was silent for a moment. "Would it surprise you to know that Mr. Molk was dead?"

For a moment, Annja considered that, wondering if she was being played. "Yeah. That would surprise me." A chill ghosted down her spine. "Is Barney dead?"

"Yes, he's dead. Someone snapped his neck shortly after he was bailed out yesterday. His body was found in his apartment only a short time ago when we sent a car around to bring him back in for questioning."

"Who did it?"

"We don't know. Only a short time ago, one of the inmates in the women's section of the jail stabbed Ms. Harp. She died before help could be given."

Unease threaded through Annja and she wrapped her arms around herself. "And you don't know who did that, either?"

"We do. We just don't know why. From what we can figure out, the woman who killed Ms. Harp had never met her."

"Why would she kill Melanie?"

Detective Connolly leaned forward and rested her elbows on the table. "The woman lawyered up immediately after killing Ms. Harp. She's got a high-priced attorney, too. Having him isn't going to help her. The woman was working on her third strike. She's not going to leave prison this time. However, killing Melanie Harp—we think—had to have been some part of an arrangement that benefited her."

"You think someone paid this woman to kill Melanie." Annja worked to get her brain around that, but she was tired and the fatigue made her thoughts slow.

"We do." Connolly's eyes regarded Annja. "What do you think?"

"Killing Melanie doesn't make any sense."

"Maybe you could tell us about the crystal and the manuscript pages Dr. Orta had," Bishop suggested.

"The crystal is supposed to be the key to a treasure of the Merovingian kings."

"Who are they?"

"They used to rule the Franks from the mid-fifth century to the late eighth century."

"The Franks?"

"Yes. What is now France and part of Germany, lands they inherited from the Gauls and later took from the Roman Empire."

"You're talking about France," Connolly said.

"Yes."

"In the past?"

"Twelve hundred years ago." Annja frowned at the detectives. "I told you this was going to get complicated."

11

"So you're out of jail?" Doug Morrell sounded bored and a little put out.

"For the moment." Annja ignored the curious stares of the people in the lobby of the Luxe Rodeo Drive Hotel. She was the only one there wearing a bright orange jail jumpsuit. Her clothes had not been returned. The well-dressed man at the concierge desk looked at her twice but said nothing.

"I've been calling for hours, since one of the interns let me know the story about your arrest and how you blew up USC was trending on Twitter."

"*I* didn't blow up anything."

"And you couldn't return my calls."

Annja took a deep breath and let it out. "They don't let you have your phone when you're arrested. And for the record, I was not under arrest. I was merely detained for questioning as a person of interest."

"Then you had your phone."

"I didn't have a lot of time to call anyone, Doug. And if I needed to make a call, I would have needed a lawyer."

"I could have gotten you a lawyer."

"I was hoping I didn't need one. I'm glad I didn't."

"Are you planning on getting arrested again?"

"I didn't plan to get *detained* this time." Annja used her room card to access the elevator to one side of the check-in desk. The people standing there stared at her with concern, and the woman working the computer frowned at her.

"You've been in police hands twice in the past twenty-four hours. You know what disappoints me?"

"No." Annja stared at her reflection in the glossy walls and stainless steel of the elevator. Her hair was blown and hung in straggles. She decided this was probably the worst she'd ever looked outside a dig.

"I barely heard any mention of our show on the news, and the Twitter posts were more about you instead of the show." Doug did sound disappointed, but a lot of it was put on. "We need all the publicity we can get these days."

Doug was still worried about the way *Chasing History's Monsters* had almost been cut from the network.

"They probably cut it. I mentioned the show."

"We were mentioned on a crawler a couple times, but who really reads those things? They just get in the way."

"I wasn't really the story, Doug. Steven Krauzer was the story, and now you've got a lot of dead people soaking up attention." Annja couldn't help thinking about the men she'd killed. So far Bishop and Connolly—and the LAPD—were convinced she'd acted in self-defense. Much of that was due to the testimony offered by Krauzer and the mysterious security agency he had called to rescue him.

The elevator stopped on her floor and she waited for the doors to open.

"How much longer are you going to be there?"

"I don't know. Krauzer's in a tizzy because his shooting schedule has taken a direct hit." Annja strode from the elevator toward the hallway where her room was. It would be safer to leave LA, but Bishop and Connolly hadn't exactly been fans of that, and she hated to leave things undone. The mystery revealed in Orta's manuscript pages was still unsolved. She wanted to believe it was solvable, but with archaeology, not all the answers turned up and sometimes a guess was the best a person could do.

Annja paused at her door, swiped her room card, listened for the locking mechanism to disengage and stepped inside.

"Have you even been out to the harbor to look for the

ghost pirates that are supposed to be there?" Doug was nothing if not dogmatic when it came to the things he wanted.

Annja sighed. "Ducking bullets? Running for my life? Did any of that get through?"

"Sure. You also told me that you didn't get any of it on film."

"No, I didn't."

"And even if you did, we don't do cops-and-robbers shows."

"Not even a haunted prison?"

"Cool! You're talking about Alcatraz? Alcatraz would be the bomb!"

Annja made sure the door locked behind her, added the second lock and tried to relax. "Doug, I wasn't in Alcatraz. I'm not going to Alcatraz. I'm going to make myself presentable and I'm going to the hospital to check on Vincent Orta."

The professor had made it through surgery and was expected to make a full recovery.

"Yeah, yeah, but think about the Alcatraz thing. I'm telling you, that could be something that—"

"Goodbye, Doug. Hanging up now. Don't call back. For hours. I'll be catching up on sleep I've missed." Annja broke the connection, dug her power cord out of her backpack and set the phone to charge, then added her tablet PC and camera out of habit. Full power for devices only happened through diligence.

She stripped out of the jumpsuit and wondered what she was supposed to do with it. Bishop and Connolly had let her leave with the garment, but someone was probably accountable for it. She dropped the jumpsuit onto the chair by the king-size bed, grabbed her toiletries and headed into the bathroom. A bath, hot and bubbly, was calling her name.

And sleep. She so needed a few hours of rest.

"Look, Sabre, I'm glad you guys rescued me. Really, I am, but—"

Sabre cut Krauzer off midsentence. "I'm pleased that

you are satisfied with our efforts, Mr. Krauzer, and trust me
when I say you've gotten your money's worth on the service
you've been paying for." He shifted in the plush chair and
tried to curb his impatience.

They sat in Krauzer's office on the movie-studio lot. The
bungalow had been built back in the 1940s during the hey-
day of filmmaking, when studios were pushing out around
five hundred movies and shorts a year.

The director sat behind a large polished walnut desk.
He hadn't yet changed out of the clothes he'd been wearing
all night, despite the fact that the midmorning sun shone
through the Viennese blinds. He had already scheduled a
couple of interviews with entertainment-news agencies and
was planning to do them in his clothing. A makeup person
had already been in to touch up his appearance, managing
to almost make him look disheveled and heroic.

His office was empty of anything that didn't reek of his
own successes, and framed posters of his hit movies hung
on the walls in full-colored glory, crying out for attention.

If Sabre hadn't wanted to know more about the crystal
and the manuscript pages Krauzer had mentioned the professor had, he wouldn't have been there to listen to all the self-
aggrandizement the director favored. Those details about the
crystal were missing pieces to the puzzle, and Sabre didn't
want to let them go.

"I just wanted you to know that, and I didn't want to
sound selfish." Krauzer checked his appearance in the
lighted mirror that sat on his desk, brushing at the stubble
filling in around his thin beard. "But those guys got my
property. I want the elf-witch crystal back."

"Mr. Krauzer—"

"Don't call me Mr. Krauzer. Call me Steven. You and
me, we've been through the war together. We've shed blood
together." Krauzer ran his fingers through his hair, muss-

ing it further. He pointed to a slightly darkened spot on his face. "Is this a bullet burn?"

"It looks like dirt."

"I think it's a bullet burn." Krauzer tapped at his face but didn't touch the mark, probably for fear it would wipe away. "Wow. I came close to taking a bullet right between the eyes." He grinned. "That should look good on *ET.* Maybe get me a booking on *The Tonight Show.*" He frowned. "Of course, that would go better if I was holding my elf-witch crystal at the time, showing people that I'd gotten it back. That would make a statement. Think we can get that done soon?"

Sabre quelled the impulse to yell at the man. Luckily, none of his men had been killed during the firefight or this session would have gone differently. Police officers had been killed, and the LAPD wasn't thrilled with Krauzer, but they would treat him with kid gloves because he was a mover and a shaker in the city.

"We don't even know who took the crystal." Sabre made himself remain polite.

"You'll figure it out, though, right? 'Cause you have people who can find stuff?"

Sabre did have people looking into the identities of the men who had attacked Krauzer, but the police weren't being forthcoming with information. He was here now to find out more information about the crystal. The Merovingian stories danced around inside his head. So much of his family's history was tied up in that time period. "I do."

"Then you should know who those guys were at any time, right?"

"Hopefully."

Krauzer's phone rang. He checked caller ID, then reached for the handset. "I gotta take this. Media people."

Sabre nodded.

Krauzer punched the speaker function. "This is Steven Krauzer. Who am I speaking with?"

As soon as the caller identified herself as an entertainment reporter and started gushing about the kidnapping and gunplay, Sabre tuned her out. His phone vibrated in his pocket. He stood up from the plush chair and walked to the side of the office that looked out over the movie lots.

Outside, studio groups were already in motion. Electricians and carpenters stood out in front of sets and warehouses where various television shows were shot. One of those housed the set that Krauzer and his people were currently working on. Luckily, whoever the mercenaries were, they hadn't struck while Krauzer and the film crew were on set.

The hit came after the crystal was stolen by Melanie Harp and the Creed woman had circulated pictures of it on the internet. That had drawn out the kidnapper-thieves. Sabre made a mental note to have Saadiya and her people check up on that. Maybe they could establish a trail.

Sabre tapped his Bluetooth earpiece and answered the call. "Yeah."

"Annja Creed is on the move." Meszoly sounded tired, but Sabre knew he could depend on the man.

"Where's she going?"

"I don't know yet."

"You're not the only one following her, are you?"

"No. I've got three others helping me watch. I was impressed with the way she handled herself. Considering how she dealt with those men, I'm wondering where she got her training and if maybe you should be offering her a job."

As far as Sabre knew, Annja Creed had never been military or covert ops. From the background Saadiya had turned up on the woman, she was just what she appeared to be: a television host and an archaeologist. However, she'd been to a lot of places around the world and dealt with a lot of conflict. Sabre was also sure not all of Annja Creed's brushes with criminals showed up. Despite her fame on the internet and social media, she was quite private. He understood and liked that about her because he was the same way.

"Good. Let me know if anything changes."

"I will. I've still got a team on the professor in the hospital, too. We're not the only ones watching Creed, though."

That didn't surprise Sabre. Only two paths remained open to anyone searching for the crystal: the thieves, who were in the wind, and Annja Creed. "I'm sure she's continuing to draw interest from the local police."

"She is, but I haven't identified all of the players yet. We've got some local law enforcement on the scene, but there are some bogeys, as well."

"Some of the men from last night?"

"We don't know yet."

That was going to be a problem. So far Sabre had kept his people on the right side of the LAPD. Over the years, he'd earned some goodwill, but he'd never had a situation go as ballistic as the one had the previous night.

"If there's a chance you can pick up one of the bogeys— quietly—maybe you should do that."

"Oh, I've got my eye out in case that opportunity presents itself. I'd like to find out who we're up against. Have you learned anything from Krauzer?"

Sabre checked the director's reflection in the window. Krauzer was talking enthusiastically to the entertainment reporter, and the story had grown since the last time he'd told it. Now Krauzer described how he'd taken up a weapon and blasted the helicopter out of the sky. Sabre was going to let the director stick with the story. That way the university people could come to Krauzer for reparations.

"I'm still working on that, but I'm beginning to get the feeling that he doesn't know anything more than he's telling."

12

"Ms. Creed, your taxi is here."

"Thank you." Annja tipped the concierge as he held open the cab's door so she could slide in. She got settled and belted in, then gave the driver instructions to take her to Good Samaritan Hospital, where Orta was currently laid up recovering. The driver pulled smoothly into traffic.

Although she'd managed only two hours of sleep, Annja felt somewhat rejuvenated after the long bath and the nap. She'd dressed in jeans, a tank top and a baggy sweater to break the chill coming in off the harbor. Her backpack rested in the seat beside her.

Connecting to her satellite internet on her tablet during the slow traffic, she checked some of the alt.history and alt. archaeology sites she visited when researching various projects for posts she'd entered about the Merovingian kings. She flicked through the entries quickly, not happy with the results because most of them had to do with Steven Krauzer and his movie more than historical whispers and rumors about the crystal. Slightly frustrated, she powered down the tablet PC and put it away, then slipped on a pair of sunglasses to keep the bright sunlight at bay. Taking a band from her backpack, she pulled her hair back into a ponytail. Excitement continued to thrum through her, a constant undercurrent because she knew the chase was still on.

"I TOLD THEM you were my girlfriend." Vincent Orta winced in embarrassment as he lay in the hospital bed surrounded by a phalanx of beeping and humming machinery. He looked small in the whiteness of the bed and his color hadn't yet come back. "That was the only way they would let you in. I apologize if I've discomfited you in any way."

Annja approached the bed and smiled. "Not a problem. I think it's flattering." She placed a vase of orchids on the small table beside the bed and sat in the nearby chair. "How are you feeling?"

Orta gestured toward the IV hanging above his head. "I'm pain-free and riding a great buzz. This stuff should be illegal."

Annja laughed even though the joke was old, remembering that it was probably Orta's first chance to use the line— and he was under the influence anyway.

"I brought you a care package." She held up the small bag she'd put together before leaving the hotel. "A deck of playing cards. A handful of thriller and science-fiction novels, in case you want the quiet instead of television. I took a guess at snacks and treats and settled on trail mix." She set the bag on the side table.

"You didn't have to do that."

"I kind of did." Annja smiled. "I'm the reason you're in the hospital. If I hadn't brought the crystal to you for help, you wouldn't have ended up getting shot."

"I wanted to see the crystal. I had my manuscript mystery to solve." Orta struggled to push himself up in the bed. "If there is any fault, it would be on both of us. But neither of us had a clue someone would be so interested in Krauzer's crystal."

"You see, that's where I am to blame. I put images up on the web and drew those people out."

Shoving with his hand again, Orta tried to find a more comfortable spot.

Annja gave him the bed controls and waited until he managed a sitting position that caused only a little wincing. She put a pillow behind his back to help him.

"Thanks. The meds help a lot, but I'm still weak and a little shaky." Orta sighed in relief. "I saw in the news that those guys who shot me got away with the crystal."

"They did."

"But you stayed with me. Thank you for that."

"I wasn't going to leave you."

Orta shook his head in disgust. "I also found out the police don't know who those men were."

"Detectives Bishop and Connolly have identified a few of them as international mercenaries. That isn't for media consumption yet, and I don't think they were exactly happy sharing the information with me, but they had to ask questions about what I knew. I made sure I was getting information, too."

Grimacing, Orta waited a beat. "Those were mercenaries? Like, take-over-third-world-countries mercenaries?"

"We didn't get into their history, but that's definitely the vibe I got from the detectives."

"Why are they so interested in the crystal? It doesn't make any sense."

"If they're mercenaries, they were probably hired."

"So someone had to hire them."

Annja smiled. "That's how these things would work."

"None of them have told the police who hired them?"

For a moment, Annja hesitated. "The police didn't recover any of those men alive."

"Oh." That news took away some of Orta's devil-may-care attitude even with the painkillers. "I didn't know the police had let you go. I called over there, to let them know you were one of the good guys, and was surprised you were released."

"They let me go because I didn't know what they want to know." Annja settled back in her chair. "I still don't."

"But you'd like to find out."

"I'd like to find out more about the crystal and those pages you found."

Orta sighed. "Me, too. Only it looks like I'm going to be on bed rest for a few days. And if I wasn't doing that, I'd be teaching class."

"How badly are you injured?"

"The surgeon told me the bullet didn't hit anything vital, nothing that's going to need reconstruction or will do any permanent damage, but I'll have to do some rehab, and I'll never wear a bikini again."

He chuckled and Annja smiled, impressed by the way he was conducting himself. The fear still showed in his eyes, though, and she knew part of his feigned resiliency was because she was a woman and he was there. Guys could be foolish at times. Getting shot was a big deal.

A uniformed police officer poked his head into the room, gave the surroundings a once-over and retreated.

"My guard." Orta shrugged and winced. "Evidently, the police believe I might still be in some danger."

"I don't think you are, but it's better to have protection and not need it than to need protection and not have it."

"True. And the police officer doesn't seem to mind being here. But I don't think he's getting anywhere with the nurses." Orta grinned, then looked more somber. "Do you still want to follow this up? The mystery mentioned in the manuscript?"

"Yes. You said you had something that might help?"

"A lead at most, I'm afraid, but I have to admit that I'm reluctant to give it to you because I don't know how much danger you're going to be in."

"Maybe those men were just after the crystal." Annja looked at Orta, hoping he wouldn't hold back, because she didn't have a definite direction to go in yet.

"Is that what you think?"

"I don't know, but I do know that I'm not ready to let this

go. With or without whatever you have, I'm going to look for answers. And the more I know…well, the more I know."

Orta nodded. "The manuscript we decoded mentions the Bibliotheca Corviniana. How familiar are you with that library?"

"I wasn't until this morning." While in the bath, Annja had used her tablet PC to consult her sources to bring her up to speed on the work listed in the hidden message.

"Ah, well, let me tell you what I know." Orta shifted on the bed again. "Matthias Corvinus put the library together sometime between 1458 and 1490. That's a thirty-two-year gap of uncertainty, and that lets you know how little we actually know of the library. The collection is rumored to have started earlier, but most scholars agree that Matthias declared the library in 1460. Agents of the king scoured the surrounding lands and picked up works written during the Greek and Roman empires and as many books written during the Renaissance as they were able. It was meant to assemble all the knowledge known to man."

"Like the Library of Alexandria."

"Exactly. People just assume so much knowledge is known, but they don't realize how hard civilizations and forward-thinking men and women have fought to hold on to it. They think since knowledge has always been there, that it always will be, and they don't realize how much learning slips through our fingers every day when records get destroyed. It is so frustrating how casually this younger generation just simply lets go of everything that has gone before. Even in our field. They develop tunnel vision and look for answers instead of learning the big picture or how to properly question something."

"That argument has probably been around since education was formalized." Annja felt the professor's pain, though. "I've seen the same kind of thing in the lectures and workshops I've been part of. Students grasp the idea of the fact there was a *before*, even nail down some of the details to regurgitate on a test, but they don't immerse themselves in those worlds."

"So you do know." Orta lay back. "What do you know about Matthias Corvinus?"

Leaning back in the chair, Annja got more comfortable. "He was king of Hungary and Croatia, and his whole reign was filled with battles and wars against Czech mercenaries and the Ottoman Empire. When Serbia and Bosnia fell, Matthias set aside his struggles against Frederick III, who was the Holy Roman Emperor at that time and the king of Germany."

"The first of the Hapsburg kings, yes."

"After Serbia and Bosnia were lost to the Ottoman Empire, Matthias made a deal with Frederick III to become king of Hungary, setting aside Frederick's claims to the Hungarian throne in 1463 after Matthias paid a fortune in ransom."

"Some call it blackmail." Orta grinned. "In any case, Matthias wasn't satisfied with his position and wasted no time beginning aggressive campaigns that netted his kingdom more lands. But that growth was difficult, and controlling all the conquered people and holding his borders against other encroaching countries was strenuous."

"He had more enemies without than friends with."

"Exactly, so he took steps to remedy that by hiring mercenaries of his own. His father, John Hunyadi, formed the core of that army in the early 1440s, hiring fighting men from other countries, but Matthias built upon that idea. As a boy, he'd fallen in love with stories about Julius Caesar's legions and military prowess. From 1458 until a few years after Matthias's death, those mercenary troops grew until they were the largest permanent army in the world at that time."

"The only other monarch to have a professional army during those years was Louis XIV of France." Annja warmed to the subject as she started spinning threads to connect everything she knew and could guess at. "As I recall, both Louis XIV and Matthias Corvinus insisted on permanent billets for their warriors."

"Precisely. Until that time, kings and royalty simply took men from their lands as they needed to. Those men worked at normal jobs until they were called into battle. There was no training, no practice and no drilling before they fought for their lives on a battlefield. Matthias's tactics and support of his army changed war and tactics in those areas for decades."

"His men also used firearms more readily than any other army at the time." Annja vaguely remembered that from her reading that morning.

"They used harquebuses, so primitive compared to today's rifles, but they were lethally effective at the time. A man had to train steadily and for years to use a longbow, which was the most dangerous ranged weapon on the battlefield in those days, but a man could become very effective with a harquebus in a matter of months. And at close range he was deadly."

Annja sat and listened, letting Orta speak because he was in his element.

"Of course, to raise and support such an army, Corvinus also had to find funding. That meant increased taxes, which no one wanted to pay, but he didn't give people a choice. There was a rebellion in Transylvania, but he quickly put that down, then started declaring wars for major land grabs. By that time, the Black Army, also called the Black Legion, was a well-honed fighting machine. Every fourth man was armed with a harquebus. Gunpowder was hard to come by and horribly expensive, but Corvinus kept his troops well supplied. As a result, his empire flourished."

Orta took another sip of water. "The military action at that time is fascinating, but that's not what you're interested in."

"I wouldn't say I wasn't interested." Annja grinned. "Military actions have shaped a lot of our history and provided numerous records and archives."

Orta smiled in return. "But we need to prioritize. The library grew as much as Corvinus's army. He guided his country into being the first to embrace the Renaissance that was only then taking place in Italy. Corvinus knew a new world was coming and he wanted to stay in step with it.

"No one knows for sure every book his library contained. There are no master lists. The National Széchényi Library in Budapest hopes to digitize what they know of the books. It's a colossal undertaking. The Turkish invasion lasted for decades, and Corvinus held out against them. After his death, though, it was a different matter. His successor, Vladislaus II, wasn't able to raise the necessary monies to keep the Black Legion together. They gradually went away and left the kingdom vulnerable. Somewhere in there, the library was ransacked and the surviving books scattered."

"We know a lot, but we don't know enough to figure out what Julio Gris was writing about in his papers."

"Gris mentioned the name of the man who had learned the story of the hidden Merovingian treasure." Orta looked at Annja.

"György Dózsa," Annja said. "It would have been nice if we could have finished reading those pages."

"Still, you have something. Do you know who György Dózsa was?"

"I'd heard of him before, but I did some research last night and his name turned up. Most historians believe he was a nobleman from Transylvania."

"Which means we have more ties to the Kingdom of Hungary, yes. That places us roughly in the same timeline as Corvinus."

"Dózsa raised an army of peasants to revolt against the nobles. He wasn't successful and ended up getting caught. He was tortured and executed by his enemies."

"Yes, and he's remembered as both a freedom fighter and Christian martyr by some and a criminal by others. Gris said he got the story of the Merovingian treasure from someone who knew Dózsa. There is a scholar I can put you in touch with. A man named Istvan Racz. He knows more Hungarian history than anyone I know. You should probably talk to him."

"Let me know where I can find him."

Frowning, pursing his lips and narrowing his eyes, Orta studied her. "Just because these people have that crystal, doesn't mean they're done with this."

"I know."

"It would be better if you just let this go," Orta stated.

Annja smiled at him. "Would you let it go?"

Wearily, Orta shook his head. "If I wasn't in this bed, I'd go with you."

"Then tell me where to find Racz."

Orta gestured. "Let me borrow your sat phone. I'll put his number into your address book."

13

With her backpack settled over her shoulders and Istvan Racz's phone number logged into her sat phone, Annja said her goodbyes to Vincent Orta, promised him she'd keep him apprised of her treasure hunt and left the hospital room. The uniformed police officer in the hallway watched her go and reached for his phone. She knew he'd be reporting her departure.

Two men in the waiting area overlooking Orta's room abandoned their magazines and took up deliberate pursuit. Despite their effort at blending in, they didn't try to disguise their interest. Or maybe they thought she wouldn't notice them because she wasn't looking or wasn't skilled enough to spot them. Either way, Annja picked up on them immediately.

They wore casual clothes with lightweight thigh-length jackets. Shrapnel scars, gray with age, stood out on the side of one man's face. The other man was smaller and biracial. Both of them moved in loose readiness and didn't make eye contact.

Deliberately avoiding the elevators, Annja increased her speed, almost jogging to the stairwell door and ducking through. The men trailed her by a short distance, but they'd sped up when they saw where she was headed.

Instead of going down the stairs, Annja reached up and caught the side of the stairs leading up to the next floor. Moving quickly, she hauled herself up and pressed herself into hiding behind the stairwell wall. The men wouldn't be fooled for long, but she didn't need much time.

Balancing on the stairwell, pressed back against the wall, Annja watched as the door swung open. She took in a long, slow breath and let it out.

The scar-faced man came through first and hesitated just a moment, looking at the next landing, the door there and then down the stairwell shaft. He slipped a cell phone from his pocket and spoke into it briefly in French. Annja overheard his conversation easily enough.

"This is Claude. She spotted Edgar and me and is running. Stand ready. She has to be coming your way." He started down the steps. "We'll take her at ground level."

The second man followed at the first man's heels, but he wasn't as locked into his notion of how Annja had disappeared. He stopped two steps down and turned to look up.

Uncoiling from her perch, Annja kicked at the man's head, driving her boot at his face. Even with surprise on her side, Edgar almost got an arm up to block her kick. His open hand curled around her calf for just a moment, tightened, then loosened as her foot caught him full in the face and bounced his head off the wall behind him.

His eyes glazing slightly from the impact, Edgar struggled to recover. One foot slid onto a lower step, but he caught his balance and remained upright. Setting himself, he lurched back up the steps at Annja.

On her feet now, Annja watched Claude reaching under his jacket for the pistol leathered there. Ducking, Annja easily avoided Edgar's lunge and stepped into him, letting his muscular arms pass over her head. Claude leveled his weapon and fired immediately. Annja didn't know if the shots were intended as warnings or if the man planned on disabling her.

Or if he simply shot to kill her and claim her possessions.

Either way, the loud crack was deafening in the stairwell, and Annja suddenly felt as though she had cotton balls in her ears. Edgar shouted a warning to his partner but the words sounded far away.

Using Edgar as a shield, Annja grabbed his shirt in her left hand and kneed him in the crotch hard enough to take the fight out of him for a moment. He staggered and nearly became deadweight that she fought to balance.

Claude fired again and the bullet chopped into the wall only inches from her head, then ricocheted into the stairwell door with a low-pitched whine. Only a few feet away, he started forward and tried to find a shot around his partner.

Annja grabbed the 9 mm pistol from Edgar's shoulder holster and pulled it free. Aiming instinctively, she fired two bullets into Claude's left knee. Yelling in pain, Claude flailed for the railing, missed it and collapsed, rolling down the steps.

Shrugging out from under Edgar just as the man was trying to rally and wrap her in his arms, Annja swung the pistol butt into his temple. His eyes rolled up and he sank to the steps.

Holding the pistol ready, hoping she didn't have to use it, Annja trotted down the steps. Behind her, the door opened. She glanced up and watched as a young man in a nurse's uniform halted halfway through the doorway, eyes wide and fearful.

"Hey!" he shouted behind him. "Hey! Help!"

Then, suddenly realizing he was a possible target, the guy ducked back through the doorway. Although muffled by the closed door, his cries for help continued.

Despite his pain, Claude turned his gaze on Annja and tried to point his pistol at her.

Annja reached out and wrenched the weapon from the man with her free hand. As she stood in front of him, she stripped the magazines from both pistols and released the slides, letting the weapons fall in pieces to the steps.

"Who are you?" Annja demanded.

Holding on to his bloody knee, Claude swore at her in French. Giving no warning, Annja stepped forward and put her foot on the man's wounded leg. He screamed in pain and tried to crawl away, but she kept the pressure on and wouldn't let him retreat.

"I don't have a lot of time here, Claude. Either your friends will arrive or the police will. Who are you with?"

Claude held his silence, except for some spirited moaning, for a moment longer, then lay still. "I work for Ligier de Cerceau."

The name meant nothing to Annja, but she filed it away. "Who is he?"

"My boss."

"What does he want with me?"

"He knows you have copies of those manuscript pages you were looking at with the crystal." The man shifted, trying to find a good position for his injured leg. "The other pages are in police hands. He can't get them."

Based on her own inability to get the pages for at least one more viewing, Annja figured that was true. "What does de Cerceau know about the pages?"

Claude shook his head. "I don't know. I just do what he tells me. Today he told me to bring you to him. Or to kill you."

A chill tingled across Annja's spine, but she ignored it. She'd been in danger plenty of times before. "Why does he want the crystal and the pages?"

"I don't know. We're not told everything."

Cunning gleamed in Claude's eyes and reminded Annja that she needed to be going. He was obviously counting on keeping her occupied until the backup team arrived.

She leaned down to rifle through Claude's clothing and had to elbow him in the face to get him to settle down. Sulking, with an obscene oath, he put up with her search. He carried his wallet in his pants pocket and she took it. She also grabbed his cell phone and Edgar's. Then, aware that time was working against her, she turned and fled down the stairs.

She entered the next floor and walked to the elevators as a security guard trotted toward the stairwell.

"Hold up, miss." The security guard raised a hand toward Annja and reached for his holstered weapon with his other hand.

Annja pointed toward the stairwell. "Be careful. There are two men in there shooting at each other."

The guard hesitated just a moment, then reached for the walkie-talkie mounted on his shoulder and reported shots fired. He looked at Annja. "Are you hurt?"

"No." Annja chafed at having to wait, but she didn't want to appear to be fleeing the scene, either. Even though she was. If the police got involved, she'd be answering questions again. She wanted to be moving.

"Good." The security guard drew his sidearm. "Go downstairs, get somewhere safe and wait until I find you."

"Sure."

Still talking on his radio, the security guard closed on the stairwell door.

Annja didn't want him to get shot, and she didn't think her two would-be kidnappers were in any shape to put up much of a fight, but she repeated her warning about the guns.

The guard nodded and positioned himself by the door with both hands on his weapon. "Security!" he shouted. "Put your weapons down!"

Annja kept moving. She felt certain that Claude and Edgar's backup team would be looking for them in the stairwells, so she had some breathing room in the elevator. After taking out her sat phone, she called a cab service and asked for one at the front of the hospital. The dispatch person assured her that a unit was en route and would arrive in minutes.

When the elevator hit the second floor, she got off,

checked the hallway and saw no one suspicious, then headed
for the nearest stairs leading to the first floor, avoiding the
stairwells at either end. On the first floor, she strode toward the ER, threading the line of patient-filled gurneys and
medical personnel streaming from that direction. A female
police officer and two male security guards ran toward the
stairwell with their weapons in their hands.

The ER was crowded with sick people waiting to see
doctors or huddling nervously with family members and
friends. Annja stood beside a potted plant with broad leaves
and stared through the window as she gazed out in front of
the hospital.

There was no cab yet, but she also didn't see anyone who
might be working with Claude and Edgar, which was a good
thing. Still, she didn't want to get caught out in the open in
front of the hospital. Whoever de Cerceau was, he had professionals working for him.

She took out her sat phone again, then retrieved the card
she'd gotten from Detective Leslie Connolly from the side
pocket of her backpack and punched the number in. The
connection was made almost instantly.

"Detective Connolly." The detective sounded professional, but there was an edge in her voice.

"Hi, Detective." Annja moved one of the plant's broad
leaves and took another look outside.

It took Connolly a moment to recognize Annja's voice.
"Ms. Creed, I'm surprised you called."

The roar of an engine and the scream of a siren carried
over the phone line.

"I'm betting you're not too surprised. I'm sure you've
heard about the shooting at the hospital."

"As it turns out, we're on our way there now." Connolly
sounded cool. "We'd heard you were involved."

Realizing the hospital nurse must have outed her, Annja
frowned. She'd had enough of the authorities for the moment.

"I was only involved to the point of self-preservation. Two men came after me. I left them behind for you."

"Alive?"

Annja held back a barbed comment. "Yes, they're alive. One of them told me they're working for a man named Ligier de Cerceau. The name means nothing to me. I was hoping you could tell me more."

"I really can't—"

"If you're not going to talk to me, there's no reason for me to hang around here."

"You're involved in a shooting."

"I was involved. *Was*. No thanks to the guard you've got covering Dr. Orta." Even as she said the last remark, Annja felt guilty. There was no way Connolly or her partner could have known she would be attacked in the stairwell. And they were after *her*, not Orta.

"We could have put a guard on you if you'd thought you were in danger."

"I can take care of myself." Annja gazed around the ER waiting room and knew that she wasn't attracting any untoward attention. Everyone was watching breaking news about shots fired at the hospital on the televisions around the room. "I thought we could compare notes. If you don't know anything about de Cerceau, we have nothing further to discuss. I'll let you get back to your day."

"Wait."

Annja held on to the phone.

"Ms. Creed? Are you there?"

"I am." Through her own grayed reflection in the window glass, Annja watched a yellow cab slide to a halt in front of the hospital.

"I thought I'd lost you." Connolly sounded relieved.

"Not yet." But that was going to happen soon.

"De Cerceau turned up on some of our preliminary reports. The men we have in custody have worked for him in the past."

"I'm betting they still are. So tell me about de Cerceau."

Out in front of the hallway, the cabdriver looked around and tapped his fingers on the steering wheel.

"The information's still coming in. We're building a better picture of the man."

"What do you know so far?"

"He works as a mercenary, but he's also done international security work for people who ship valuable artwork and artifacts. Some auction houses around the globe do regular work with him on high-end pieces. He has a reputation for being quite formidable."

Annja considered that, knowing that work in those fields would allow de Cerceau to move around fairly easily and know a lot about expensive pieces, as well as the collectors who bought them. She wondered who wanted the crystal. And why.

"There are two men down in a stairwell." Annja shifted her backpack over her shoulder. "One has been shot, but there's no danger of him bleeding out. The other will probably still be unconscious. He got hit pretty hard. If you look around, I think you'll find more people working for de Cerceau who will be concerned with getting those men out of there."

"All right. Where are you going to be?"

"With any luck?" Annja smiled. "Gone." She broke the connection on the sat phone, kept it in one hand and exited the ER room through the admittance door.

Outside, Annja stayed focused on the waiting cab and watched the surroundings for movement as she walked toward the vehicle. Two other cars sat in the waiting area in front of the hospital's main door. People got out of the cars. An older man in a wheelchair propelled himself toward the entrance. Two young women trailed in his wake.

Reaching the cab, Annja opened the back door and slid inside.

The driver, a young man wearing a Jack White concert T-shirt, looked over his shoulder. "Are you the one who called about the cab?"

"That's me."

The driver nodded at the hospital. "Visiting someone?"

"A friend." Annja glanced at the entrance and spotted three men who looked as though they might have been friends of Claude and Edgar nervously searching the lobby. One of them started out of the building, trying to get a better look into the cab, which had tinted windows.

"I hope the person's doing all right."

"He is. Thanks. Could we go? I'm kind of in a hurry. I overstayed."

"Sure, sure." The driver turned to the wheel and took his foot off the brake. The cab slid forward, dodging the waiting cars and heading toward the street. He pulled to one side to allow an LAPD patrol car to roll by with lights flashing and siren howling.

"Something's going on." The driver hesitated long enough to let a second police car go by, as well, then accelerated out into traffic.

"Something's always going on in this city." Annja took out the captured cell phones and tried to get into them. Both were password protected, which bothered her only a little. She had other means of getting information. She turned them off, took out the batteries and dumped them both back into her backpack.

"It might even be a movie or television stunt, though they usually block the streets off for that, which can be a real pain." The driver looked up at her in the rearview mirror. "Where do you want to go?"

"Santa Monica." That was where Orta had told her Dr. Istvan Racz lived.

"Okay, I can take you there. Do you have a destination?"

Annja consulted her phone and found an internet café in Santa Monica. She gave the driver the name and address, then punched in Istvan Racz's number and listened to the phone ring.

14

"I'm surprised you got out here without Krauzer tagging along." Meszoly sat behind the SUV's wheel and watched the police action in front of the Good Samaritan Hospital.

"He wanted to come." Sabre focused through the camera's telephoto lens and snapped shots of the men the uniformed police officers were guiding out of the hospital. "I reminded him he had a blockbuster to shoot and told him this probably wouldn't turn out to be anything." He pressed the button again and the camera whirred in response, taking a quick series of five images. "Do you recognize any of these men?"

Meszoly slipped off his sunglasses and consulted the tablet PC lying on the seat between them. He flicked his finger across the touch screen and went through the images Sabre had captured.

"No. A couple look familiar, but you do this kind of work, people in our business start to look the same unless you really know them."

Shifting the camera, Sabre captured images of the two detectives he'd spotted working the crime scene, as well. Identification had been made simpler by the television reporters on-site who shoved microphones into the detectives' faces and left the uniformed patrolmen alone.

The small television monitor in the SUV's dash picked up the live news feed on a ten-second delay. Crawlers beneath the scene identified the detectives as Bishop and Connolly.

Putting the camera down for a moment, Sabre used a stylus to make quick note of the names on an app on the tablet.

Then he emailed the names to Saadiya, who would gather background intel on the detectives, following up with the camera images. He felt certain all of the information would ultimately end up being useless, but he had been trained to be thorough by his father and then by his mentor, who had taken over his training after his father's death.

"I know Krauzer pays us well, and I know that he's a high-profile client, so doing due diligence by him is a good public relations move." Shifting in the seat, one hand still on the steering wheel and the other hand near the pistol on his hip, Meszoly kept his eyes trained on the hospital.

For a moment, Sabre remained silent. Meszoly wouldn't press him on the matter out of respect and past experience that Sabre wouldn't answer until he was ready to. But he wanted to talk about this, just to make sure he wasn't going too far in the matter. With all the stories he'd been told during his childhood, it was easy to get caught up in everything. He sighed when he thought of his brother and how that history had separated them. He didn't want to turn out like his sibling.

"The crystal and those pages and, ultimately, wherever they lead, are important to me." Sabre lifted the foam container of hot oolong tea from the cup holder and took a sip.

"Have you ever wondered why I named this security business the Black Legion?" Sabre asked.

A grin spread across Meszoly's lips. "Figured it was because it sounded sexy as hell and looked good on the website."

Sabre chuckled. "Not quite." But he had to admit both were true. "Have you ever heard of the Black Legion?"

"Some kind of German death squad back in World War II?"

"No." Reconciling himself to telling the story, at least as much of it as he would let himself at this time, Sabre took another sip of tea and leaned back in the seat.

"Back in the fifteenth century," Sabre stated, "there was a Hungarian king named Corvinus who assembled the largest professional army of its era. Until that time, in times of war, kings simply sent the word out that soldiers were needed and men gathered from fields and farms, from docks and shipyards, and from wherever men were to do their work. They came because the king called them to battle. And when that war was over, those that survived went home.

"At the time, Hungary was in a world of hurt." Sabre returned his gaze to the hotel, letting the police and media circus there soak up his attention. "The country was in the middle of hotly contested land grabs, and Corvinus constantly had to rob Peter to pay Paul to keep his seat on the throne. To ensure his position and to protect the future of his country, Corvinus wanted to flip the script and create a war machine the likes of which had never been seen before. He got his professional army, but the problem was the cost."

"Professional fighting men cost money. You don't spill blood—yours or anyone else's—without getting paid."

"Unless you're a patriot."

"Which is another word for underpaid, underequipped and unappreciated."

For one silent moment, Sabre thought of all the patriots he'd seen die and those he'd killed. He'd signed up as regular Army for the Afghanistan action, come out, then gone back in as part of the private sector with DragonTech security services. His father had died shortly before he'd signed up for the Army. He'd been twenty years old and hadn't known what to do with himself. He'd learned the United States military hadn't been the way to go. DragonTech had provided an education and a mentor.

"I suppose you got all of this from the History Channel?"

"Actually, no." Sabre grinned. "I got these stories from my grandfather. And he got them from his father before him.

There's a family book, a collection of books, actually, that have been handed down almost six hundred years."

"All of them telling the same story over and over?" Meszoly shook his head. "Must make for some boring reading."

"Those books tell the story of my ancestors' search for a lost treasure."

"A lost treasure?"

"Yeah."

Meszoly's eyebrows rose from behind his sunglasses. "Why have we never had this conversation before?"

"Because of the way you're looking at me right now."

"It's a little out-there, buddy."

"I know how it sounds." Sabre breathed out and lowered the camera. He'd captured everything worth seeing. Whatever was going on in the building, the police had shut it down or boxed it in. "It is out-there. My father had a problem with the stories, too. That's why he was never the one to tell them to me. It was always my grandfather. My father didn't believe a word of those legends. That caused a problem between him and my grandfather."

"Is there some reason this story is important now?"

"During the time I was talking to Krauzer—"

"I find it hard to believe anyone can have a conversation with that blowhard."

Sabre nodded. "While I was *listening* to Krauzer talk, he mentioned that the woman and this professor believed the crystal and some documents they had might lead to the lost treasure of the Merovingian kings."

"They were the kings of Hungary?"

"No. They were the kings of the Salian Franks. They ruled over what we know as France and parts of Germany. Too much history goes by, borders tend to float on from where they actually were."

"That's a long way from Hungary."

"Not so far in some ways. The point is, the Merovingians were believed to be gods, or—at the least—near gods. They were deposed in the eighth century by Pepin the Short. That started the rule of the Carolingian kings, but that's not what my family was interested in."

Across the street, the police cars and media trucks were starting to pull back from the hospital and move along.

"One of my ancestors served in Corvinus's professional troops. It was sometimes called the Black Army because they wore black armor, but it was called the Black Legion just as much. My ancestor, Vilmos, was one of the top generals and was with Corvinus until the end."

"Corvinus died?"

"He was forty-six or forty-seven at the time. Guys didn't live as long back then."

"Especially if they're trying to hold on to a country a lot of people wanted."

"There's some question as to whether Corvinus died from a stroke or from poison. Vilmos thought Corvinus died from a heart attack."

"That's a better story when the guy you're supposed to be protecting dies on your watch." Meszoly grinned. "If it was me, that's the story I would tell."

Chuckling, Sabre nodded. "The point being, Corvinus put together this huge library. Outside Italy, Hungary was in the largest Renaissance period in the world. Art. Dance. Literature. Music. Corvinus wanted all of those things brought to his kingdom. He wanted to be cutting-edge."

"Wow. Ambitious guy. Supporting a professional army and being a patron of the arts would break most people."

"True. We've seen it happen. After Corvinus died, the feeding frenzy began. The throne was supposed to go to his son, but Corvinus's wife, the prince's stepmother—"

"It's always a good story when there's a wicked stepmother."

Sabre grinned. "Long story short, the Black Legion fell on desperate times as they got fragmented by the infighting. Most of them ended up siding with other people, hoping they could continue getting paid."

Meszoly snarled an oath. "You and I both know how that usually works out. Generally, everything's okay if you back a winner, but not always. And when you end up on the losing side, you're screwed."

"No one could pay for the Black Legion. Those men ended up having to rely on themselves to survive."

"So they stole from whoever was around them, even the people they were supposedly there to protect, because, in the end, an army has to eat." Meszoly sighed. "Man, we have lived that story."

A few times, when they'd been trapped behind enemy lines without support, Sabre and his men had been forced to resort to similar tactics.

"Gradually, the Black Legion members ended up getting executed, imprisoned or scattered," Sabre said.

"I'm assuming your ancestor was one of those."

"He was. And he was the one who started my family's search for the Merovingian treasure."

"Do you know what it is?"

"Jewels. Paintings. Gold." Sabre shrugged. "No one knew for certain. Vilmos and Corvinus evidently talked about the possibilities a lot. There was a rumor that Pepin the Short was outwitted by Childeric III, the Merovingian king that he deposed, that not all of the Frankish swag was accounted for. Some of the rumors stated that the Merovingian magic was tied up in the treasure, too."

"What magic?"

"The Merovingians were noted for having red hair and for wearing it long. Legend had it that as long as a Merovingian warrior wore his hair long, he couldn't be killed in battle."

"How true was that?"

"Merovingians died. You and me, we haven't met anyone who's unkillable."

"You don't believe that one?"

Sabre shook his head.

Meszoly studied Sabre for a time. "But you believe that treasure's still out there? That it's even real?"

"I do." He paused. "I've never gone looking for it. Not once. I've read through the books plenty of times, and I hung on to my grandfather's stories, but I think that was because he was raising us while my father was off fighting in whatever war would have him and my mother had left when I was really young. I don't even remember her." He tapped the tea container. "But I remember my grandfather. He believed those stories."

"So you want to follow up on this?"

Sabre nodded slightly. "Yeah."

"Why?"

"Because last night that legend came to me. I didn't go looking for it. It came to me." Sabre thought about that some more, realizing how true that statement was. "That's not something I can ignore."

Meszoly snorted. "You and your superstitions."

Sabre smiled, but he couldn't help feeling excited. What he'd said was the truth. All of those events last night had joined together to put him on this path. He couldn't just walk away.

"So," Meszoly said, "what do you want to do?"

"We're going to have to try to pick up Annja Creed's trail. I've got a feeling she knows a lot more about this than we do."

"Do you plan on going over there in that hospital and asking her?"

"She's not in that hospital." Sabre packed the camera away and powered down the tablet PC and shut down the Wi-Fi satellite dish.

"How do you know that?"

"Because two of de Cerceau's guys came out bloody. Who do you think wrecked them?"

"You think she's that good?"

"She survived against de Cerceau's people last night. That wasn't luck."

Meszoly flicked a thumbnail across his stubbled chin. "Maybe the police are holding her inside."

Sabre shook his head. "No. She's long gone. Let's get back to headquarters and see what Saadiya's turned up."

As Meszoly put the SUV in gear and pulled out into traffic, Sabre's mind was elsewhere. He remembered sitting on the wooden bench in his grandfather's woodworking room. He'd watched the old man build furniture, turning out chests and chairs and tables like clockwork. Sometimes he'd allowed Sabre to help. But he'd always smoked his pipe and told those stories.

Sometimes Sabre's brother would sit on the bench and listen, too, but his brother had never worked with the old man. He'd just sat there and listened to the stories. Occasionally, afterward, they would talk about the stories. Sabre had been fascinated by what had taken place, but his brother had always been caught up in wondering what the treasure was.

Reaching into his pocket, Sabre removed a special padded case that held a single coin. He took the coin out and touched it reverently, feeling the smooth texture of the worn sides. Despite cleaning, the coin still looked ancient and discolored. It held the raven shield that had been the mark of Matthias Corvinus.

The coin had been struck sometime during Corvinus's reign, and it had been—according to family legend—one of the first denars the king had paid Vilmos after employing him. Like the stories and the books, the coin had been handed down from father to firstborn son.

Only this coin had been refused by Sabre's father, and

his grandfather had given it to Sabre, though he was his father's second child. Tradition had been broken.

Meszoly glanced over. "That old thing?"

Sabre squeezed the coin in his fist, feeling the solidity and the heaviness of it. "Yes. It's always brought me luck."

"I've known times it didn't."

"If it was a sure thing, it wouldn't be luck, now, would it?" Despite the tweak of irritation, Sabre smiled at his friend. The coin was a point of contention between them. Meszoly didn't like trusting luck, and he liked trusting Sabre's luck even less.

Sabre's cell phone trilled for attention. He punched the connection button and put it on speaker function.

"I see you two have finally quit skulking on the local constabulary," Saadiya said. She sounded chipper. "Boring?"

"It's always a treat to watch our tax dollars at work," Meszoly said.

"Well, while you two lads have been out on a lark, you'll be happy to know that your brilliant computer support has been busy, and *successful*, I might add. I managed to ID two of de Cerceau's men inside the hospital from police reports I accessed. I don't know if the identities are the actual real names of the men, but they've been listed in police reports."

"I'm waiting to be impressed," Meszoly said.

"All right. Here it comes, then. It appears one of those lads, Claude Matisse—"

"Not his real name," Meszoly interjected.

"—also has a prepaid mobile registered in his name. I took the liberty of accessing his phone records and tracing his calls. I'm building a map of potential malevolent creeps, one of whom has already turned up on the attack on the college last night, so we can get some insight into our opponents' network. As I was doing that, I noticed that Matisse's mobile just lit up two minutes ago."

"The police took him into custody," Meszoly said.

"That they did, but his mobile is not on him. It was there at the hospital, but now it's not." The smile in Saadiya's voice carried over the connection. "You know where he is. Now, would you like to know where his mobile is?"

Grinning triumphantly, Sabre showed the denar to Meszoly, listened to his friend's irritated curse and put the coin away. "I would like to know."

"It's in an internet café in Santa Monica. I'll send the address to your vehicle's GPS. Cheers."

Sabre hung up. A moment later, a text flashed onto his screen with the address of the internet café. He punched it into the SUV's GPS system.

"You're thinking the Creed woman took Claude Matisse's cell phone." Meszoly pressed harder on the accelerator and guided the big vehicle through the traffic.

"Do you know anyone else who would take it?"

"Perhaps one of Matisse's mates got away in the confusion."

"And took his phone, leaving him there?"

Meszoly shrugged, then sighed and nodded. "Okay, the Creed woman took his cell."

"And now we can find her." Sabre shifted in his seat and wished the traffic would thin out. Anticipation squirmed in his stomach.

15

The man was a fake, and Ligier de Cerceau didn't want to swallow the prickly ire he felt at the arrogance of whoever was behind the deception. He had laid his life on the line to get the crystal for his unknown employer and getting handed off to a go-between was intolerable. Controlling his anger, the mercenary commander sat in a back booth in the overpriced deli restaurant in Beverly Hills and planned his next move.

The crystal had drawn too much attention for him to simply walk away.

He glanced around, wondering if his true employer was sitting somewhere inside the restaurant or if he—or *she*—had set up in one of the buildings across the street to observe the meeting from afar. Maybe that person had just settled for listening in on the conversation.

The diner was as much a celebrity as the movie industry in the city. Actors and actresses, producers and directors and writers all went there to pretend they were ordinary. And to be seen.

Waving away the young server, de Cerceau glared at the man across the table from him. "I don't have time for lies."

The operation at the hospital had not gone as planned. Not only had Annja Creed escaped, but his men were compromised. Even now the LAPD was questioning two of his people. There would be questions concerning the attack on the university and Melanie Harp's death. Chances were good that he wouldn't be able to work in the United States for a time, possibly years. Someone was going to pay for that. De Cerceau seethed inside but covered it with an icy demeanor.

"Do you have the crystal?" After a brief hesitation in the face of de Cerceau's anger, the man tried to be authoritative, almost blustering, but the veneer was a sham, so thin the cracks were already showing.

Over six feet tall and in his late thirties, the impostor looked like someone who could handle himself in a physical confrontation. He was broad and capable, and he looked as if he hit the gym regularly. The musculature wasn't just for show. Calluses lined the man's palms, badges that promised he had gained his size through hard work, not just a lucky roll of the genetic dice.

Barely containing his anger at the deceit, de Cerceau forced himself to be civil. He leaned back in the booth and tapped his earpiece to open the frequency. "Bring the car around."

Gerard answered immediately. "I am on my way."

"I have the crystal." De Cerceau leaned back toward the man. "Would you like to see it?"

"Yes, very much." The man who was supposed to be SEEKER4318 nodded happily. He sat there waiting expectantly, as if de Cerceau was going to pull the crystal from his pocket.

De Cerceau silently cursed the man, partly because the fool had been ill prepared, for all his good looks, and because it was likely he would have no information. Still, questions had to be asked.

On the other side of the glass, Gerard pulled the Mercedes sedan to a halt out in the parking lot. "I am here, Colonel."

"I have the crystal out in the car." De Cerceau pointed at the Mercedes.

The man glanced at the car, took a breath, then looked back at de Cerceau. "Can't you bring it in?"

A smile ricked the corner of de Cerceau's mouth. "No. I

want a chance to count all of the money, and I'd rather not reveal what's in that briefcase you brought."

The man clasped the handle of the briefcase in the seat beside him. "I assure you, the contents are all there."

"This is how I do business. You understand."

Nervously, the man adjusted his tie and nodded. "Of course. Do we have time to get something to eat?" the man asked. He touched the menu hopefully.

Sliding out of the booth, de Cerceau shook his head. "No."

"Perhaps something to go?"

"You can eat after we finish our business."

"Of course. Getting a booth like this again will be a problem, though." Sadness shone in the man's eyes. Evidently, he'd been looking forward to eating at the diner.

De Cerceau led the way outside. He had two men inside the restaurant who would cover his six. They had gotten there before he had. He had no worries about the impostor trying anything.

As he crossed the parking lot, de Cerceau knew that was the most vulnerable point. A sniper on the roof might take him out if the shooter tried for a head shot because de Cerceau wore Kevlar under his clothes, but Gerard would be safe inside the armored car. De Cerceau felt his chances were good that whoever was seeking to trick him wouldn't risk losing the crystal.

No, the better plan would be to attempt to lock down the Mercedes in the parking lot. De Cerceau had prepared for that, as well. Two SUVs, driven by his men, were already in motion, ready to run blocker for any kind of interception.

Gerard stayed inside the vehicle but popped the locks.

De Cerceau opened the right rear door and swept a hand inside. He smiled at the impostor. "Please. Get in."

The man peered into the back of the car for a moment, then straightened. "I don't see a crystal."

"I'm not going to flash something like that in the parking lot." De Cerceau waved to the car again. "Get in."

The man glanced back at the diner, but he didn't appear to be searching for anyone in particular. "All right." He got into the sedan and held the briefcase in his lap.

De Cerceau closed the door and walked around to the other side. As he slid into the seat, he nodded to Gerard. Immediately, the Mercedes accelerated into motion. Gerard handed de Cerceau a pair of black surgical gloves and he pulled them on.

"Where are we going?" Sweat drenched the impostor's cheeks and he suddenly didn't look so debonair as he watched de Cerceau slip on the gloves.

"For a short drive." To keep things moving along and cut down on the time the man had to think, de Cerceau leveled a forefinger at the briefcase. "Let's see the money."

The man hesitated, then shook his head, trying desperately to recover his aplomb. "That's not how this is supposed to go. First show me the—"

De Cerceau backhanded the man. The impostor sagged back against the door. Blood spilled from his split lips. Before the man could recover, de Cerceau covered his prey's head with a big hand and searched him as he squalled in protest.

Claiming the man's wallet, cell phone and key ring, de Cerceau leaned back in his own seat. Gerard passed a bar towel back from the glove compartment, which de Cerceau took and handed to the man.

"Don't bleed on my seat."

Gasping in pain, the man held the towel to his mouth and stared fearfully at de Cerceau.

Casually, as Rodeo Drive passed him on either side, de Cerceau searched the man's wallet. He matched up the man's driver's license and screen actor's card to his features.

"Your name is Jason Boone?" De Cerceau stared at the man.

"Yes." The man mopped at his lips again, wide-eyed with fright. "I mean, yes, that's my name."

"You're not SEEKER4318?"

Boone frowned at that, and the effort made him wince in pain. "I don't know who, or what, that is."

De Cerceau tried again. "You're not the man who hired me."

"No. *I* was hired."

"To do what?"

"To meet you. To deliver the briefcase and get the crystal."

"Who hired you?"

"I don't know."

De Cerceau drew back his hand and Boone flinched.

"I don't know! I swear!"

"Tell me how you were hired." De Cerceau lowered his hand.

"Through my booking agent."

"Who's your agent?"

"Seymour Goldfarb."

The name meant nothing to de Cerceau, but the man's words rang true.

"Look." Boone winced in pain. "I don't even know what this is. I was told it was a tryout for a pilot on Netflix or something."

"What were you supposed to do with the crystal when you got it?"

Boone shrugged. "The person who hired me was supposed to call."

Picking up Boone's phone, de Cerceau went through the address book and found no entries. He glanced at the actor. "This isn't your phone."

"No. It's a burner. It came with the job."

Wary that someone might be tracking the phone's GPS, de Cerceau took the battery from the phone and deactivated it. "Does your agent know who hired you?"

Boone shook his head. "Seymour told me not to take the job, because he couldn't track down the agency or the guy who called it in."

"The caller was a man?"

"Yes."

"Why did you take the job?"

"It paid five hundred dollars. I didn't care where the money came from. I needed it." Boone's lower lip trembled. "Please. I don't even know what's going on."

Thinking rapidly, weighing his options, de Cerceau glanced up at Gerard. "Pull over."

Immediately, Gerard sliced through traffic and pulled in front of a small coffee shop. The car slid smoothly to a stop.

"Let me have the briefcase." De Cerceau reached for the item, took it from Boone and quickly examined it for any booby-traps. He didn't think there would be any. Whoever had sent the actor wouldn't want the crystal harmed.

Satisfied all was well, de Cerceau opened the briefcase. Stacks of hundred-dollar bills sat inside, and he knew he'd been paid his asking fee. At least that was something. He gave the briefcase a cursory inspection but didn't find any tracking devices. Satisfied for the moment, he closed the briefcase.

Boone licked his bloody lips nervously. "Is it all there?"

"Yes."

"Thank God." He blotted his lips again. "Can I go now?"

"Of course." De Cerceau even smiled. "Our business here is concluded."

Hand shaking, Boone reached for the door release and pulled. The lock popped open, and he swung the door open a few inches. Without a word, Boone opened the door farther and stepped out.

"Mr. Boone? There is one other thing you can do."

The actor hesitated, frozen like a mouse beneath the shadow of a hawk. Slowly, he turned. "Yes?"

De Cerceau pulled a pistol from his shoulder leather and pumped two silenced 9 mm rounds into Boone's face. Shot dead, the actor fell back spread-eagled on the sidewalk. De Cerceau took out his cell phone with his free hand and took a picture of Boone lying on the ground. He pulled the door shut as Gerard drove away from the curb.

16

SEEKER4318 cursed as he left the building across the street from where the actor he'd hired had left the diner with de Cerceau. He felt conspicuous even among the small group of office workers that had departed the building with him. He'd deliberately waited for them to leave. Dressed in a suit, he looked like one of the mindless drones who worked at the call service, the insurance agency and the other inconsequential jobs housed within the structure.

This should not be happening. The meeting should have gone smoothly. The woman's death the previous night in the hotel room had indicated that fortune was with him.

He didn't understand. He'd done everything right. Hiring the actor, especially with the way things had turned out, was a bit of brilliance. He was certain that de Cerceau would question the man. There was nothing to discover, though. The man knew nothing.

Still, it meant the crystal remained out of his reach. There was no way he could take it from de Cerceau. Worse, given the mercenary commander's actions just now, de Cerceau was also pursuing the treasure.

SEEKER4318 had no doubts that de Cerceau's efforts would go unrewarded. The man was ignorant of what was at stake. He was a blind hog rooting for an ear of corn. Whatever de Cerceau had heard, whatever he'd guessed at, whatever he thought he knew, that information wouldn't be enough to lead him to the Merovingian fortune.

Controlling his breathing to keep himself calm, SEEKER4318 walked another three blocks, then flagged a cab. After he clambered into the rear seat and gave his destination, he pulled out a burner cell phone he'd purchased just to contact the actor. He couldn't even remember the man's name.

He punched in the number and let it ring. No one picked up.

Silently, SEEKER4318 cursed de Cerceau's greed. Then he checked another of the phones he carried, turned it on and viewed the email address he'd set up to work with the mercenary. There was one new message, posted only moments ago.

Almost hypnotized, he opened the message and found an attached image. He opened it, as well, watching as the picture filled out and revealed the actor lying dead on a street. Blood pooled on the sidewalk beside his face.

While he was still frozen, the phone dinged again, indicating the arrival of another email message. He opened that, too.

The police are already hunting me, the message read. With this man's death, they'll be hunting you, too. Pray that they find you before I do.

Anger filled SEEKER4318 as he stared at the words. He hadn't anticipated this turn of events. There would be a trail potentially connecting him to the dead man, even with the false name he'd used. The police cyber unit would keep pounding away to find out who had sent the actor to his death. De Cerceau had thought of an angle that he himself had not considered. Still, even if the police somehow found him, they would have to prove he'd hired the actor, and he had nothing to do with the man's execution.

Then, realizing he wasn't safe with the phone still active, he switched it off and removed the battery.

He called to the driver and got his attention. "I've changed my mind about my destination." He pointed at a small Cuban restaurant that featured outside dining. "I'd like to stop there."

"Okay." The driver pulled next to the curb.

SEEKER4318 checked the total fare on the meter, added a modest tip and walked toward the restaurant. As he passed a public trash can, he wiped both of the burner phones and the batteries and tossed them inside the receptacle. With luck, they would turn up in a sanitation burial ground and never be seen again.

Luck.

That was supposed to be on his side. He remembered cutting the woman open and seeing the portents and possibilities. De Cerceau's actions were a bad turn, but he still had luck coming. He believed that, but the hunger to know what lay before him now with this latest turn of events became a burning ache within him.

He took a seat at one of the outside tables under a gaily colored umbrella that ruffled in the breeze. Now that he was outside in the breeze, he felt calmer. Things were still doable. The prize could still be his.

The secret held within the crystal had lain hidden for hundreds of years. Only that woman, Annja Creed, had shown up and somehow found the beginning of the trail. SEEKER4318 hadn't even known the trail lay in two pieces, the crystal and the pages Dr. Orta had found.

"Would you care for something, sir?"

Surprised, SEEKER4318 glanced up at the young server standing before him. She'd slipped up to him undetected. She had dark features and startling blue eyes that he suspected were contact lenses. All the women in this city tried to find some way to distinguish themselves.

"Some lemonade, perhaps?" He was too unsettled to eat, his mind whirling madly as he thought of de Cerceau finding the treasure and making off with it.

"Of course." The server folded her pad and walked away.

His personal phone vibrated inside his jacket pocket. With some trepidation, he pulled it out and looked at the screen. He didn't recognize the number, but he knew the 212 area code was from New York City. He tried to think of people he knew in New York. The list was almost nonexistent.

Then he realized that the person didn't have to be calling from New York. These days people could keep their phone numbers no matter where they lived.

He almost answered the call, but his indecision let it go to the answering service instead. He resolved to wait a few moments and let the message be recorded.

A police siren cut through the air.

Looking over his shoulder, SEEKER4318 watched a patrol car speed as quickly as it dared through the street. He guessed that the unit was responding to the discovery of the dead actor. De Cerceau hadn't gone far before he'd killed the man.

Anxious to know what was going on, SEEKER4318 opened the web browser on his phone and checked a Los Angeles news affiliate's site for breaking news.

The death of the actor, Jason Boone, came in at sixth place, but probably wouldn't rest there long. There was nothing unusual about the murder.

The discovery of the dead woman in the hotel room held third place. Seeing that one bothered SEEKER4318, but he'd killed before and knew that he'd left no trace of himself behind at the room. He dismissed the possibility of discovery even though the story relayed that "LAPD's top sex-crimes unit" had been assigned to the investigation.

He returned to the story concerning the dead actor.

"—witnesses here report that they don't know why Jason Boone was gunned down in broad daylight," the female reporter said. She stood a few feet from the dead man as uniformed police officers rolled out yellow crime-scene tape. "According to a witness I talked to, Boone was initially released from a dark blue luxury car, then was called back to the vehicle only to be shot dead by a man seated in the back."

The server returned with a tall glass of lemonade. SEEKER4318 paid her immediately, adding a tip, so that he wouldn't be further bothered.

"Hi. Are you here by yourself?" The husky voice belonged to a woman in her late twenties. SEEKER4318 started to berate her and send her away, but then he caught sight of the necklace lying in the valley of her breasts. The bronze medallion held the image of a dog barking at its own curled tail.

He chose to take that as a sign and further examined the woman.

She was dressed in bright orange yoga pants, a psychedelic midriff shirt and a yellow pullover. The hoodie corralled most of her ginger-colored hair that had to have come from a bottle. Bright pink lipstick framed her mouth.

"I am alone." SEEKER4318 smiled.

The woman stuck out her hand. "I'm Destiny."

He took her hand and felt the anticipation growing within him. His luck still held. It had brought this woman to him at a time when he felt as if he was at a crossroads. He had questions he wanted answered, and here was the divining rod he wanted. She could put him on the right path once more.

He gave her a false name, one he had not previously used. "I'm happy to meet you. Although I must admit that I'm flattered Destiny came calling for me."

The woman chuckled. The humor was artificial, part of her act, but that didn't matter. She was here, and she could be his with little effort on his part.

"Blame my parents for that name. I do." She laughed again. "Would you mind some company? I'm new to LA."

"Of course." SEEKER4318 stood and graciously pulled out a chair for her to sit in.

She thanked him and sat, smiling amiably. Only a short

time later, she mentioned that seeing the sights wasn't all she planned to do while in town and mentioned that she knew of a nearby hotel where they could have a more intimate conversation—if he was willing to pay.

He agreed that he was so inclined, and he followed her with sharp anticipation. Soon the secrets of the future would once more be laid bare.

17

"It's gonna take me a couple minutes to break the pass codes on these phones, Annja, and while they're live, there's a possibility that someone can track them to you."

Seated in front of the rented computer at the internet café, Annja smiled at Daquain Stevens's image on the monitor. He was young, in his early twenties, with a shaved head and thin beard. His dark skin was unblemished except for the small blue tattoo on his right cheek.

"I'm ready for that." Annja glanced around the building. She wore her sat phone's earpiece so at least half of their conversation was private. Not that she thought anyone else was paying any particular attention to her.

The computers had a lot of clients, most of them gaming internationally with local friends or other gamers online around the world. Nearly all of the screens were filled with various explosions, military operations or giant robots.

"I hope you're ready." Daquain frowned. "Because those two guys you had me research for you are seriously hardcore people."

He was talking about Ligier de Cerceau and Sabre Race. Annja had forwarded their names to Daquain when she'd called him to ask him the favor. It hadn't taken him long to gather information from the databases he had access to.

"I know."

"That guy de Cerceau has got a dozen arrest warrants out on him in Europe and Asia. And Sabre Race has been sued a dozen times for assault. He was even photographed hanging a guy out of a tenth-story window."

"How are either of them still free?"

"De Cerceau is clean in the United States. At least, he was. Looks like LAPD is filing charges on him now. And the bodyguard guy has expensive lawyers and settles stuff out of court sometimes."

"Sometimes? What happens the rest of the time?"

"Guys he's beat on are guilty of stalking, robbery, blackmailing and the like. He's mostly good."

"Mostly."

"Yeah."

"I'll keep that in mind."

"My advice is don't tangle with either one of them. It'd probably be best if you got out of California."

"De Cerceau is chasing me. I don't think that's going to change."

"Why is he chasing you? The crystal thing?"

"That's my best guess."

Daquain sighed and frowned. His eyes stayed locked on the screen in front of him, but he wasn't seeing her. He was watching websites he was sorting through. "I'm still checking into that, too."

Annja felt guilty for involving Daquain. He was one of the outside social media gurus Doug Morrell had hired to promote *Chasing History's Monsters*. She had met Daquain and immediately found a bond with him over Marvel superhero films and other interests.

"You sure I can't talk you out of this?" Daquain looked hopeful.

"These people are chasing me. I need to figure out how to stay ahead of them, and the only way to do that is to figure out where this trail leads. In the meantime, I need to know everything about them I can."

Daquain sighed. "You could go to the police. They're already involved."

Annja smiled at him. "Would you go to the police?"

Daquain frowned. "No, but the police and I have a history. Okay, let's do this. Hook up that first phone and turn it on. You turn it off when I say so."

"Deal." Annja picked up the first of the captured phones she'd taken from the men at the hospital and plugged it into the wires Daquain had told her to purchase from a local computer store. "I'm connected."

"Turn it on."

Annja switched on the phone, watched it power up and studied the screen as it lit with the instrument's manufacturer's advertisement. Then the image scrambled into indecipherable numbers and letters and symbols. For a moment, she watched because part of her field of study included symbology, but this was beyond anything she was familiar with.

And it was fast.

She glanced outside but saw only what looked like normal traffic on the street and passersby out for a walk or a shopping excursion. Turning her attention back to the phone, she looked at the monitor, then shifted a little in her seat to make sure the reflection there showed the front of the café and the entrance. Over the top of the monitor, she could clearly see the emergency exit at the back of the room.

Nothing showed on Daquain's face. It was as though he'd been sucked into the internet and only his body was left behind. But his upper arms moved slightly, letting her know he was coding, pushing past the security on the phone.

"Done." Daquain glanced at Annja. "Hook up the next phone. Power that one down first."

Instead of powering the phone down, Annja opened the back and removed the battery. She reached for the second phone, connected it and powered it up.

Long minutes passed.

"This one has more info." On the screen, Daquain grinned in delight. "Guy who used this was more active. I'm getting phone numbers."

"Any names?"

"Looks like code names. Gimme a minute and I'll see if there's anything deeper. Even these prepaid cells can be jumped up by someone who knows what they're doing."

Lines of code flashed on the computer screen, matching what was coming up on the cell. Annja couldn't make any sense of the display. It was all gibberish.

"They're still tracking, Daquain." Annja hadn't wanted to interrupt, but she knew how she sometimes got lost in a process and forgot about time passing. The thought that someone could be tracking the cell phone's signal and the possibility that it would be the men from the previous night left her anxious.

"I know. I know. I almost got everything."

Then the phone's screen went ballistic, going dark, then exploding with light. The symbols, numbers and letters flashed even faster on the computer monitor.

"Shut the phone down, Annja!"

She reached for the phone and ripped the battery out of it. The screen went dark again.

SABRE BRACED HIS FOOT against the SUV's floorboard and reminded himself that Meszoly was one of the best drivers he'd ever worked with. Meszoly had driven jeeps along narrow mountain trails along the Hindu Kush with rockets tearing craters in the landscape around them. The man had driven through a minefield outside Bogotá while Eric Magloire had performed CPR on a rescued kidnapping victim with cartel gunners on their tail.

He could handle Los Angeles traffic.

Meszoly cursed and lay on his horn, blasting the Audi sports car ahead of them. The Audi driver hung an arm out the window and gave him the finger.

"Sabre." Saadiya's voice sounded agitated over the cell phone mounted on the SUV's dashboard.

"What?" Sabre braced himself with one hand in the window as Meszoly cut a corner sharply and zipped past the Audi.

"I just lost signal on the phone," Saadiya said.

"Why?"

"The Creed woman has someone connected to the phone. Whoever it was put up firewalls and the phone dropped off the cell towers."

"They found you?" Sabre couldn't believe that. Saadiya's middle name might as well have been Stealth.

"Not me. Someone else was tracking the phone connection, too. They got in ahead of me and alerted Creed."

Sabre breathed out a curse.

"Who is it?"

"I'm backtracking them now. They're still on the line."

"It's de Cerceau." Meszoly took a fresh grip on the steering wheel and whipped the vehicle hard to the left. Rubber screamed as the big SUV roared through the next intersection. "That guy's not letting any grass grow, either."

"Meszoly's probably right." Saadiya sounded cold, distant, the way she did when she was working in the zone. "If it is de Cerceau—"

"They're on their way to Santa Monica, too."

"Copy that." Sabre thought quickly, glancing at the GPS on the dash and figuring they were only minutes out from their destination. "Do de Cerceau's people know you're in there?"

"Not yet. Whoever their computer guy is, he's concentrating on breaking into the phone. He doesn't see me."

"Good. Keep it that way as long as you can."

"Will do."

Sabre glanced at the GPS map again and saw that they were almost on top of the destination. "Where are they?"

"Almost to you. Coming hot on your heels."

"Understood." Sabre pulled his pistol and set it in his lap, holding it with one hand across his thigh.

"WE'VE GOT A PROBLEM on this one." Daquain leaned forward, more intent on the keyboard now. "They had people waiting on this one to go live again. They tracked that phone and they know where you are. Whoever it is, they're good. They got into my hack. Almost managed to track me back."

"But they didn't find you?" Unease threaded through Annja, making her feel as if dozens of strings were attached to her, pulling her in various directions. But she didn't want Daquain involved in her current situation.

"Not as far as I know, but you've got to get out of there quick."

Already standing, Annja slung her backpack over her shoulder. "I'm leaving the computer at this end up and running."

"Good." Daquain furrowed his brow as his fingers clicked across the keyboard. "That can buy you a little more time to get out of there. They won't know you're not online, and I can keep their computer guy busy chasing his tail until they get someone on the premises."

"Thanks, Daquain. I owe you another one."

The hacker shook his head. "You don't owe me. Get moving. And let me know you're safe when you can. Otherwise I'm gonna tell that cop you hang out with that you're in trouble."

Annja smiled, but Bart McGilley was another person she didn't want mixed up in this. "Give me a little time to get back to you."

"Thirty minutes. Then I hit the panic button."

"Deal. Thanks. I'll square things with you when I get back to the city."

"You don't owe me anything. We're friends."

"Something for your little sister."

"Okay. Hit me up when you can after you're out of there."

Annja headed for the front door and halted just as a black SUV braked to a sudden stop in front of the building. Her heart rate kicked up to a higher level. She waited long enough to see four armed men get out of the vehicle, then streaked for the back door.

18

"I've hacked into the traffic cameras around the internet café," Saadiya said.

Sabre picked up his tablet PC as Meszoly took another hard right. "Can you push the feeds to my tablet?" He eyed the SUV's GPS and saw that they were still four minutes out from the destination.

"Of course I can. Coming to you now."

As the image formed on the screen, Sabre took in the strip-mall layout. In addition to the internet café, a Caribbean diner, a shoe outlet, an electronics store and a recycled-sports-equipment business occupied spaces there. There wouldn't be a lot of civilians on-site, but there would be some. As he watched, people wandered past the businesses.

"Is Creed still inside?" Sabre wished he could see inside the internet café, but brightly colored gaming posters filled the windows.

"The computer she was using is still up, but the phone signal is still dead."

"You can't ping the phone?" Usually, even though a phone was turned off, the GPS could still be pinged. Law enforcement investigators had to get a court order to ping phones, but Sabre wasn't constrained by the same privacy laws. And Saadiya was good at her job.

"Negative." A trace of frustration sounded in the cyber specialist's response. "She must have deactivated the phone."

"She knows we're onto her."

"She knows *someone* hacked into her phone. I don't think

she knows it was me. She'd have to be really good with computers to trace me. I'm a ghost."

"Or she'd have to know someone who is good with computers." Sabre blinked and watched the screen, feeling the seconds tick down. He had a distinct feeling Annja Creed was on the move. Despite his own annoyance at the situation, he couldn't help feeling a growing admiration for the woman.

"She knows someone, and she was connected to that person through the internet."

"Track that."

"I tried. Whoever it is, they have some mad skills."

On the screen, a woman walked to the front door of the internet café and stopped. She peered out for a moment and Sabre recognized Annja Creed. Even with the distance and the street camera's sketchy resolution, he could see that she was beautiful.

"Is she waiting for someone?" Sabre glanced at the cell phone and saw less than a minute had passed. They were still too far away.

"I don't know. But Dyson and his team are a minute five seconds out from site." A second green dot flared to life on the SUV's navigation system. "I've marked him for you."

"Thanks." Relief unthreaded some of the knots in Sabre's stomach as he matched the ETA against the countdown on the vehicle's GPS. Dyson was good, and Saadiya had the woman on the street cams. Annja Creed could run, but she couldn't hide.

"We've got trouble." Saadiya cursed.

"What?"

"Looks like someone is going to beat us to the prize."

The scene on Sabre's tablet PC shifted and focused on a black SUV hurtling off the street and roaring across the parking lot toward the strip mall. The view shifted again, including the internet café as the SUV slid to a stop in front of the building.

"Who is it?"

Four armed men got out of the vehicle. Annja Creed disappeared from the glass door and the men broke into a run.

"They're de Cerceau's people." Saadiya's words were clipped with urgency. "One of their phones was connected to Matisse's phone."

Sabre glanced at Meszoly and the big man nodded. Switching his gaze back to the navigation system, he watched Dyson's vehicle closing on the target. "Connect me to Dyson and let him know he's rolling in hot."

"Copy that."

Reaching to the rear seat, Sabre grabbed his Kevlar helmet and Meszoly's. He pulled his own on and kept the driver's ready.

THE FIGHT-OR-FLIGHT REACTION hardwired into Annja's body shot into overdrive, but she kept it under control and used the extra adrenaline. A few of the gamers noticed her sprint through the lines of computers and watched with interest, but most of them remained buried in their virtual worlds.

She hit the panic bar across the door, opening the exit and setting off the alarm, which squalled in her wake just as the first armed man came through the door with an assault rifle to his shoulder. Evidently, the idea of keeping everything low-key had been jettisoned.

Outside, her options were limited. A long parking lot stretched to the left and right and was four lines deep. Beyond the parked cars, a six-foot-high wooden privacy fence fronted what looked like a residential area. There were a lot more trees than roofs, so Annja hoped the population in the neighborhood was sparse.

She reached the first line of cars before the alarm suddenly shrilled louder from inside the internet café to let her know the door had opened. She didn't know if some of the gamers had followed her out or the first of the armed men had reached her.

The back windshield glass of a car parked to her right suddenly exploded.

Annja resisted the impulse to go to ground. If she stopped running, they'd have her. Instead, she kept her pace, lifted a foot to catch the bumper of the sedan ahead of her and threw herself forward in a headfirst dive. She skidded across the top of the car as gunfire erupted again.

Bullets chewed into the back of the car with metallic shrieks and hammer-like impacts.

Sliding slightly sideways from her momentum, Annja gave in to her forward impetus and rolled down onto the car's hood. She dropped below the front of the vehicle just ahead of the onslaught of bullets that ripped through the front glass. If she'd hesitated, they would have hit her.

Breathing rapidly, thinking even faster, she regained her feet and stayed low as she plunged forward to the next row of cars. She didn't think the men could see her as she sprinted between the parked vehicles. At the end of the next car, she turned left and continued running, passing three large vehicles that offered more cover, before turning right again and heading for the fence.

Getting across the fence was going to be the problem. Thankfully, the final row of cars was parked next to it, providing her cover until she reached it. Staying low, she kept moving forward.

MAKING HIMSELF STAY RELAXED, knowing there was nothing he could do from where he was, Sabre watched the action play out over his tablet PC. Saadiya managed to pick up a camera that provided a view of the parking lot behind the internet café.

Annja Creed was good. From the way she disappeared

into the parked cars and darted through them, picking a broken path toward the privacy fence instead of heading straight for it, Sabre could tell she'd been under fire before. Having gotten a briefing about her from Saadiya, he'd known she'd been involved in volatile situations, but she moved like a pro.

Sabre thought if they hadn't been on opposite sides of this situation, he'd have liked to get to know her better.

He glanced up at the GPS and saw that Dyson's vehicle was arriving. "They're at the back of the internet café. Creed is trying for the privacy fence to the east."

"Copy that." Dyson's reply was professional, short and ready.

The SUV rolled into view of the camera and instantly drew the attention of de Cerceau's mercenaries. One of the mercenaries opened fire on Dyson's vehicle, maybe recognizing the arrival as a threat or wanting to frighten away an interloper or possible means of escape for their quarry.

Dyson leaned from the passenger seat as the driver pulled the SUV hard to the left.

"You've got citizens in the field," Sabre reminded him.

"Affirmative." Dyson held his position. "I have the shot." He fired a quick double tap that hit the mercenary.

The man's head snapped back and his lifeless body sank to the ground.

The SUV pulled to a stop at an angle and the four men inside deployed in two-by-two formation.

"You still have three on the ground." Sabre scanned the tablet PC and spotted two of the mercenaries forming up to the south. "I have two of them to your south. Eighty feet out behind a large gray pickup."

"Copy that." Dyson stayed low and trotted down the line of cars with his assault rifle pulled against his shoulder.

"Third man's in the wind." Sabre searched for the missing mercenary but couldn't find him. He'd lost Annja Creed, as well.

Then she popped up near a van parked next to the fence. South of her position, less than forty feet away, the third mercenary slid up over the top of a vehicle and took deliberate aim.

Sabre opened the radio channel again and spoke over his headset. "Dyson—"

AWARE THAT ANOTHER VEHICLE had joined the first and those men also wore tactical gear, Annja knew she was out of running room in the parking area. Feeling more desperate, she sprinted alongside a large van that was covered in colorful advertising wrap for an upcoming movie.

The fence was only a few tantalizing feet away, and beyond it were the tall trees that promised refuge.

Gunfire broke out behind her, full auto that set off shrilling car alarms followed by a distinctive double tap.

Then, for a moment, there was no gunfire. The car alarms continued, and in the distance police sirens keened.

Annja considered her options, thinking that maybe no one knew where she was. If that was true, she could possibly hold her position until the police arrived and saved her.

The idea of being saved was not something she looked forward to. Saving herself was more how she handled things. Furthermore, if the police, especially Bishop and Connolly, took her into custody, there was no telling when she would be free again.

Whatever secrets the crystal and Vincent Orta's borrowed papers had almost revealed would be discovered by someone else.

That was intolerable. She'd spent nearly all of her adult life ferreting out historical secrets.

She moved forward, past the van, and halted at the front of the vehicle. She hitched her backpack into a better position, then took a quick breath of air to ready herself. Moving fluidly, she stood and raised a foot to the van's bumper, kicking out to thrust herself up. Her hands reached for the top of the privacy fence, which was now only a little more than waist high on her.

Her fingers clutched the rough, weathered wood and she pulled her weight over in a vault, using the van's suspension for added thrust. From the corner of her eye, she spotted the gunman hovering behind a parked car down the row.

Committed, she shoved herself over the fence as bullets ripped into the wooden planks and chewed splinters from the irregular surface. The roar of the gunfire filled her ears, pierced by the police siren and howls of neighborhood dogs.

On the other side of the fence, the land fell away into a bowl-shaped depression four feet deep. Caught by surprise, Annja managed to land on her feet, but the soft ground and the leaves gave way under her, causing her to fall backward. She slid down the hill as bullets continued to hammer the fence and knock holes through the planks.

Another rifle, this one more piercing, blasted a quick tattoo and the first rifle ceased firing.

At the bottom of the depression, Annja got her feet under her and ran. The grade smoothed out and rose again into a small forest of trees that quickly hid the fence and the strip mall from view. She followed the terrain for a bit, stretching her legs to get up to speed.

To either side of her, more privacy fences cut off one- and two-story houses from the trees. Dogs barked constantly and the police sirens grew nearer.

But she was free and running.

Less than a hundred yards farther on, she reached a street and flagged down a cab. While the driver made his way to her, she took off her backpack and brushed the debris away as best as she could. Then she dusted herself off and climbed in.

"Are you okay, miss?"

Annja flashed him a reassuring smile. "I am. I was sightseeing. Taking pictures. I stopped watching where I was going and tripped in the woods."

The driver smiled and nodded. "These things happen. Where would you like me to take you?"

"The pier."

"Of course. A delightful place for taking pictures." He signaled and pulled into traffic.

Glancing behind her, Annja looked to see if anyone had followed her, sweeping the sidewalk in front of the small forest with her gaze. No one was there. Remembering her promise to Daquain, she dug her sat phone from her backpack and called him.

He answered in the middle of the first ring. "Hey. You good?"

"Yeah, I'm good." Annja took a deeper, more relaxed breath and shrugged out of her backpack.

"I'm tracking the story at the internet café."

"Reporters are already there?" That amazed Annja.

"Nah. Social media, girl. That's where the real news is these days. By the time the professionals get there to wrap the story, the peeps with smartphones have already uploaded the 411. The action there is trending pretty heavy."

"Anybody mentioning my name?"

"Not yet."

"Did anyone get a picture of me?" she asked quietly.

"Haven't seen any good ones yet. They got some, but you were doing the Whac-a-Mole thing through the cars, then jumping the fence. No way they could get zoomed in."

"That's good."

"Traffic cams are gonna be a problem. I'm looking at those feeds, too, and the police are going to be able to clean them up and know who you are."

Annja sighed, thanked Daquain, ended the connection and wondered if anything was going to go right. Then her sat phone buzzed for attention. Checking the phone screen, she recognized the number immediately as the one she'd dialed earlier for Dr. Istvan Racz, the history professor Vincent Orta had recommended her to follow up with.

"Hello?"

"To whom am I speaking?" The voice sounded vaguely European in inflection.

"My name is Annja Creed, Dr. Racz. I was referred to you by Dr. Orta regarding a matter he assured me you would be interested in."

"What matter might that be?"

"The Merovingian kings. I was told you were an authority in the field."

"I consider myself to be that." Racz hesitated.

Annja knew the man was probably wary of wasting his time. Being an archaeologist or a historian was a lot like being a medical doctor. Instead of asking about ailments, people queried about historical stories they'd heard, treasure ships lost by pirates and what parts of the Indiana Jones movies were based on real events.

"I have information regarding the possible location of the Merovingian treasure." Annja spoke as quickly and as professionally as she could. She summarized her involvement with the crystal and with the papers Orta had contacted her about. "I'm sure if you could give me just a few minutes of your time, I could convince you of the veracity of the story, Dr. Racz."

"Where are you?"

"I'm in Santa Monica. I was hoping to meet with you."

"Do you feel like meeting me at my house? Or would you prefer some other venue?"

Annja glanced up at the street cameras at the intersection the cab was crossing. She didn't know if Bishop and Connolly had, or would, put a BOLO out on her, but she didn't want to meet in a public place.

"I can meet you at your home."

"Splendid." Racz gave her the address. "I will see you when you arrive, Ms. Creed."

Annja thanked him, told him she would be there soon and hung up, then relaxed into the seat. Ahead, she spotted the tall Ferris wheel at Santa Monica Pier. Beyond it, the Pacific Ocean lapped at the beach where sunbathers lounged in chairs and on blankets. A few colorful sails dotted the rising horizon.

Now, maybe, something was going right.

19

Sabre Race stared at the police fest taking place in the parking area behind the internet café. Nearly a dozen black-and-whites had converged on the area, and there were three undercover detective cars that he'd identified.

"Drive by." He waved a hand to Meszoly, who rolled past the scene.

"Is there any sign of the Creed woman, Dyson?" He watched as Dyson and his men laid down their weapons, knelt and put their hands on top of their heads.

"Negative. There's a bunch of trees on the other side of that fence. I didn't see any blood that showed she might have been hit. I think she got away clean."

The woman's luck was incredible. Alone and unarmed, she'd escaped de Cerceau's mercenaries.

"What about the opposition?"

"All down for the count."

A half-dozen armored policemen trotted forward, barking orders that transmitted over the phone link.

"Good job. Just sit tight until the attorneys get the charges dropped." There would be some resistance to that and maybe some fines, but that was all part of the business they were in. He kept attorneys on retainer in most of the surrounding states who could represent him and his people in instances like this.

"Copy that."

One of the police officers grabbed one of Dyson's hands and pulled it behind his back. That was the last Sabre saw of the man before they rolled out of the parking area.

"Guy's got a phone headset here," someone said.

"Give me that." The connection rattled and cracked for a moment. Then the second voice came over the phone louder and gruffer. "This is Sergeant Burchard of the Los Angeles Police Department. Who is this?"

Sabre committed the name to memory and hung up. "Saadiya?"

"Here."

"Sergeant Burchard of the LAPD—find out who he's working with and what he does with our guys."

"On it."

"And light up our lawyers. I want them waiting when our people walk into whatever precinct they end up at."

"Already done."

"Any luck tracking Annja Creed?"

"No. She's vanished. I checked the surrounding streets, but by the time I accessed those cameras, she must have already been gone. I'm checking with the cab companies. One of them reports picking up a fare near there only a couple minutes ago."

Excitement flared inside Sabre, but he kept it in check. "Did you get a destination?"

"Santa Monica Pier."

Sabre cursed. "What about a lock on her phone?"

Saadiya's smile was evident in her voice. "Now, that is something I'm having some success with. I checked through the cell towers surrounding the internet café, thinking she'd probably be using her phone. I'm still checking through all the numbers, but I'm going to have an answer soon."

"Good. Let me know when you have it. In the meantime, Lajos and I are headed to the pier. Send two other teams to search with us."

"Roger that."

"How much do we know about the Creed woman?"

"She's a television host. Book author. Archaeologist. Pretty much what we've been told."

Sabre shook his head, not agreeing with that. "She's more than that. She moves too well out there. I was thinking last night was a fluke, that she just happened to get away. But she took out two of de Cerceau's mercs by herself, and now she's been able to get away from us and de Cerceau. Find out more about her. Dig deeper. We're missing something."

"Copy that."

Sliding his cell phone back into his pocket, Sabre reset the navigation console for Santa Monica Pier. He felt certain Annja Creed had gone there to lose herself, and it was a good plan. He hoped Saadiya tracked the woman's number first.

"ANYTHING SPECIAL YOU WANT, miss?" the clerk behind the counter at the communications shop asked.

Annja surveyed the sat phones that were in stock and picked a brand she'd used before. The unit wasn't as good as the phone she carried, but it would do.

"Good choice." The clerk grabbed a plastic bag.

"I'll take it with me." Annja took cash from her pocket. She usually traveled with currency because she didn't like using her ATM card everywhere and she liked the idea of leaving a trail even less.

"Great." Using a box-cutting knife, the clerk slit the plastic casing and extracted the phone. He turned it on and the screen filled with data. "See? Already has part of a charge, but I'd power it up as soon as you can."

"Okay. Does it come with a charge cord?"

"It does indeed." The clerk pulled the cord from the box like a magician. "Ta-da!"

"How much?"

"Do you know how to swap out SIM cards? If you don't, I'll be happy to do that for you. Free of charge."

"I can do it." Annja had no intention of swapping out the

cards. The whole idea of buying the phone was to escape being tracked.

She left the communications shop and walked down the line of businesses. Volleyball players roared in raucous behavior farther down the beach and fishermen congregated around the pier. She chafed to get moving, but she knew she needed to lose the people she suspected were following her electronically. Sabre Race and de Cerceau were both too well connected to technology not to be able to pursue her.

Her phone had rung almost incessantly. Doug Morrell had called a few times, so she suspected she'd been mentioned in the news again. Then there were phone calls from Orta, Krauzer and the two homicide cops, Bishop and Connolly.

She chose to avoid Doug's calls a little longer because she had nothing to tell him, the same with Krauzer, but she'd called Orta at the hospital and told him she was going to be off the grid for a while and she'd be back in touch as soon as she could be. He hadn't liked it, but he'd understood.

Then she called Detective Connolly.

"Where are you, Ms. Creed?" The detective's tone was no-nonsense, implacable.

"Look, I don't have a lot of time, so I'm going to do the talking or I'm going to hang up. Are we clear?"

"Ms. Creed—"

Annja hung up and kept walking down the line of stores.

Turning left at a surfboard rental shop, Annja walked between it and an ice-cream novelty shop with a small crowd at the counter. She hit Redial.

Connolly answered on the first ring. "I'm listening."

"Good. I know you guys are tracking the phone. You're probably not the only ones. I wanted to let you know I was going to be out of touch for a while and I'll call you when I can."

"That's not acceptable. There are a lot of—"

Annja raised her voice. "There are a lot of people trying

to kill me. If you don't think so, take a look at that parking lot near the internet café, then tell me how safe I am."

"Are you going to stay in Los Angeles?"

"I don't know."

"You can't just—"

"Do you want to tell me how safe I'll be with you guys? Want to explain Melanie Harp's death to me?"

Connolly didn't say anything.

"This guy de Cerceau has got some really deep connections."

"What is this about?" For the first time, Connolly sounded human and frustrated.

"Like I told you, it's about treasure."

"No one knows that it's even real."

"That doesn't keep people from killing each other over it." Annja ended the call, took the SIM card from her sat phone and tossed the unit in the next trash can she passed.

She stopped at another communications kiosk, this one occupied by a harried woman dealing with a teen's technology problems, and bought a prepaid card for phone minutes. She paid in cash again. Once she disappeared online, she suspected Sabre Race or de Cerceau might try to find out if she'd bought another.

The blond guy might remember her, but the woman who sold her the prepaid minutes card wouldn't. She walked to a bus stop and boarded when the big vehicle arrived and opened its doors.

TWO CHANGES OF cabs later, one going each way, Annja debarked three blocks from Istvan Racz's home and walked to his address in what was referred to as the North of Montana district.

The house was a two-story brick structure that looked as if it had been built in the 1930s. A small circular drive surrounded a fountain. A wrought iron gate-blocked entrance, and tall fences covered in blossoming hibiscus surrounded the estate.

Annja guessed that the house had at one time belonged to old Hollywood royalty, and she wondered how Racz had afforded the place on a professor's salary.

A midsize security sedan rolled up to a stop behind Annja as she stood at the gates. The passenger window sank into its housing to reveal a large older man sitting behind the steering wheel.

"Are you lost, miss?"

"No, I'm here to see Dr. Racz. I was about to buzz."

The guard waved to let her know she could help herself. He waited.

A call box was to the right of the wrought iron gate. Annja crossed over to it and pressed a red button. The camera mounted above it swiveled into position to view her.

"Ms. Creed?" The man's voice sounded tinny over the intercom.

"Yes."

"You're not driving?"

"I took a cab."

"Ah, I see. Please come ahead."

With a small squeak, the wrought iron gate pulled to the side. Annja waved to the security guard, who nodded and rolled up his window as he took his foot from the brake and continued on his way. After Annja passed through, the gate closed behind her.

She walked around the gurgling fountain and crossed to the half-dozen wooden steps leading to the front door. The porch was wood, solid and well cared for. Before she could press the doorbell, the door opened.

"Ms. Creed?" The man was about Annja's height, built slender and wiry. His complexion was dark enough to pass as Hispanic, but his last name indicated a Hungarian heritage. She guessed that he was in his midforties.

"Dr. Racz?" Annja offered her hand.

"Yes." Racz turned aside and swept a hand toward the interior of his house. "Please. Won't you come in?"

20

Istvan Racz escorted Annja to a sunroom at the back of the house. The large plate-glass window overlooked a sprawling backyard equipped with a water feature that formed a moat around a small medieval stone castle. A flotilla of brass sailing ships bombarded the castle with water cannons and the spray created rainbows that danced in the breeze.

Everything looked neatly tended. Brightly colored flowers in startling oranges, yellows and reds bordered stone paths that meandered through the trees. Annja couldn't help staring and wondering again how a college professor could afford the house and grounds.

"I know, I know." Racz laughed good-naturedly. "The house is a little showy. My grandfather was a wealthy man who indulged my grandmother. She had a green thumb and tended everything herself when she was alive. Now it takes a small army of landscapers to keep everything just so."

"It's very beautiful."

"It is, but I felt some explanation was in order because this place, as you know, is far beyond anything I could afford on a professor's salary. I come from old money. Very old money. I don't feel guilty about that. Still, I sometimes wish I had the will to just let it all die. But I can't." Racz waved to one of the plush chairs in the room. "Please. Sit."

"Maybe we could sit somewhere else." Annja gestured to her jeans, stained with dirt from her scramble from the parking lot. "I had an accident this morning."

"I promise, all of this can be cleaned."

"I'd feel better if we did this somewhere else."

Racz nodded. "If you insist. My office is outfitted with leather and wood. It can be easily cleaned."

Annja thought she would have felt better if it had come outfitted with vinyl and imitation wood, but she followed him.

THE OFFICE WAS smaller than the sunroom and reeked of ancient pipe smoke. A mahogany desk claimed one end of the room. Floor-to-ceiling shelves held books and maps and objects from around the world. Most of the items had come from Europe—medieval coins, fired clay figures that looked like animals, but the majority of the display consisted of beaten metal rings and headbands from medieval times.

"Your grandfather was a collector." Annja bent to look at a collection of gold plates, bowls and pitchers behind the glass of a display case. "Ninth-century Magyar period?"

Racz joined her beside the case. "You've got an excellent eye, Ms. Creed. Of course, you should. I have to admit, after I got your call, I looked you up on the internet. It turns out you're quite famous."

"Not so famous. Especially in this town. Most people here wouldn't give a cable show a second glance."

"Be that as it may, I'm impressed. And I wasn't talking about the television show. I was referring to your work in the field."

"Well, thank you." Annja straightened. "Your grandfather must have traveled a lot."

"He did." Racz waved her to a leather chair in front of the desk. "The money came from a several-times-removed grandfather down the line who made a fortune in shipping. From what I understand, he began accruing his wealth while working opium fields in India in the early nineteenth century. The Indians there raised the poppies so the British, the Americans and the French could sell it to China markets."

"I know." Annja sat and put her backpack at her feet. She

liked the fact that Racz wasn't embarrassed about his family's wealth or how they'd acquired it.

"Times were different back then." Racz took his seat behind the desk and looked comfortable. "Those days I would be called a narco-baron or something."

"Several members of the House of Lords in London tried to cover up where they'd made their money at the time. And some of today's pharmacological corporations would like to pretend they didn't get their start from those profits."

Racz leaned back in his chair with his elbows resting on the arms. "History has a way of catching up to us. It always has. From what I've read, you've had a lot of luck in that area yourself."

"You can call it luck if you want, but there's a lot of hard work that goes into making that luck happen."

"Of course. Please don't think I meant any offense or intended to denigrate your skills."

"I don't." Annja dug inside her backpack for her computer. "Dr. Orta said you might be able to help me with a project he and I turned up."

"I'd be happy to, though I'm surprised he didn't come with you."

"He…had an accident." Annja saw no need to get into details with Racz. Hopefully, he would just point her in a direction and she would take it from there.

"That's unfortunate." Racz's dark eyes looked sorrowful. "I hope he will be all right?"

"He will be. He just can't join us now." Annja booted up her tablet PC. "Do you mind if I use your internet?"

Racz gave her the visitor's password and she placed her computer on the edge of the desk. He leaned forward in his chair to look at the images she and Orta had captured with the crystal.

"How did you get these?" Racz stared at the images with rapt attention.

Quickly, Annja explained about the crystal Krauzer's set designer had found, the pages Orta had gotten from his student and Julio Gris's journal.

"Are these real?"

"We believe so."

Racz gazed at the images. "May I put these up on a larger screen?" He reached behind his computer monitor and unplugged a cord. He passed it over to Annja.

She had to dig out a converter to make the connection to the tablet's video output, but she had one and the job was done easily enough. While she was doing that, Racz pushed a button on a remote control and a large screen dropped down from the ceiling over the bookshelves.

"Not my grandfather's addition." Racz smiled. "Though he used to watch film he'd shot in other countries at dig sites. I just upgraded."

Annja pressed the commands to show the images on the screen, which had to be 120 inches diagonally. Abandoning his chair, Racz walked to stand in front of the screen with his hands in his pockets. "Can you read this?"

"I read Spanish fluently."

"How is your Romanian?"

"Not as good as my Spanish, but I can make do."

Racz smiled. "Then I must ask you, how is your Hungarian?"

Annja shook her head. "When it comes to reading? Lacking. Put me in a Hungarian culture, I can order food and make my way around, but the written language is presently beyond my capabilities."

"Then you're going to need me."

Annja took a breath and thought about Dr. Racz running from the likes of Sabre Race or de Cerceau. She didn't think the security leader would be a problem once they got out of California, but the French mercenary wouldn't give up so easily. And de Cerceau had zero need to hang around

California—or probably even the United States after everything he had done.

"You really don't want to go with me, Dr. Racz. Some really bad people are after me and what they think I know."

Hands still in his pockets, Racz turned to face her. "What do you know?"

Annja shook her head. "Only what I've told you."

A gentle smile framed his lips. "Which is not enough to help you find what you're looking for."

"No. Not even close."

"And these people won't believe that without taking extreme measures to satisfy themselves."

"Probably not."

"So you remain in danger." Turning back to the image on the large screen, Racz grinned more broadly. "My grandfather was forever going on about his adventures around the world. When he started in on one of those tales, my grandmother would throw her hands in the air, go get her shears and walk out to her garden. My brother and I, though, we would sit and listen to those stories and our heads would fill with all of the exciting things we might do and see if we ever followed in his footsteps." He paused. "I have never had a true adventure. I've traveled to other countries, of course, and even taken part in digs, but mostly my life has been presenting one paper after another at some boring conference. You know what I'm talking about."

Annja had been to a few of those conferences, as well. Generally, there wasn't a whole lot of new information being discussed. She preferred to be in the field.

"I do."

"This is my opportunity, Ms. Creed. My chance at adventure. I don't plan on missing it." Racz paused. "In addition to my desires, you're going to need me in your quest, and you know that."

"I can find my way through historical materials quite well enough."

With a shrug, Racz pursed his lips. "I'm certain that you can, but the trick is to do it before the men chasing you catch you."

Annja had no argument for that.

"As it happens, I know quite a lot about the time periods we're discussing, and I know a great number of people who collect things from those eras." Racz straightened himself with military precision. "The truth of the matter is that you need me if you intend to succeed in your endeavor." He grimaced. "I realize that is rather bold, but there you have it."

Gazing at the man, Annja thought maybe de Cerceau would scare Racz off soon enough. If he didn't get killed during an encounter. That would be the difficult thing to avoid. And as much as he might slow her physically, there was every chance that he could help with the necessary research.

Racz extended his hand and smiled hopefully. "Do we have a deal?"

Reluctantly, Annja took the man's hand. "We have a deal." She hoped that she didn't regret her decision.

"Good." Racz took his hand back and retreated to his desk. After he opened a locked drawer with a key hanging on a chain around his neck, he took out a leather-covered journal that showed years of hard use. He displayed the book with obvious pride. "My personal book of the Merovingian treasure. My grandfather helped me start it when I was only seven." He chuckled. "I have to admit to several delusions of grandeur because of this thing."

"Is there anything in there that helps us know where to go next?" Annja returned her tablet PC to her backpack.

"I know that without consulting the journal." Racz slid the book into a pocket of his slacks. "We need to go to Ordizia."

"Spain?"

"I know of no other."

"Why Ordizia?"

"A small museum there houses a grand collection of Friar

Andrés de Urdaneta's ships' logs and charts. Have you heard of him?"

Annja had to dig through her recollection of recent research, but she had the name. "He was an Augustinian friar, and he was responsible for the second world navigation. He sailed with Miguel López de Legazpi, the commander of the expedition. Philip II arranged for the people and the ships."

Racz's eyes sparkled with excitement. "You are quite knowledgeable."

"I remember the names from research I did yesterday and this morning."

"Then you know that de Urdaneta was considered one of the finest navigators in the known world at that time."

Annja nodded and stood, swinging the backpack over one shoulder. "Why are we going to Ordizia? If the maps are online, we should be able to access them."

"We can access the maps and logs the museum is willing to show the public, but there are several that are part of a private collection." Racz scratched at his chin. "Unfortunately, the person who owns that collection will want something in return."

"To go with us?" Annja didn't plan on adding to her party and the prospect left her frustrated.

"No." Racz laughed. "Sebastian would never want to do something like that. He's not a big risk-taker. He will be looking for financial remuneration."

"If it's not too much, we should be able to deal with that."

"Excellent." Racz smiled even bigger. "Shall we make air reservations?"

"I'll handle that. You go pack a bag."

"Very well." Racz nodded and departed.

Taking a burner phone from her backpack, Annja dialed a number she knew and surveyed the room. The phone rang and rang.

21

Sabre glared impassively at the people walking the sidewalks in the neighborhood near the internet café where Annja Creed had last been seen. Impatience seethed within him. They had practically been on top of the woman—now she was in the wind and Dyson was going to be out of action for at least a few hours until the attorneys got him off the hook. After all, they were legally empowered as security agents to try to get property back for their employer. Sabre was certain Krauzer's attorneys would weigh in, as well.

"Maybe it's time to reach out." Meszoly spoke softly because he knew Sabre didn't react well to someone telling him how to do his job, but he also knew when to offer counsel. "We've got more access to intel through other sources than what Saadiya can give us in a short amount of time."

Sabre knew that Meszoly's assessment was true, but he also knew he hated calling in favors. Especially from the man Meszoly referred to. They'd both worked for the contact as mercenaries before forming their own security firm, and truthfully, they'd learned a lot while working for the man. Leaving DragonTech had been hard because they'd been paid well and the training had been ongoing. But Sabre liked the idea of managing his own clientele and the personal freedom. More than that, though, his past employer sometimes shaved laws too thin to suit Sabre's tastes. The man was dangerous.

Meszoly took the next corner slowly and they both looked around for Annja Creed even though they knew they weren't going to find her. They trolled along another sedentary neighborhood street, passing a patrol car that was probably assigned to do the same thing and was doubtless accomplishing just as little.

Maybe Saadiya could track Creed through the taxi services, but Sabre wasn't holding out any faith in that area. The woman knew what she was doing. He had to give her that. She'd proved herself the previous night and again today by taking out de Cerceau's men in the hospital and escaping the trap that had nearly closed on her at the internet café.

His estimation of her had risen dramatically, and part of him relished the hunt. When two people were equally matched, only luck separated them. He was willing to bet that his fortune was better than hers.

Finally, knowing the clock was now working against them, Sabre picked up the cell phone and dialed. The overseas connection picked up after one ring and a woman's sultry voice answered in a professional German accent.

"DragonTech Securities. How may I help you?"

"Who is this?" Sabre spoke English. All of the people on the end of that connection spoke several languages.

"I am Heike."

"It's a pleasure to speak with you, Heike." He oozed charm, hoping it might have some effect. "My name is Sabre Race. I'd like to speak to Mr. Braden."

"I'm so sorry, Mr. Race, but Mr. Braden doesn't take unscheduled calls. Perhaps you would like to leave him a message?"

Sabre curbed his anger. Allowing his temper to slip loose now would be a mistake. "Please forward my message immediately. It's important, and I know Mr. Braden would want to hear from me."

"I will, Mr. Race."

Ignoring the itch to ask if Garin Braden was in the building, Sabre thanked the woman and hung up. Staring at the phone in his hand, he willed it to ring. Luck would be with him.

IN THE SHADOWS of the multicolored cargo containers that lined the working docks of Rio de Janeiro, Garin Braden looked at the ninety-eight-foot statue of Christ the Redeemer perched on the Corcovado Mountain in the distance.

Garin didn't care for the statue, and he regretted his need to personally take care of the business that brought him to the city. Brazil was too hot and humid this time of year, though that was welcome respite from those northern climes. He could have handed the matter off to one of his subordinates.

And every time he looked at Christ the Redeemer, Garin thought of Joan of Arc. Some thought she was a warrior called by God and some believed she'd been a master strategist.

He hadn't known her well. Joan had spent more time in Roux's company than Garin's. He'd kept away from Joan because Roux had wanted it that way. He'd been her champion, after all. Not Garin. Despite Roux's efforts, and directly because of his distractions, she'd ended up tied to a stake and burned alive.

Garin's final memory of her was of that horrific scene, forever etched in his memory by the stink of burning flesh. Not that he hadn't seen such brutality before. His own father was a cruel man who hadn't cared for his son except as a potential worker. His father had held a lot of resentment because he wasn't certain he was Garin's father. Garin's mother had had a wandering eye when her husband wasn't around.

Once his father had learned he could sell that son to Roux, he hadn't hesitated. Even Garin's mother hadn't fought the transaction. Whatever money trickled into her husband's purse could potentially end up in hers.

So he'd gone off, wrapped in rags and cold in the harsh winter, when Roux had decided he needed an apprentice. For the next few years, Garin had made fires and suppers and done whatever scut work the old man had decided needed doing. Their relationship even then had been strained, but there were occasions when it had been pleasant.

Sometimes Garin thought about those, but not often. More often, as with this day, he thought of himself and his business ventures.

And this day, he was in Brazil to kill a woman.

Standing well over six feet, Garin looked like a dockworker with his broad shoulders and massive build. Genetics and a harsh, active life had led to the physique, but he worked at it, too, because he liked women. It was one thing to be rich, but athletic prowess allowed him to enjoy his conquests even more.

His black goatee squared off his broad face. Faint scars showed on his features, but so much time had passed that they'd almost faded. Only the latest acquisition, a pink worm that curved across the right side of his neck, stood out. When the time was right, he had a laser surgeon who was particularly gifted in his craft who would remove the scar.

Dressed in cargo jeans, work boots and a black tank top that showed off his bronzed skin, Garin knew he easily passed for one of the dockworkers. He watched as massive hoists lifted the cargo containers onto waiting ships. The resounding booms of the containers settling onto metal-plated decks echoed around Garin and punctuated the droning noise of diesel engines. "I have her," Sidnei Portinari reported over the comm link Garin wore in his left ear. Portinari was the leader of the DragonTech team based in Rio de Janeiro and spoke in Portuguese.

Garin slipped his smartphone from his pants pocket and looked at the screen. He touched the streaming app he'd had written for the operation and brought up a video link.

One of Portinari's men had secured a position atop a container and focused on a narrow lane between containers. The view showed a gunmetal-gray Aspid GT-21 that rolled slowly along the lane, approaching the hidden camera. Sleek and swooping, the exotic car looked like something out of a science-fiction movie with its various angles and hollows.

"You have confirmed the woman is in the car?" Garin opened his fingers on the smartphone's screen to magnify the view and still couldn't see through the dark glass.

"Yes. Our people picked her up at her home. She has not stopped."

The woman was Tarsila Innecco. She had given Garin the new scar. Even thinking of her now, he remembered the jasmine scent she favored and her taut, muscular body.

"Is she alone?" Garin continued watching. Sunlight splintered across the sports car's sloped windshield.

"No. She's accompanied by her second."

Garin grinned in anticipation. Tarsila was dangerous on her own. Having Victor Volpi there heightened that danger. But Garin wouldn't have had it any other way. Volpi was Tarsila's lover and a lethal man in his own right. They'd never met, but the investigators who had found Tarsila Innecco and her little hideaway had uncovered Volpi, as well.

On the small phone screen, the car rolled to a stop near a light blue cargo container. For a moment, no one moved.

"Sir." Portinari spoke softly and politely. "We can take care of this for you."

Garin's response was immediate. "No. Not this time. This is personal. But thank you."

"As you wish. We will be on overwatch."

"Of course." Overwatch wouldn't be necessary. Garin monitored the screen.

After another moment, an old man stepped from the shadow of the container and waved at the sports car. Dressed in faded gabardine pants and a plaid work shirt with the sleeves hacked off to reveal tattooed arms that had withered with age, the old man looked harmless. Gray whiskers dotted his lined face, and the left cheek was pockmarked by burn scarring.

The old man stopped twenty feet from the car and waved again.

Slowly, the passenger-side door opened and Volpi got out. He was in his early thirties and wore an expensive blue pinstripe suit and sunglasses. His dark blond hair was gelled into submission and looked black in places. Lean and muscular, he moved like a cat. And like a feline, he was aware of his presence. His hands moved automatically to straighten his clothing, though the fabric fell naturally into place.

From the camera angle, Garin saw Volpi speaking, but there was no audio pickup.

"Volpi— Where is it?" The translation came from Aasta Thaulow, the Norwegian linguist and lip-reader monitoring the meeting.

The old man stepped back and gestured to the container.

"Garcia— Here. It is here."

Emil Garcia was a local fence, a man who auctioned off cargoes that were "lost" and needed to be "found" by others willing to pay for them. Portinari had recruited the man for the operation.

What he'd supposedly found today was a shipment of pharmaceuticals. The cargo was actually provided by one of the shippers DragonTech provided security for. The goods would be returned before anyone knew they were missing.

Pharmaceuticals were the fourth-largest item selected by cargo hijackers. A single tablet of OxyContin went for twelve times the original value on the street. The cargo container provided a $7 million haul for someone who had a supply network. Volpi had friends and Tarsila was greedy.

"Volpi— How much do you want?"

"Garcia— As we agreed. Four million in US dollars."

Volpi shook his head.

"Volpi— That's too much.

"Garcia— You can double your money.

"Volpi— Only after weeks or months of trafficking it. I will give you two million."

The bickering went on for a short time and Garin's irritation grew. The sun was hot.

Finally, Garcia settled on $2.6 million, enough of a discount to make Volpi think he'd gotten a good deal. Satisfied, Volpi turned and nodded toward the car.

A moment later, Tarsila Innecco climbed from the car wearing brown leather trousers, strappy sandals and a sleeveless yellow blouse. Her red hair was gathered and tied back so that it flowed over her shoulders and down her back. The round-lensed sunglasses hid her hazel eyes. She carried a Versace handbag just big enough for the Taurus M45/410 revolver she favored.

Garcia waved them to the container as he reached for the locks.

Trusting that Volpi and Tarsila would be focused on their windfall, Garin pocketed his smartphone and strode forward.

Portinari made one last attempt. "Sir—"

"No," Garin snarled. He slid a hand into another pocket, through the cutout to the holster strapped to his leg, and brought out a suppressor-equipped AMT .45 ACP subcompact pistol. His hand swallowed the weapon's small frame.

By the time he reached the cargo container, Volpi and Tarsila were inside. He stepped up his pace because there was every chance they would kill Garcia if they thought they could get the pharmaceuticals without paying for them. They might wait to see if Garcia had anyone watching them.

"Move!" Portinari's sudden command cracked over the earwig.

Instantly, Garin dived to the hard-packed earth. His

breath puffed a cloud of dust. Then he rolled against another container as a bullet whined from the target container. The hammer-like impact bonged inside the container.

"Sniper!" Portinari called out commands to his team. "Those two didn't come alone."

Neither did I, Garin thought.

"Where is the sniper?" Edging up against the container where he'd taken shelter, Garin peered around the corner. Another bullet slammed into the container's edge and drove heated steel splinters into his cheek. He ducked back and watched the front of the pharmaceutical container.

22

"I may have something." On the tablet PC, Saadiya looked pleased with herself.

Her call wasn't the one Sabre had been waiting for, but he took it. "Tell me."

"I managed to hack into the phone records on the satellite phone Annja Creed discarded."

"What do you have?"

"A telephone number and address she called right before she disposed of the phone." Saadiya took time to make a couple keystrokes. "I just sent it to you."

Sabre's phone dinged with the arrival of the text. He stared at the name in disbelief and couldn't help feeling his luck had turned. Sickness twisted in his stomach.

The name Istvan Racz was followed by a telephone number and an address that Sabre knew well.

"I'm doing some background on Racz." Saadiya kept typing. "On the surface, it looks like he's a college professor specializing in Hungarian history. As I get more intel, so will you."

"Thanks, Saadiya." Sabre didn't bother telling her what he already knew or that the man was familiar to him. He leaned forward and plugged the address into the GPS unit. Looking at Meszoly, Sabre pointed a forefinger at the map as the unit traced their new journey for them. "There. Now."

Meszoly nodded and pressed his foot harder on the accelerator.

Sabre sat back and wondered if the revelation was good luck or bad.

He felt certain it was bad.

ANNJA'S PHONE RANG as she was leafing through one of Frigyes Racz's journals of his exploration of Translyvania while following up on information relating to King Géza II's attempt at colonizing that country. At the outset, the transplanted Germans were supposed to protect and patrol the southeastern border of the Kingdom of Hungary.

The journal was enticing reading. Frigyes Racz was a good raconteur and hadn't been afraid to go into dangerous places. The man's writing had a good blend of ancient history and his own adventures while tracking artifacts. After reading some of the passages, Annja was surprised the man had lived as long as he had.

"You called?" Roux spoke in French.

"I did. I have a favor to ask." Annja felt as if she was on thin ice with that. She didn't like relying on Roux or Garin, though all three of them were tied because of the sword.

Roux growled irritably. Calm voices sounded in the background, and there was a televised presentation of at least three horse races that she could identify. Roux didn't bet on horses much, but he favored Texas Hold'em, sitting in on games around the world.

She pictured him in her mind dressed in a conservative suit, his white beard trailing to his chest and his blue eyes piercing above his thin nose. There was something grand and almost mystical about him.

"And what might this favor be?"

"I've got to get out of Los Angeles—Santa Monica, actually—and was hoping you might arrange for a jet that I could use."

"Contrary to your view of me, I don't just carry around jets in my pockets."

Annja knew he was being short with her because she hadn't been able to hide her judgmental reaction. Still, if a man was going to live five hundred years, it would seem he would gain some good sense and a little propriety.

"No, but you can arrange for a jet." Annja didn't want to have to ask again. They didn't keep markers between them, so no one owed anyone anything, but she didn't think she should have to ask twice.

"So can you."

"It would be better if I didn't do that. I don't want my name showing up anywhere."

Roux's tone changed, became more interested and a little protective. "Are you in trouble?"

"Nothing I can't handle."

"With the police?"

"They're on the periphery of things. They can't keep me here, but they do want to talk to me. However, if they slow me down, the other people looking for me can catch up."

Roux paused, and for a moment, Annja thought the connection had dropped.

"You have been busy." He sounded distracted.

"What do you mean?"

"There's a considerable amount of information about your present situation on Twitter and Facebook. Murders. Suspicious deaths. Shoot-outs. Chases. Questioning by the authorities. Mercenaries. Bodyguards. And some kind of missing artifact?"

Sighing, Annja glared at the artifacts in their glass display cases. Things had been so much simpler back then, when social media didn't tune into everyone's lives. Back then, the only worry had been gossip.

"The last two days have been…interesting."

"And you're all right?"

"I am."

"You sound tired."

"I am tired." Annja felt uncomfortable when Roux started acting in the least bit paternal. "Look, is this jet going to happen? If not, I could still call Garin."

She didn't want to do that, though. Things with Garin

had gotten complicated. She didn't quite trust him, because he always took care of himself first but didn't bother telling anyone when that was going to happen. And he was far too attractive. Garin was confusion incarnate some days.

"Calling Garin won't be necessary, and it might complicate the situation, actually."

That made Annja immediately suspicious. "Complicate the situation how?"

"Never mind about that. Where would you like your jet to pick you up and deliver you?"

Roux probably had more money than Garin had, but he didn't flaunt it. The old man liked to play in the shadows, while Garin seized the limelight when he could. That would eventually catch up with him, though, because he couldn't keep reinventing himself. Eventually, he'd have to retreat to the shadows, too. There was no telling how he would take that.

"There's an airport here in Santa Monica. We can be there within minutes."

"'We'?"

"I'm traveling with a companion. A history professor who's helping me."

"So just the two of you?" Beeping at Roux's end of the connection probably came from notes he was putting into his smartphone.

"Yes."

"And where will you be going?"

"Ordizia, Spain."

"Lovely city. For what reason?"

"Research." Annja expected Roux to pry because he was often nosy, though he would never admit to it.

"This isn't the number you usually call from."

"I had to get rid of my phone."

"Probably a wise move. Will this number be good?"

"Until I let you know that it isn't."

"Give me a few minutes to make arrangements."

That was one of the things Annja struggled to comprehend. Roux and Garin moved through the world as though there were no international boundaries. She couldn't imagine what a life like that would be like.

"Call me back." Annja pressed Disconnect and pocketed the phone, about to return her attention to Frigyes Racz's journal as something to focus on. Her mind had a tendency to clutter when she didn't keep it busy. And she had plenty to think about at the moment.

Still, why would calling Garin complicate matters? That bothered her because it meant Roux knew something about her present situation that she didn't know. She wanted to call Roux back and demand an answer, but she knew that would only delay what he was doing for her.

Before she could open the journal, rumbling sounded out in the hallway and Racz stepped into the room towing a luggage bag behind him.

"We have a problem," he said quietly.

"What?"

"I believe someone tailed you here." Racz crooked a finger at her to follow him.

Annja stepped forward and joined him at the desk.

Racz tapped his computer keyboard and security video popped up on the monitor screen. In the sixteen views afforded, three of them showed uniformed men circling the house with slow, methodical precision.

"Do you know who they are?" Racz rocked a little as he stood there. A tight grimace pulled at his mouth. "They are obviously not the police."

"I can't be certain, but I think they're with the Black Legion security people. Their uniforms look right." And they didn't come in guns blazing, she thought. That was something Annja felt certain de Cerceau's mercs would do.

Racz's nostrils flared and his breathing quickened, though

whether in fear or irritation Annja wasn't certain. "I assume they share our interest in the secret message in the crystal."

"Oh, I'm willing to bet they have an interest in it, and they won't stop to find out what we know about it."

A man in the lower left quadrant of the computer screen took a glass-cutting tool from his vest. He knelt and worked quickly, inscribing a five-inch circle in a pane of glass with quick confidence. He tapped two fingers against the scored section and the glass dropped to the tile floor inside.

The *tink* of glass striking the tile and shattering sounded a long way off.

Racz looked at her. "What do you want to do?"

"Not be here when those guys get inside. They're not here to talk. Not politely, at any rate."

The professor nodded. "Agreed. They haven't yet broken into the garage. Perhaps that is a possibility for our escape."

"Can we get there from here?"

"Of course. It's attached." Racz picked up his luggage and sprinted from the room.

Heart hammering in her ears, Annja followed him through the house. She didn't like that she couldn't see the progress made by the men breaking into the house, but she was certain the cordon around them was tightening.

She and Racz raced through the large, spotless kitchen and saw a uniformed man standing near the door leading out into a small courtyard. His head turned as he tracked them and he spoke sharply. Even though she couldn't hear the man's words, Annja knew someone could. He leveled his assault rifle, but they were past him before he could fire. If that was what he intended.

The door off the kitchen led to a remodeled utility room filled with gleaming technology. Racz walked through that door and pulled a set of keys from his pocket as he stepped out into a neat, well-kept garage that contained a small dark blue SUV and a red 1950s Corvette convertible. She wondered fleetingly if the sports car was something Grandpa Racz had left behind along with his house and journals.

Racz used the key fob to unlock the doors and the mechanisms thunked dully. He started to haul himself up into the vehicle, but Annja shouldered him aside and plucked the key from his hand.

"What are you doing?" Racz glared at her as if she'd gone mad.

"Have you ever had to escape in a vehicle before?" Since he wasn't moving, Annja shoved him into motion.

"No, of course not." Racz trotted around to the other side of the SUV.

"Trust me. Today isn't a day you want to learn. There's not going to be a do-over." Annja pulled off her backpack and tossed it into the backseat. She slid smoothly behind the wheel, inserted the key and switched the ignition. The powerful engine blared to life, but the muffler subdued most of the noise.

Racz fumbled with his luggage for a moment, trying to heft the bag into the vehicle, having trouble in the narrower confines on his side.

"Leave it." Annja pulled the transmission into gear.

Scowling, Racz dropped the luggage and clambered in. He was breathing hard and his eyes were wide.

"Buckle up." Annja followed her own advice and pulled the seat restraint into place.

Racz fumbled for the seat belt and pulled it down.

From the corner of her eye, Annja spotted one of the uniformed men running toward them from the utility room. He had a machine pistol in his hands and was shouting something.

Hoping that the man had no orders to shoot to kill, Annja took her foot off the brake and dropped it onto the accelerator, aiming the SUV at the closed wooden garage door.

23

Pinned down by sniper fire, Garin watched in helpless frustration as Victor Volpi and Tarsila Innecco sprinted from the cargo container. Both of them had pistols in hand and were running crouched over to make smaller targets of themselves.

Ignoring the sniper fire for a moment, Garin leaned forward, took deliberate aim and squeezed off a shot at Volpi. The man saw Garin at the last moment and tried to take evasive action, but it was too late. The bullet caught him a glancing blow on the hip, lower than Garin had intended because at that distance pistol accuracy wasn't a sure thing.

The impact partially spun Volpi and he stopped to regroup a few yards from the sports car. He pressed a hand to his side and his fingers came away wet with blood.

"Surrender," Garin ordered, holding the pistol steady before him. If he could recover the money he'd lost, that would be fine. But it wasn't necessary. Still, recouping his losses would add injury to insult for them. Not that the feelings would last long afterward.

Volpi glanced up and took a fresh grip on his pistol, raising it to fire.

Garin settled his sights over Volpi's midsection again, cursing the pistol's lack of range. If things had gone as Garin had hoped, he would have been shooting Volpi and Tarsila up close and personal, giving her time to see death coming for her. Her subterfuge had cost him a few million, wealth that he didn't have to have, but the blow to his ego had been far worse and he wouldn't suffer that. He didn't like thinking of himself as weak or feebleminded.

And over a woman, at that.

He started to squeeze the trigger, staring down the barrel of Volpi's gun and trusting the Kevlar body armor he wore under his clothing. Then a sledgehammer blow struck him in the ribs, knocking the wind from his lungs. Already falling, he managed to scramble back into the safety of the cargo container. The bullet had struck too fiercely to have come from Volpi's weapon. The round had come from the unseen rifleman.

"Sir?" Portinari's concerned tone cracked over the comm link.

"Get that sniper." Garin sipped his breath back into his lungs. The Kevlar had kept the round from penetrating into his body, but only just.

"Yes, sir."

Knowing he had no chance at the sniper, Garin turned his focus to Volpi, who staggered toward the car. Ignoring the pain in his side that threatened to squeeze the breath from him again, Garin fired once more, this time catching Volpi in the upper arm. The man's gun dropped to the ground.

Tarsila leaned over the sports car's roof and took deliberate aim. Her first round burned through Garin's hair and caught the top of his left ear with a hot, burning kiss. Warm blood trickled down his cheek as he took a step to the side and fired another round, this time aiming at the woman.

Coolly, Tarsila held her position as both of Garin's rounds skimmed across the hood of the car. Her next shot caught Garin in the same side as the sniper round, only a few inches higher. Spots danced in Garin's vision as he forced himself to move again, barely escaping her follow-up round.

Volpi staggered into her field of fire as he reached the door to open it. After succeeding in pulling open the door, he sank down inside and began yelling at Tarsila. "Let's go!"

Tarsila fired the final rounds from her pistol in rapid succession, barely missing Garin with her fusillade of shots as he retreated along the cargo container. When her weapon was empty, she clambered into the car and slid behind the wheel. The rear tires spun and screeched against the pavement as she floored the accelerator and came at Garin.

Trapped between the rows of containers, Garin knew he couldn't have outrun the sports car even if his lungs had been pumped with oxygen and his ribs weren't burning with pain. He drove himself forward and managed to reach a narrow opening between two stacks of cargo containers an instant before the vehicle overtook him.

The car's fiberglass fender shredded as it kissed the rough hide of the corrugated cargo container. The deafening noise hurt Garin's ears until Tarsila steered away from the shipping box.

He leaned from the opening after the car rushed past. Settling the pistol's sights over the vehicle's rapidly retreating rear, he emptied the magazine. Holes appeared in the back windshield but he was certain Tarsila and Volpi had escaped unscathed.

Ignoring his wound, Garin raced through the opening between the cargo containers. The path Tarsila had taken ended only a short distance farther on. A stack of three blue containers marked the area where an opening had been left for service vehicles to get through. She would have to turn back to him.

"The sniper is down," Portinari reported.

"Good," Garin growled as he stared at the immense loading crane standing high above the cargo containers two rows over. He ran for the crane, reached its base and sprinted up the steps leading to the control center. At the top, he pulled open the Plexiglas window and threw himself inside.

A squat man in jeans, a T-shirt and a soccer ball cap sat

in an abbreviated seat at the controls. He stared fearfully at Garin when he leveled the pistol at him.

"Go!" Garin ordered in Portuguese, gesturing with the pistol, indicating the man should exit through the door.

Eyes wide, the man abandoned his post immediately, crouching against the wall in the small space until he was through the door. Then he slid down the rails on his palms and hit the ground running, never once looking back.

At the far end of the rows of containers, Tarsila gave the sports car too much acceleration and skidded out of control around a tight corner. She backed away from the container she'd collided with and left pieces of fiberglass in her wake. Then she was shooting forward again, gaining speed as the tires found traction.

Garin hated that he didn't get to tell the woman that she deserved what was coming, that the only person she'd truly managed to fool in the long run was herself. But he knew she would get the message all the same. He hoped that she still felt as if she was going to get away with her life, that she had no idea of the fate that awaited her, right up until her last dying moment.

After holstering his weapon, Garin familiarized himself with the crane's control levers.

The crane shivered like a great beast as he moved it around more suddenly than he should have. The forks at the end of the thick cable held a long green cargo container. If events had been within his control, Garin would have liked to have dropped the container on his prey. But that wasn't as certain as he would have liked.

Instead, he swung the container into a collection of other metal cargo units and managed to topple them over with a loud *bong* followed by a series of harsh clangs. For an agonizing minute, Garin thought the impact wasn't going to be enough to knock the stack of containers sideways.

The cargo containers slid but didn't immediately fall. It

looked as though Tarsila and Volpi were still going to get away, barely escaping under the avalanche Garin had hoped would block their path.

Then the containers succumbed to gravity and toppled like a child's toys onto the expensive car. The vehicle came to an instant stop, flattening under the weight of the containers that had hit it.

Getting out of the crane's seat, Garin left the machine and slid down the boarding rails on his palms just as the operator had. When he reached the ground, he kept moving, lengthening his stride because events were uncoiling quickly. The pain in his side was already lessening and he thought maybe nothing was broken.

"Sir, patrols are en route," Portinari stated.

"Slow them if you can, but prepare for exfiltration."

"Affirmative, sir."

Garin wasn't overly concerned, as long as the official didn't shoot first and ask questions later. He kept law firms on retainer for sticky situations like this. The case could be made that he was protecting his goods as long as reparations were made for property damage. He was willing to do that if necessary.

He took the AMT .45 pistol from his leather and exchanged the spent magazine for a fresh one. He tripped the slide release, and the pistol stripped the first round from the magazine and seated it as it slid forward. Keeping the weapon at his side, he trotted toward the wreckage of cargo containers two rows over. One of the cargo containers near the top of the heap lost its fight with gravity and balance and slid down. Gashes opened in its side as it caught a corner before burying into the asphalt.

The sports car's right side was crushed under a corner of a container. One of Volpi's arms hung outside a window that had clamped down like teeth. Blood ran down his arm and rained down onto the ground, soaking in on contact.

Keeping the AMT trained on the front of the car, Garin stared through the shattered windshield at Volpi's bloody face and blank, staring eyes. He was dead and gone, an empty shell.

Tarsila, on the other hand, remained still very much alive. Bloody and fearful, she sat pinned in her seat by the front section of the car where it was crushed by a cargo container. One of her eyes was nearly swollen shut and her nose was broken. Taking in the blood-covered face and the panicked eyes, Garin moved toward her.

"Tarsila?" Garin spoke softly even though warning sirens were going off.

She stared at him and raised her pistol in a shaking hand. "Garin?" She smiled and blood leaked from the corner of her mouth to her jawline.

"I'm here."

She spit blood as she held her pistol steadier. "I knew I shouldn't have left you alive after I took your money. I knew you were a dangerous man."

"I am."

Sirens closed on their location and the sound shimmied between the rows of cargo containers.

For a moment, sympathy touched Garin. During the past five hundred years, he'd been reminded again and again how fragile life was. He couldn't even guess at how many lives he'd taken over the centuries.

Tarsila Innecco had been fun, intelligent and vivacious. He'd known it wouldn't last. These affairs never did. Human life was too fleeting. He'd become used to enjoying what he could of them.

"You shouldn't have betrayed me." Garin looked at the pistol in her hand and felt certain he could move before her finger tightened on the trigger.

A thread of blood spun from the corner of her mouth to

her chin and hung there for a moment before a drop splashed onto her shoulder. In her hand, the pistol shook.

She tried to smile, but her face was bruised and swollen, and the expression looked twisted. "Under other circumstances, maybe I wouldn't have betrayed you." She blinked and struggled to concentrate. "You never loved me."

"If I didn't, you wouldn't have been able to do what you did."

She tried the smile again, but she had less control over it. Her eyes glazed slightly and she had trouble focusing. "Maybe you did love me, but you wouldn't have stayed in love with me."

Garin thought about lying to her, offering some final comfort, but he knew she would recognize a falsehood immediately. "No. It's not you. It's me. I have issues."

"So here we are."

Garin shrugged.

"Sir," Portinari said into his ear. "We have to go. Now."

"I've got to leave." Garin holstered his weapon. Watching her die made him feel sadder than he'd thought it would. Until he'd seen her so broken and helpless, he'd thought of her only as an enemy that needed to be put to death.

Tarsila tried to take a fresh grip on her weapon, but it almost slid through her fingers. "I could kill you."

"No." Garin shook his head. "You can't. You're already too far gone."

Anger firmed her jawline and a fresh trickle of blood spilled from her mouth. She squeezed the trigger.

Even from only six feet away, the shot went wide, plucking at the loose folds of Garin's shirt as it passed. The recoil knocked the pistol from Tarsila's hand. Frustration tightened her eyebrows for just a moment. Then her head fell back against the seat as she relaxed in death.

Garin tapped the comm in his uninjured ear. "Get me an escape route." He turned from the car and ran back between the rows of cargo containers, where the police vehicles couldn't go.

Following the directions given to him by Portinari, Garin fled through the maze.

SEVERAL MINUTES LATER, a few streets in back of the harbor, Garin stepped off the corner in front of a clothing consignment shop catering to blue-collar workers and met the black Land Rover coming down the street. The driver halted long enough to allow Garin to enter, but Garin got in so quickly that the vehicle never completely came to a stop. He slid into the backseat across from Portinari, who checked his employer for signs of injury.

"Bruises and a nicked ear." Garin shifted slightly in the leather seat. Pain still laced his ribs and made breathing an irritating chore. "Nothing more."

Portinari nodded. "I am glad that you are well."

"Thank you."

"Will there be any blowback from the woman or the pharmaceuticals?"

"Some, perhaps, but nothing that can't be rectified with money. I'll make sure your working account has enough capital in it to smooth over anything that might be a problem."

The driver took an easy course in the direction of the small airport where Garin had a private jet waiting. He drove just under the speed limit.

Portinari produced a small attaché case and opened it in his lap, revealing a new pistol, a satellite phone and all of Garin's personal identification. Garin swapped out the things he had, knowing the pistol he'd used to ambush Volpi and Tarsila would end up in the bottom of the Pacific Ocean before the sun set.

There was only one missed message on the phone, so something had hit the network that couldn't be handled at his offices. He held the phone to his ear and played the message.

"Mr. Braden, I have received a phone call from a man named Sabre Race, who says the nature of the call is important."

Garin knew that the call would be important. He and Sabre had been close for a time, still were in some respects but were now separate. Sabre wouldn't call unless he had a problem.

"As you know," the message continued, "you flagged Mr. Race's name for your personal attention. He is calling in regards to Annja Creed, who is also flagged similarly." The woman went on to give Sabre's phone number.

The information startled Garin. Sabre and Annja didn't know each other. He placed a call to his information desk and it was answered on the first ring.

"Mr. Braden, how may I serve you?" Heike sounded upbeat and positive.

Garin hadn't met her. He didn't put much effort into his phone assistants, because he rotated them regularly. No one needed to know as much about his business as he did. Usually the people who served so close to his personal needs were placed within other companies he owned, where they could not confer with each other. Maintaining compartmentalization was challenging.

"Where's Annja Creed?" Garin moved gingerly in his seat, trying to find a position that wouldn't bother the bruised ribs.

"In and around Hollywood, sir. It's difficult to say. She's moving a lot, according to the news."

Hollywood potentially put her in Sabre's sandbox, but Garin didn't know how the two of them could have gotten involved.

"Send me all updates on her." Garin kept tabs on Annja when he could. She changed venues often, but he held it in his best interests to know where she—and that sword—were whenever he could. Since the sword had come back into the world, Garin felt more threatened and less secure.

After five-hundred-plus years, he recognized that change was inevitable, but he still guarded against it and controlled it as much as he could. Wealth afforded that privilege.

"Yes, sir. I'll email them to you."

"And connect me with Sabre Race." Garin settled back into his seat and knew he couldn't plan his next move until he knew what was going on. He had never thought Sabre's life would intersect with Annja Creed's, and he wasn't certain what he was going to do about that.

Or whose side he would take.

24

Just before the SUV barreled into the closed garage door, Annja raised an arm to protect her face in case the windshield shattered. The safety glass would fragment into cube-shaped pieces that would be mostly held by a substrate layer of plastic film.

Unless something came *through* the windshield.

And then the air-bag deployment became a problem.

The safety feature erupted the moment the SUV's front end tore through the garage door. Bursting out of the steering-wheel housing, the air bag slammed into Annja's upraised arm with bruising force. Despite the fact that she'd been prepared for the air bag, that she had leaned as far back in the seat as she could to escape the effects, the fabric ovoid drove her arm back against her chest and slammed into her face.

She struggled to peer through the webbed windshield over the airbag. She thought there were uniformed people scattered across the yard. Maybe only three or four, maybe as many as a dozen. Her senses reeled from the force of the blow and she knew she wasn't operating at her peak.

For a moment, she was afraid she'd hit one of the uniformed men, which she was loath to do because—by all accounts—Sabre Race and his people were legitimate security people. Before the SUV struck him, he rolled to the left in a loose tangle of limbs, but she saw him come up on his knees in the side mirror when she checked.

A handful of bullets peppered the SUV's rear window and back, but none of the rounds came through to the front seats. And the shooter stopped immediately. Whoever had fired had done so out of instinct, then must have gotten called down by the team's leader.

She reached into her pocket and pulled out a small lock-back knife, flipped out a blade with a thumbnail and stabbed the air bag, which deflated rapidly. She dropped the knife between the seats and placed both hands on the steering wheel as she tried to see through the windshield. Only a hole in the middle of her view provided her any true clarity.

Ahead, the wrought iron gates loomed formidably. Annja wanted to scream out in frustration because she'd forgotten about them. Then she glanced up and spotted a small black transmitter clipped to the sun visor. Only a few yards shy of the gate, she stabbed the red button and hoped it was for the gate, not the garage door, or that the device operated both of them.

The gates slid into motion. Knowing they would never open enough in time, Annja let off on the accelerator and tapped the brake. The tires screeched in protest, and the SUV struggled to stand on its nose for a moment before the antilocking feature kicked in. Annja corrected the vehicle's direction and managed to put the SUV between the gates, which had opened just wide enough to allow the vehicle to pass through. The passage cost both side mirrors, which detonated on collision with the gates, and long scratches ripped down the passenger side of the vehicle with shrill squeals. The various crunches and squalls of mistreated metal reverberated inside the SUV.

A car passing in front of the estate gates veered to the side as Annja hauled the steering wheel to the right. She barely evaded the other vehicle and swerved from side to side for a moment before getting the SUV under control.

Air blasted in through the small hole in the windshield. The webbing obscured her view. Reaching forward, she slammed her left palm against the windshield and forced it free of the molding, turning it into a flap of broken glass that folded and beat against the other side. She struck again and again, finally succeeding in knocking the glass loose enough that the wind caught it.

With the view in front of her unimpeded, she reached in back of the seat and took her sunglasses from her backpack. She pulled them on and felt instant relief from the sun and the wind. Glancing over her shoulder, acutely aware of how blind she was without the side and rearview mirrors, she spotted the two black SUVs closing the distance behind her.

Beside her, Racz struggled with the passenger-side air bag. The professor was trapped against his seat, unable to fight free. Shifting hands on the steering wheel, Annja picked up the knife between the seats and stabbed that air bag, as well. It deflated instantly, releasing Racz.

His nose bleeding and his lips split, his lower face turning bloody, the professor appeared dazed. He blinked against the wind and looked over at her. "Did we get away?"

"Not yet." Annja tapped the brake again and cut the wheels hard to the right. The seat belt tightened around her as the SUV skidded around the corner. She held the horn down, blaring a warning to everyone ahead of her.

Pedestrians caught out in the street scurried quickly to safety.

Annja tried to figure out where they were, but she didn't know the city. "Where's the airport?"

Racz held tightly to his seat with both hands and stared at the traffic at the intersection ahead of them.

Annja reached over to the man and punched his shoulder hard enough to hurt.

Drawing back, Racz looked at her as though she had gone mad. "Why did you hit me?"

"The airport. Where is it?"

Racz blinked in puzzlement for a moment, then nodded ahead of them. "Next intersection. Take a left. It's not far.

Stay away from Venice Boulevard. It'll be packed with traffic at this time of day."

The light at the next intersection gleamed red and the street was jammed with waiting cars.

Pulling to the left, Annja slid into the oncoming lane, which was thankfully empty, and raced toward the intersection, still leaning on the horn.

"You've got to stop." Racz braced his feet against the floor.

Annja glanced over her shoulder and saw the lead SUV was even closer. "Can't." She focused on the traffic ahead of her.

FIRED UP BY the chase, Ligier de Cerceau sat in the rear seat of the black Lincoln Town Car and watched the two SUVs in front of him jockeying for position as they trailed after the dark blue vehicle ahead of them. There was no mistaking the ravaged vehicle as it careened down the street. If the damage hadn't made it stand out, the erratic steering would have.

De Cerceau cursed the situation. If he'd only had a few more minutes, he would have been able to close in with his own team, men who were far better trained than his earlier troops. He would have killed Sabre Race and his people, and Annja Creed would have been his.

He fisted the pistol in his hand and listened to the radio communications between the other four cars in his operation. They were in pursuit, as well, trailing the action along side streets.

"Units two and three are ahead of the lead vehicle," Jamal Orayyed said rapidly, his anticipation showing.

"Show me." De Cerceau glanced at the tablet PC lying on the seat beside him.

The monitor showed the street they were on, as well as the surrounding streets. For the moment, Orayyed had all the players in view from a satellite feed he'd piggybacked.

The lead SUV was marked with a red dot and the two SUVs following it were designated by orange dots. De Cerceau's five vehicles were marked with blue dots.

"Have units two and three intercept the woman at the intersection." De Cerceau glanced at the street ahead, knowing it would all happen quickly.

"Yes, sir."

SABRE CURSED AS Meszoly raced through the streets. He still couldn't believe Annja Creed had escaped from the house, but he realized he was liking her more and more. If only she didn't have information he needed.

Meszoly tapped the brake, staying just scant feet off the bumper of the SUV ahead of them. He was relaxed, smiling even. "She's good."

"Yeah, but her being good doesn't help us now." Sabre flinched slightly as Meszoly shot by a parked car. If there had been another coat of paint on either vehicle, Sabre felt certain they wouldn't have made it.

"It does keep things interesting, though, doesn't it?"

Sabre stared ahead, thinking about trying to shoot out the woman's tires, but there were too many pedestrians on the streets.

And there was no guaranteeing that Annja Creed would be able to stop her vehicle without hurting someone.

Sabre sat up straighter and called over the comm to the driver in the vehicle ahead of them. "Glanz, get up next to her and force her off the street."

"Will do." The SUV ahead of them accelerated and darted into the oncoming lane, going out wide to pass the target vehicle.

Before Glanz could reach an optimum position, a black SUV shot out into the intersection and T-boned him, driving the vehicle sideways. The loud impact rattled around inside Sabre's vehicle and drew a curse from Meszoly.

Sabre fisted his seat belt restraint as Meszoly hit the brakes. "Was that one of ours?"

"Negative," Saadiya replied. "That one's unidentified. I'm accessing street cams now."

"Tell me that wasn't a bystander." All of Sabre's instincts told him the SUV belonged to someone who'd dealt themselves into the play, but his gut still rolled slightly at the thought that a bystander might have gotten hurt.

The two wrecked vehicles skidded sideways and blocked the street on the other side of the intersection. A second unidentified SUV roared through the street and narrowly missed the twisted hulks of the two vehicles. It slid slightly with the tightness of the turn, then regained acceleration in pursuit of Annja Creed's vehicle.

Two men popped open the rear doors of the SUV that had struck Glanz and his team. Both men carried assault rifles and closed in on the other vehicle.

"They're not bystanders," Meszoly said drily.

"Stop," Sabre ordered, but his colleague was already braking so they could offer assistance.

The two men turned to the approaching vehicle and brought up their rifles.

Sabre stared through the windshield and held his assault rifle at the ready. "Saadiya…" He didn't want to fire on someone who might turn out to be a law enforcement person, although he felt strongly these men weren't policemen.

"I have facial recognition on one of the men." Saadiya spoke rapidly. "Mathieu Callot. French mercenary. Known to affiliate with de Cerceau."

"Affirmative." Sabre ducked as high-velocity rounds spiderwebbed the bullet-resistant windshield. Opening the door, he slid out and used the door for cover, leaning around it to aim at the shooter. Thinking the man was probably wearing Kevlar under his jacket, Sabre fired two short bursts into the gunner's legs.

When his legs crumpled beneath him, the man went down. Before Sabre could move, two more vehicles roared around them in hot pursuit of Annja Creed. Neither of them were part of his security effort. For just a moment, Sabre glimpsed de Cerceau sitting in the back of a luxury sedan. The Frenchman grinned wolfishly. Sabre barely restrained himself from opening fire.

"I can't raise Glanz," Saadiya reported. "He's not responding."

Realizing they were under fire, the second man wheeled around to take aim. Meszoly fired once and put a bullet through the man's face. The corpse took one step backward, collided with the wrecked vehicle behind him and slid to the pavement.

Focusing on containing the battlefield, Sabre trotted forward and inspected both men in the two front seats. The driver stared with unseeing eyes, his chest crushed by impact with the steering wheel. The passenger was unconscious, covered in broken windshield glass.

"They're out of it," Sabre told Meszoly.

Meszoly held the wounded man down on his stomach with a knee in the middle of his back. He whipped out a plastic restraint to secure the groaning man's wrists behind his back. "De Cerceau just drove by us."

"I know. We can't do anything about that yet. Saadiya, are you still on Creed?"

"I am."

"Stay with her."

"Affirmative. I've called in emergency rescue services to your twenty."

"Thank you." Sabre reached the SUV and tried the door, but it was locked or jammed. It was dented enough that opening it was going to be a problem anyway. Cupping a hand, he tried to stare through the window, but the glass was broken and frosted with cracks. "Glanz!"

There was no answer.

Sabre stepped back, then rammed an elbow into the glass and broke through.

Glanz lay back in his seat, still strapped in and supported by the air bag. A pulse showed in the hollow of his throat. In the passenger seat, Chelsea Cantor was just stirring.

Another Black Legion SUV raced toward them. Meszoly waved it down and it came to a rocking stop only a few feet away.

"Stay with our people," Meszoly ordered. "The area's secure. Keep it that way until the authorities arrive."

Harkness, the young man behind the steering wheel, nodded and got out. Emergency flashers around the vehicle flared to life.

Sabre sprinted back to the SUV and Meszoly beat him by a hair. He barely had time to buckle in before Meszoly had the SUV speeding in pursuit of the other vehicles.

"Do we know where Creed is going?" Sabre asked over the comm.

"Looks like the Santa Monica Airport," Saadiya replied.

"Unless she has a plane waiting, she's not going far." Sabre settled into his seat and mentally prepared himself for the coming confrontation.

25

As she steered her commandeered vehicle, Annja glanced over her shoulder to see the black SUV bearing down on her. She didn't know who was in it, but she knew whoever it was boded ill for her. The near miss at the intersection had been unsettling. Her hands shook slightly, but she kept herself calm. A dark blue Mercedes weaved back and forth, jockeying for a position behind the lead chase car.

"Do you know who is in the Mercedes?" She shot Racz a look.

The professor twisted in his seat, smearing blood on the shoulder of his shirt, and shook his head. "No. Why would I? You brought this to me, remember?"

Annja had, and she felt bad about that. "Look, they're after me." She hit the horn and froze a car that had been about to pull out in front of her. "You don't have to be part of this. I can let you out."

"Let me out?" Racz shook his head and groaned in exasperation. "If you slow down, they'll have us, and I don't think they'll just want you at this point. No, I like my odds better with you. You're lucky, and I believe in luck. That collision back at the intersection could have been us."

Annja nodded grimly. The vehicle had been practically on top of them. "Okay. Keep watch on that SUV. Let me know if they try to come alongside."

"I will. Several other vehicles appear to be following, as well."

Annja risked a look over her shoulder and spotted the additional vehicles. She concentrated on the fact that the airport was only a short distance away, according to the signage.

Her phone rang and she fished it from her pocket. She put it on speaker and hoped it was good news. Talking to the police at this moment wasn't something she wanted to do.

"Annja?"

Recognizing Roux's voice, Annja almost sighed in relief. "Tell me you have good news."

"You have a jet waiting for you at the airport."

"Thank you, but you might want to let them know there could be a problem."

"I did. I know there's a problem. One of the local television stations is monitoring your chase through the city."

"What?" Annja looked out the side window and scoured the airspace, spotting the news helicopter sailing through the cerulean sky.

"Evidently, you've become quite the news item."

Racz pointed desperately at an intersection just ahead. "Here! Turn here!"

Annja pulled on the wheel and followed the signage toward the airport entrance.

"I've arranged for you to have permission to drive onto the tarmac to the waiting jet." Roux sounded totally calm. "You will be waved through the security checkpoints."

"If I even slow down for those checkpoints, we could get taken." Annja saw the final turn into the airport coming up quickly. To her right, planes filled the airport and a few of them flew overhead.

"That has been taken care of."

"How?"

Suddenly, a van pulled into motion only a short distance from the airport turnoff. For a moment, Annja thought it was one of the people who followed her, either de Cerceau or Sabre Race, and prepared to take evasive tactics.

But the van sped past her and turned suddenly to block

the street behind her. Armed men with weapons boiled out of the vehicle.

In a way, Annja wasn't surprised that Roux had prepared so well. The old man had been around a long, long time, and he never quite embraced halfway measures when a show of force had to be mustered. When push came to shove, the body count exploded.

The lead SUV tried to steer around the van, but one of Roux's band fired a rocket launcher at it. The warhead detonated against the front right wheel and flipped the vehicle over in a slow roll that left it upside down. The SUV spun on its top while flames licked out around the ruined wheel. Black smoke trailed up from the burning rubber.

The dark blue luxury sedan slid to a stop a couple car lengths back. Annja saw that as she made the turn into the airport security area.

"There." Roux sounded pleased with himself. "That should make things easier."

"Thanks, Roux." Annja rolled toward the checkpoint and ignored the looks of disapproval and disbelief directed at her.

"You're welcome," Roux said. "I have to admit, your present situation is…interesting. There have been several rumors of the Merovingian treasure, but I never believed in them. Garin always seemed interested, though. Have you heard from him?"

"No." Annja continued to slow and watched as the security guards spread out at the checkpoint. "I've got to go."

"Of course. Be safe. I will see you soon."

Ignoring the impulse to ask Roux what he meant, Annja hung up the phone and replaced it in her pocket.

"Who are those men?" Racz peered through the side window at the new arrivals.

"Friends of a friend." Annja got out her identification and asked for Racz's.

The professor took out his passport and handed it over.

He pulled a handkerchief from his pocket and pressed it to his nose and mouth. "I suppose it's good to have friends."

"Some days." There were times, though, when Roux and Garin had worked against Annja. She never knew for certain which way they would end up regarding different events. She stopped at the checkpoint and raised her hands, then smiled as disarmingly as she could.

"GET US OUT of here." De Cerceau glared at the battered SUV trundling across the airport tarmac. He'd hoped it would be held up by security for a time, but it hadn't been. Annja Creed had been almost within his grasp and had somehow managed to get away. It was galling.

Gerard turned the car quickly, pulling around the SUV that had followed them. "We may be in for some trouble, Colonel." He left one hand on the steering wheel and reached for his pistol with the other.

Down the street, two SUVs pulled into view and stopped. Although de Cerceau couldn't see inside the vehicles, he felt certain Sabre Race would be in one of them.

"Let's avoid them if we can." De Cerceau watched the cars. "Take a side street and see what they do. They're more interested in the woman than us. Have the SUV with us stay between us and them."

Gerard communicated the orders and tapped the accelerator to get them going again. He pulled into the nearest side street. Neither of the Black Legion vehicles tried to follow.

De Cerceau gazed back at the airport as police cars with flashing lights arrived on the scene. He opened up his comm to Orayyed. "The woman has made it to the airport. Evidently, she has a flight scheduled out of there. Can you find out her destination?"

"I am trying."

"Let me know the minute you do, and find out what Sabre Race is doing, as well. He may know more than we do at this point. Otherwise he would be focused on retrieving the crystal." Recognizing that made de Cerceau uneasy. The crystal possibly was no longer the main artifact in the search for the treasure. Whatever the key was now, it lay in Annja Creed's head. And Sabre Race already knew that.

"Of course." Orayyed hesitated. "You should also know that the Los Angeles Police Department has issued a warrant for your arrest."

That wasn't surprising, but it made staying in the United States problematic. De Cerceau chose to focus on Annja Creed. Wherever she was going, he felt certain she wouldn't be staying in America. All he had to do was follow her out of the country.

"THE ONLY THING I can confirm is that Annja Creed has a private jet waiting for her."

Frustrated, Sabre Race watched the satellite feed of Annja Creed getting out of the battered SUV and walking toward a sleek Gulfstream jet. "You don't know who owns the jet or where it's going?"

"Not yet, but give me time. Ownership is hidden behind several shell companies."

Sabre let out a breath and hung on to his self-control. After all these years, after all those stories, to know that the Merovingian treasure was out there and he didn't know where it was proved almost unbearable. The woman was hot on the trail of it, following leads he had no way of knowing.

And Istvan was there with Annja Creed.

His phone rang but he didn't recognize the number. However, the area code confirmed that the call was coming from a German registered number. Heart beating a little faster, and feeling a little more hopeful, Sabre answered.

"Hello?"

"Sabre," a deep voice said. "It's been a while."

Smiling, Sabre nodded as Meszoly drove them away from

the airport. Watching the jet take off would have only provided more frustration. "Mr. Braden. Thank you for calling me back. I would never have reached out if it wasn't something important."

"It's always good to hear from you."

Sabre felt that Garin Braden was telling the truth, but there had been some harsh words spoken during the time Sabre left DragonTech. Mr. Braden, and that was how Sabre thought of him, was a good employer who rewarded loyalty. Unfortunately, loyalty didn't allow for someone to leave to start his own business. Getting over that had taken a while.

"Tell me what's going on," Braden said.

"Have you ever heard of Annja Creed? A television personality with a cable show?"

"I have."

Sabre wasn't surprised. Braden kept abreast of many things, which was why he was so good in business. "She's on the trail of the Merovingian treasure. Do you remember me telling you about it?"

For a moment, only silence sounded at the other end of the connection and Sabre thought the signal had dropped.

"Mr. Braden?"

"I'm here. I do remember what you told me. Have you discovered that the treasure is real?"

"I didn't, but Annja Creed has. I believe she's on her way there now." Sabre clenched his fist. "I don't want to miss the opportunity to recover that treasure. You know what it means to me and my family."

"I do, and I'm going to help you. Just let me know what I can do."

Sabre glanced back at the airport and watched as a jet screamed into the sky. He didn't know if it was the one that carried Annja Creed as a passenger, but one of them would. Or had.

"I need to know where she's going," Sabre said.

"I can find that out." Braden sounded coolly confident, as though he knew something Sabre didn't. And that had been true more times than Sabre could count.

"WELCOME ABOARD, MS. CREED. I am Ian." An elegant young man in a fashionable pinstripe suit stood in the open doorway of the jet. His blond hair lifted gently in the breeze and his smile was brilliant. His accent was British.

"Thank you, Ian. It's a pleasure to meet you." Annja pulled herself up the rolling metal stairwell to the door, acutely aware that she was an open target for a sniper. "I wasn't expecting a jet this big."

"Mr. Roux wanted to ensure you would be traveling in comfort. The flight to Spain will take just over twelve hours. He thought you might not want to lay over anywhere."

"I don't." Annja felt guilty at being so demanding. The flight was expensive, and it wasn't her jet to begin with.

"Understood. We have extra fuel tanks to ensure that we can safely travel that distance." Ian nodded happily. "May I take your bag?"

Annja kept hold of the backpack. "No, thank you. I can manage."

Ian peered past her at the damaged SUV sitting on the tarmac. "I take it there is no other luggage?"

"We're traveling light today." Annja stepped past Ian and into the jet. She looked into the pilot cabin and saw two young women seated there talking to the tower. "You're not the pilot?"

Ian smiled again and shook his head. "You wouldn't want me to be the pilot. I'm simply here to make sure your flight is comfortable."

Racz stumbled after her, still holding his handkerchief to his face.

"And you are Dr. Racz?" Ian placed a hand on the man's arm to steady him.

"I am."

"Welcome aboard, sir. We have just a few minutes before we clear for takeoff. May I help you clean up and make you more comfortable? I'm also medically certified, if you should need any emergency attention."

Racz nodded and allowed himself to be led toward the back of the jet.

"Please sit anywhere, Ms. Creed." Ian waved at the wide, comfortable-looking seats that made Annja suddenly realize how tired she was. "There will only be the two of you. If you require a shower, there's one in the back. We've also made up two bedrooms. They're small but comfortable. If you want to sleep."

"Thank you."

"It's no problem." Ian reached into a pocket as he passed her with Racz in tow. He took out a satellite phone and handed it to her. "Mr. Roux asked me to make sure you called once you were safely aboard."

Annja put her backpack in one of the seats and took another for herself, grateful for the plush cushioning as she settled into it. She punched in Roux's number from memory.

"Annja?" Roux sounded slightly tense. "Are you all right?" He spoke in French and she responded in the same language.

"Thanks for the jet, Roux." She tried not to think about how odd it was to say that, but she couldn't help it.

"My pleasure. You are all right?"

"Yes. The men you sent are well trained."

"They're paid to be."

Annja leaned over to the window and stared out at the street scene. LAPD patrol cars blocked either end of the street and a standoff appeared to be going on. "They're also going to be in trouble with the police."

"Nonsense. Those men are security personnel going

about their business. It'll just take time to get it all sorted. I have lawyers for that. No need to concern yourself."

Annja leaned back in her seat. She didn't know what was more alien about Roux: his seeming immortality or his ability to throw money at problems without a care. Nothing seemed to faze him.

"The flight crew is exemplary, so they'll get you to your destination safely," Roux continued. "However, given the inconvenient lack of privacy in this modern world of yours, there is every chance that the men following you will be able to find you shortly after you arrive in San Sebastián."

"San Sebastián?" Annja hadn't even had time to consult a map. She took her tablet out of her backpack and powered it up. "I need to be in Ordizia."

"There are no airports in Ordizia. Thankfully, there are a couple dozen airports around that city, so the men following you won't be able to watch them all. Still, they may figure out where you're heading. Be careful."

"I don't have to do anything for the next twelve hours or so."

"Try to remember that and get some rest."

"I will." Annja broke the connection and focused on the tablet, looking for anything that might have turned up on her search sites.

A few minutes later, Ian reappeared with Racz in tow. The professor's wounds had been cleaned and he looked much better, though his nose and mouth were still swollen. He was also wearing a fresh shirt that replaced the blood-stained one he'd had on.

He sat down gingerly across from her, and Ian made sure the professor was belted in.

"Ian." A woman's voice broadcast in English from an overhead speaker.

"Yes?" Ian stood waiting.

"We're leaving now."

"Very good. Thank you." Ian turned to Annja and Racz. "Would you care for anything to drink? We have a fully stocked bar and an impressive selection of wines."

Annja asked for water and Ian nodded.

Racz asked for whiskey. Ian disappeared as the jet trundled down the runway to set up for takeoff. He returned only a moment later.

Settling in with the bottle of water, Annja stared out at the tarmac, where the police officers had men from all the vehicles lying facedown. Even if those people weren't arrested, she hoped they would be detained long enough to allow her and Racz to quietly disappear at the other end of the journey.

26

Not only had the jet come equipped with a shower and bedrooms, but there had also been a selection of clothing in Annja's size as well as Racz's. Ian had shown her the small closet when he'd turned down her bed. She supposed he had done the same for Racz and had also offered him a selection of clothing. That explained where the shirt had come from earlier. Roux was nothing if not thorough.

Despite her efforts to stay awake, Annja had finally given in to the need for sleep. She'd talked to Racz briefly, but he'd told her he didn't know anything more than he'd already told her. She had the definite impression that he was holding something back, but she didn't challenge him. She wasn't always forthcoming with her information, either. Part of the thrill of discovering lost history was being the one to do it.

She'd showered and slept and now felt almost human again in fresh clothing after a generous breakfast.

Annja stared out the window at the sparkling waters in the Bay of Biscay. San Sebastián occupied a stretch of the coast and lay only twelve miles west of France. Pleasure boats sped and sailed across the blue-and-green watery expanse. Even though they'd left Santa Monica just over twelve hours before, it was still afternoon when they arrived but was a full day later because of the time change.

Red tiled roofs covered the houses and buildings that ringed the bay. A tan stripe of beach separated the city from the water. Green vegetation clung to the low hills under a flat layer of fluffy white clouds that held the dark promise of impending rain.

"Beautiful city." Racz leaned over Annja and stared through the window, as well. Deep purple bruises ringed his eyes, and she knew that was going to be a problem because people would notice them wherever they went. "Have you been here before?"

Annja nodded. "A few times. I was always in a hurry, though. I've never spent much time here."

"You've missed a lot."

"You've been here?"

"Several times." Racz pulled back and returned to his seat across from her.

"Were you searching for the treasure those times?"

Racz smiled. "No. Despite the excitement you've seen in me since yesterday, I haven't lived my life looking for the treasure. My grandfather did that." He frowned. "In the end, that anticipation robbed him of much of his life. I know my grandmother would have been happier if he'd stayed home more." He paused and took a breath as he recollected. "I came out here because I was in love. Spain is a country I love to fall in love in. The Spanish women are exciting and different. And there is nothing comparable to a Basque woman."

Annja smiled. "I'll take your word for that."

"They have long ancestral ties to this area. They're believed to be indigenous people, here long before the French or the Spanish."

The pilot called back over the speakers that they were beginning their final descent.

After she buckled her seat belt, Annja felt the descent push her against the straps. She watched out the window as the jet swooped closer to the bay.

"I HOPE YOU enjoyed your flight with us." Ian stood to one side of the jet's doorway.

"I did."

Ian handed her a small valise. "Some more clothes and sundries for you, should you need them."

"Thank you." Annja took hold of the valise. She'd planned on getting extra clothing soon since she'd left her other clothes in Los Angeles, but this would work, and it would save her time and trouble later on. She settled her backpack across her shoulders and looked down at the hunter green Jaguar XF waiting only a few feet away. "Who's in the car?"

"Your driver."

"My driver?"

"Mr. Roux thought it would be best if you had a car while in the city and didn't have to depend on public transport. And renting a car would leave an electronic trail."

Annja wasn't sure about that. It was often easier to vanish while taking public transport than driving a rental.

"I can drive myself." It was one thing to be flown into the country, but Annja wanted some control over her movements.

"I'm sure you can, Ms. Creed. However, I don't think you know the local terrain well, correct?"

Reluctantly, Annja agreed.

"I assure you that you're in good hands with your driver."

Whoever was sitting behind the wheel impatiently blasted the horn a couple of times. Evidently, the good manners maintained aboard the jet were now going to be forgotten.

"I can take your bags for you if you'd like," Ian offered.

"No. You've done more than enough. Thank you." Bag in hand, Annja strode down the walkway.

Racz thanked Ian, as well, accepted another luggage care package and trailed after Annja.

On the tarmac, assaulted by the roar of jet engines and airport cargo handlers yelling orders to each other in a handful of languages, Annja headed for the Jaguar driver's door. She was *not* going to put up with a driver, no matter how much better that person was at driving through the neighborhood.

Before she reached the car, the driver's window rolled down and a weathered arm curled over the vehicle's roof and pointed imperiously to the other side. "Passenger seat," a familiar voice ordered.

Annja's worry disappeared for the most part, but her irritability rose drastically.

The trunk sprang open. Taking the cue, Annja deposited her new valise in the space but kept her backpack.

Racz paused at the rear of the Jaguar. "This driver could be anyone. We might be better off arranging our own transportation."

"*This* driver can't be anyone. Put your bag away."

Grudgingly, Racz did as he was told.

Annja walked to the passenger seat and the door popped just as she reached for it. She opened the door wider and slipped into the leather seat.

Roux sat behind the steering wheel, looking like a curmudgeonly grandfather on vacation. His mostly cranberry Hawaiian shirt featured 1950s rocket ships and ray guns and stood out against the white duck pants, but the leather sandals fit right in. His white hair and beard looked vaguely unkempt, but that might have been from being out in the wind. He wore wraparound sunglasses that covered his eyes.

"You look like someone who should be playing with ZZ Top." Annja strapped herself into the seat.

"I sat in on a few of their sessions when they were just starting out."

Roux's weathered face was blank and she didn't know if he was serious. "What did you play?"

"Badly." Roux waited until Racz was settled in the backseat, then accelerated from the private jet. Annja was certain there was a speed limit on the tarmac, but Roux ignored it.

"Has anyone followed us?" Annja asked.

"That's an interesting question." Roux shot ahead of a baggage cart and zipped toward the exit. "Did you call Garin?"

"Not after you told me you could get me out of California. Why?"

"It appears he's taken an interest in your latest treasure hunt."

"Why?"

Roux shrugged. "Your guess is as good as mine."

"Garin is following me?"

"He is."

"How do you know?"

"Because my people caught his people tracking you."

During the five hundred years they'd lived, Roux and Garin had had an on-again, off-again relationship. They'd journeyed together for a while after Joan had been burned at the stake, but they had gone their separate ways, as well. Roux sometimes referred to the separation as a natural outgrowth of a young man standing up to his father, and Annja saw that kind of challenge and resentment between them on occasion.

But after five hundred years, with no one else truly capable of sharing their history, the two men had been drawn again and again into each other's orbits during difficult or lonely times. After all, there was no one else they could tell their stories to.

Except that five hundred years was a long time, and Annja had already discovered Roux and Garin didn't share *all* their stories.

"Where is Garin now?" Annja asked.

"Close," Roux mused. "Getting closer." He pulled out onto the street and merged with traffic.

"Excuse me," Racz called from the backseat. "Who is Garin?"

"No one," Roux answered.

"A treasure hunter," Annja said, because that was the best explanation she could come up with that would explain the situation.

"And he's following us, too? In addition to everyone else?"

Racz sounded put out and Annja didn't blame the professor. The situation kept getting more complicated.

"He is." Annja took her tablet from its place on the floorboard between her feet.

"Is this man dangerous?"

"He can be," Annja said, and she wondered where Garin's interest in the search for the treasure came from and how much of a problem he would be.

27

"Istvan, it is so good to see you again!" A vibrant woman in her late thirties bustled up to Racz, took him in her arms and enthusiastically kissed him on both cheeks. A colorful dress sheathed her generous curves. Her black hair was cropped at the jawline and framed a sun-bronzed face that held dark blue eyes. She wore only a little makeup, letting her natural beauty show. A dimple in her left cheek twisted the corner of her lips slightly but added character. Finished with her bone-crushing hug, she stepped back and took Racz's hands, examining him from head to toe. "The years have been good to you."

Racz grinned broadly. "Evita, you are more beautiful than ever."

Evita shrugged. "Always with the compliments. You are as incorrigible as ever. I assume you are still turning the heads of young women?"

"When I can." Racz stepped back and waved to Annja and Roux. "May I present Dr. Evita de Elcano, professor of European history with specialization in circumnavigators. Evita, these are new friends of mine. Annja Creed and Mr. Roux."

Annja took the woman's proffered hand and matched her smile. "Dr. Elcano? Any relation to Juan Sebastián d'Elcano, the Basque captain who sailed with Magellan?"

"If there is a relationship, I'm afraid those ties were muddied centuries ago. I like to think, however tenuous, that such a connection exists." Evita beamed. "I have to admit, I'm impressed. Many people don't remember Juan Sebastián d'Elcano." She turned her attention to Roux. "Mr. Roux, a pleasure to meet you."

"The pleasure is mine, dear lady." Roux's sudden change to courtliness clashed with his outfit, and that chameleon-like ability still caught Annja off guard. Roux could switch from an old-world dandy to an alley hoodlum in a heart-beat, though crotchety seemed to be his most natural mode.

Evita blushed a little, and Annja noted that Racz frowned in response. Annja had no doubt that Evita had been one of the women Racz claimed to have fallen in love with while in Spain, and she immediately wondered who had ended the relationship. She dismissed that idle speculation and con-centrated on what had brought them there.

ANNJA AND THE OTHERS stood in one of the great rooms of the library in Ordizia's downtown. The building had once housed apartments, but it had been renovated decades ear-lier. The outside appearance hadn't changed, and the inte-rior sported an art-deco look.

Large Mercator projections from various historical pe-riods hung on the walls. One of them showed Magellan's voyage as well as Viking raider routes. Tiffany lamps hung from the high ceilings and gave off a soft light. There were no windows because sunlight would have faded the doc-uments. Shelving filled the walls, and workstations with computers created islands over hardwood floors. More bur-geoning stacks stood at attention in neat rows throughout.

That old familiar thrill of being in a place soaked with history filled Annja as she looked around. Library, souk or catacomb—all offered chances to explore what had been.

Stepping back, Evita gestured to the massive library room around them. "I know that Istvan has told you of Andrés de Urdaneta's collection of ships' logs, but he hasn't told me exactly what it is you're looking for." She shot him a mock frown. "He likes to keep his little mysteries to himself."

"I'm not the only one guilty of that," Racz replied.

"True, but if I may be of any help, please allow me. I have taken the liberty of requisitioning the library for your use this afternoon so you can work without being bothered. Since you're also newly arrived, I arranged for a light lunch to be served." Evita waved to a table in the corner where a small buffet had been laid out.

Roux stepped forward and glanced at Evita. "I haven't eaten in hours. Perhaps you'd care to join me at the buffet."

"You're not here to look at maps?" Evita looked surprised.

"No. I came here to look after Annja."

Annja frowned at that. She didn't need looking after. Roux was just using her to better sell himself. It was irritating but not worth the hassle of challenging.

"She is family?" Evita asked.

"Yes," Roux answered.

Probably the old man said that because it was the easiest answer to give, and maybe it was a little more ingratiating to their hostess, but Annja couldn't help feeling a little pleased at the announcement. She didn't let Roux see that, though.

"Family is important," Evita said, "and tending to familial needs is admirable."

Roux managed to look modest in a way that made Annja want to roll her eyes.

Evita looked at Racz. "You know your way around." She linked her arm through Roux's and they walked toward the buffet table together, already lost in conversation. Roux had her laughing before they reached the food.

Racz furrowed his brow at the two of them. Then he made a concerted effort to get focused. "Juan Cabrillo's logs are this way." He started across the room and Annja followed.

"Not all of these logs are originals." Annja stared at the shelves filled with bound ships' logs and felt frustrated. "They're copies." Even Urdaneta had been forced to replicate some of the maps and journals that he'd lost to the Portuguese after being captured in the Spice Islands.

"But they're *good* copies." Racz stood beside her and glanced through one of the tomes. The book was roughly eighteen inches tall, fourteen inches wide and three inches thick. The pages were good vellum and pristine for the most part. "Whatever information was in the original ships' logs will be in these."

"Not if it was hidden."

"What? Do you mean like written in invisible ink?"

"Sounds cartoony when you say it out loud like that, but yes. I've found documents that were layered beneath other documents. And written in invisible ink. Julius Caesar invented the first code that was used in military operations. Hiding information has a long history."

Racz pursed his lips and nodded. "Caesar reputedly invented the transposition code. Substituting one letter for another. I know that."

"If the Merovingian treasure exists, especially if it hasn't been found, you can bet it's not going to be in plain sight."

"There's every possibility that it doesn't exist. My grandfather never found it."

Racz's constant wavering between believing and not believing was irritating Annja. She understood the man not wanting to get his hopes up after all these years, but no matter how things turned out, the leads had to be tracked down.

Annja took down another thick book and opened it. "It would have helped if Julio Gris's journals had been kept separate from Cabrillo's." They'd already checked and discovered that, although Gris was referenced occasionally, there was no book dedicated to him.

From time to time, Racz stepped around the end of the stack for a moment. Annja knew the man was checking on Roux and Evita. Racz's jealousy would have been at least slightly humorous if she hadn't been preoccupied with finding the information she needed. She picked up the sandwich Roux had prepared for her and took another bite.

A short time later, Roux appeared with Evita on his arm. "Since you don't need our help, Evita has graciously offered to show me some of the highlights of Ordizia."

Annja looked at him and lifted an eyebrow. "You've never been to Ordizia before?"

"Of course I have, but I haven't seen everything here. Evita herself is proof of that."

Evita smiled in response to the compliment. Evidently, she didn't mind Roux's company at all.

"What if we need something?" A trace of irritation echoed in Racz's voice.

Evita smiled at him. "Simply call me. You have the number."

Roux led her away.

Racz grumped away to another library shelf.

Grinning to herself at the professor's apparent displeasure, Annja continued her search.

ALMOST THREE HOURS LATER, Annja discovered one of the ships' logs that held a sizable section written by Julio Gris. The entries had been written while at sea after Cabrillo's unfortunate death.

I have constructed my device and left it in the New World not far from where we buried poor Captain Cabrillo. It exists solely so that the trail to the Salian Frankish treasure, if not clearly marked, is at least still there, a signpost to someone clever enough to find it.

"He's talking about the Merovingian treasure." Racz read the manuscript over Annja's shoulder. "They were the Salian Franks."

Annja knew that but didn't bother to point that out. She continued reading.

I wonder if I will live to see my home again. Things have gone so badly on this voyage. Captain Cabrillo was a friend and a confidant. Had he not died, I am certain he would have gone with me to seek the fortunes that persistent myths say are there. Now there is no one I truly trust to watch over me while I undertake this task. Treasure hunting must ever be a solitary pursuit. Greed turns even the best of friends into mortal enemies when a fortune hangs in the balance.

I will take up the trail upon my return, and I will hope that my knowledge and bravery are rewarded. If they are not, and I am somehow unable to finish my chosen quest, there still exists a map created by György Dózsa's pain. It can be found in the third casting of the Virgin Mary that was created by Father Janos Brankovic.

After that, Gris wandered for a bit in his narrative, writing down memories and thoughts about family members and about the inevitability of the cruel sea. Annja thought the man sounded lonely. Having a close look at mortality during Cabrillo's lingering death would cause a person to take stock. Annja had seen similar things happen on digs after someone died or was killed.

Those brushes with death often put weaker archaeologists and relic hunters off their game.

"What casting of the Virgin Mary is Gris referring to?" Racz asked. "Dózsa was a warrior, a soldier of fortune who served whoever paid him more."

"György Dózsa was also a crusader." Annja walked to the table of food and helped herself to another glass of water. Her brain clicked and spun like a machine as facts threaded together in her thoughts. "In the early 1500s, Tamás Bakócz, the Hungarian chancellor working as an agent of Pope Leo X, raised an army against the Ottoman Empire. The paper he brought from the Holy See allowed him to raise an army and appoint a commander to lead it."

"I know all of that," Racz declared impatiently. "The army Dózsa raised wasn't supplied, and the soldiers eventually went rogue after the landlords the *kuruc* had previously worked for began brutalizing their wives and children because they wouldn't return to the fields. The war effort became a mission of vengeance."

"Yes." *Kuruc* was supposed to have been created from the Latin word *cruciatus*, which meant crusader or cross. There were some who believed the word merely meant rebel. "Do you know what happened to Dózsa when the Crusade failed?" She sipped the chilled water.

"He was killed." Racz shrugged, obviously through talking about Dózsa. "He went from potential hero to revolutionary leader."

Annja didn't see Dózsa's plight so simply. The military leader had landed in a hard spot, trapped with an army and possessing no means of taking care of his warriors or using those forces as they'd been intended.

"Dózsa did the best that he could. In fact, he worked hard to make certain that many of those noblemen and landlords were *not* killed. He helped some of them escape. Unfortunately, many of his warriors tracked those people down and put them to death."

"What does this have to do with the Virgin Mary casting?"

"I'm getting to it. Dózsa was eventually defeated by a heavy cavalry of noblemen. His amateur warriors couldn't stand up to them. After the battle at Temesvár, the noblemen captured Dózsa and took him prisoner. Later Dózsa was tied to an iron throne that had been heated hot enough to burn. He was also forced to wear a heated crown and given a scalding scepter to hold."

Racz frowned and shifted impatiently.

"Nine of Dózsa's men were brought before him while he was held captive and dying in the seat," Annja went on. "Dózsa's brother was in the lead, and he was immediately killed and cut to pieces. Afterward, the torturers pulled bits of Dózsa's flesh from his body with red-hot pliers."

"I haven't heard anything about the Virgin Mary."

"During Dózsa's torture, monks who were there to observe that justice was being done said they saw the image of the Virgin Mary in Dózsa's ear."

"That's just so much balderdash." Racz scowled skeptically, but there was a gleam in his eye that told Annja he wanted to believe the story. "They couldn't have seen the Virgin Mary in Dózsa's ear. What would be the point of that?"

"I don't know, but Vilmos Szekely and György Kiss designed and built the statue of the Virgin Mary based on that sighting. It was erected in 1865 on the site where Dózsa died on that iron throne. It's a symbol of the unrest between the serfs and the landed gentry that was taking place at the time."

"If the statue was built in 1865, it can have no bearing on our search." Bitter venom echoed in Racz's words. "It's much too late. There can't be any clues related to it that tie back to the Merovingian treasure."

"Agreed, but Gris said that the map was on the third casting created by Janos Brankovic. That came before the statue."

Racz shook his head. "The name means nothing to me outside its mention in Gris's log."

"You know who Pal Kinizsi was."

"Of course. He was the Hungarian general who defeated

the Black Army when it went rogue after Matthias Corvinus died."

"Right, and he was also cousin to Janos Brankovic."

"How do you know that?"

"I ran across Brankovic's name while I was doing research on the Black Army." Annja remembered a lot of history, but the most important thing about research was remembering where it was found. "I think we need to find Father Janos Brankovic's third casting of the Virgin Mary."

A forlorn look darkened Racz's eyes. "How?"

Annja reached into her backpack and took out her tablet PC. "The old-fashioned way." She paused. "Not exactly the old-fashioned way. The old-fashioned way never included the internet."

She sat down and made herself comfortable. The answers were out there. That was what made the hunt for them so compelling. Finding things out was just a matter of asking the right questions.

Even if finding out about Janos Brankovic wasn't the exact right answer she needed, finding out what she could about the artist put her one step closer to the right question.

28

SEEKER4318 stood in the dark room and tried to remain calm. Too many things were happening all at once, and he felt what little control he had left to him slipping away. This was his search. Whatever the Merovingian treasure was, it belonged to him.

He forced himself to take a deep calming breath.

In the streets, he spotted some of the men from the Hollywood security team. Somehow those men had managed to trail after Annja Creed in spite of her friend's private jet.

Or maybe the old man was part of the plot to snatch away the treasure. That thought left him alarmed. His bloodlust rose in him. If there had been time, he would have sought out a young woman and found the answers to these problems within her flesh. That need burned within him so hot that he was barely able to suppress it. He banked it for the moment, telling himself there would soon be time and that he would find the answers.

The Merovingian treasure was right there, almost within his grasp. He just couldn't reach out and close it in his hand. Not yet. But soon. He peered out at the city on the other side of the window. He was alone now, but he wouldn't stay that way. Events were pushing everything in on top of him.

He closed his eyes and remembered the woman crying before him in the hotel room, begging for her life. He had killed her because he'd needed the answers that she had held locked up inside her.

Gradually, he'd peeled her open and discovered the promise of the good fortune that would soon be his.

What he sought would soon be his and his alone. Despite all the odds against him, he knew that there could be no other outcome regarding the Merovingian treasure. He just had to choose his allies carefully.

He smiled, knowing that flesh and blood never lied.

He took out his cell phone and called, then listened to the connection ring. In the back of his mind, though, he heard the cries of all the women he had left scattered in pieces around this city on earlier searches. All of them had been false oracles. They had put him on the trail of different pursuits, but they hadn't located the Merovingian treasure for him.

Ligier de Cerceau answered at the other end of the phone connection. "Hello."

"You need to hurry. The Creed woman has discovered the location of an artifact that may reveal the treasure's whereabouts."

When the mercenary leader responded, he sounded sour and short-tempered. "Getting here took time. We're behind the Hollywood people. If we'd had more information sooner, that would have helped us. Don't complain when you're unable to keep us on task."

Impatience grated at SEEKER4318 like a saw-toothed blade. "Get ahead of them. I'm not paying you to come in second best." He ended the call and glared out into the street as the black-clad security team closed in.

DE CERCEAU TOOK a deep breath and put the sat phone back in a thigh pouch in his pants. He cursed his unknown employer.

"Is there a problem, Colonel?" Gerard looked at de Cerceau through the rearview mirror of the SUV he drove.

"Not for much longer. Once we get our hands on the Creed woman, we can wash our hands of the idiot we're doing business with." De Cerceau looked forward to that moment. In the beginning, he'd been happy taking the man's money—until the operation began running so rocky. After the exposure at the university, he would have backed out of the arrangement and not risked further legal attention.

But now there was the possibility of treasure in the offing. Too many people were involved for something not to come of it.

"Stop there." De Cerceau pointed at the alley only a short distance away from the map museum.

Gerard eased the SUV to a stop in the narrow alley and remained behind the wheel as de Cerceau and three armed gunmen got out.

"Audio check," Jamal Orayyed called over the headset.

The team quickly responded, confirming that all of them were linked in to the frequency.

"Control, can you pick up the other team's communications frequency?" De Cerceau jogged along the alley, turning left at the end and moving along the street. Like the rest of his team, he wore a long lightweight coat that covered his body armor and weapons. He kept a fist on the H&K MP5 slung at his right hip.

"Negative. I've attempted to breach their firewall but I haven't gotten through."

Three blocks down, two red, yellow and blue police vehicles blocked the street. Traffic had come to a standstill in front of the police cars. Some of the drivers honked their horns in frustration, but others found ways to double back the way they had come.

"Why are the police here?" De Cerceau kept to the shop fronts, drawing attention as he went, but no one tried to interfere. Soon, though, someone would call out to the local law enforcement because he was moving toward the hot spot, not staying back from it.

"A private security outfit called DragonTech set up the operation. I just cracked through the local police department's firewall and found that out."

The name seemed familiar to de Cerceau. "We know these people."

"We've dealt with them tangentially before. They usually handle big corporate jobs. Both times we've encountered them, they were providing security for people other than our targets. They're very good at what they do."

"Today we're going to be better. Get sniper teams up on the roofs." De Cerceau's heart rate elevated. He remembered DragonTech now. It was a big-money, high-powered mercenary corporation that catered to wealthy clients.

"On their way," Orayyed replied.

"Do we know why DragonTech is here?" De Cerceau took a left into an alley, mentally charting his course to the museum and knowing he could never reach the building on foot without being seen. But there was another way.

"Negative, but I have learned that Sabre Race used to work for DragonTech."

De Cerceau stopped at a manhole cover in the middle of the alley. He gestured to two of the men behind him, pointing to the manhole. "How did you miss that?"

"Sabre Race wasn't the name he used while working for DragonTech. Or while he was in the American military. He changed his name to Sabre Race just before his arrival in Los Angeles." Orayyed paused. "I wasn't looking into his background. Sabre Race wasn't our target."

"Well, he's one of them now. Find out what you can."

"Of course."

The two men lifted the manhole cover and shifted it aside. The heavy iron wheel clanked slightly when they placed it on the ground.

De Cerceau unclipped a flashlight from his bulletproof vest, flicked it on and shone it into the utility hole. A sour stench reached his nostrils from below. He stopped breathing through his nose and opened his mouth.

The beam trailed across iron handrails set into the stone

at the side. The utility-hole floor lay nine or ten feet below. The area looked at least six feet wide, leaving plenty of room, but he didn't like the idea of being trapped in a tunnel.

However, approaching the museum along the street would have been costly.

"I'm looking at an access tunnel at my twenty." Orayyed would know where de Cerceau was. "Will it take me to the museum?" He was certain it would. All of the utilities would be tied in together in this area, but he didn't want to go stumbling around clueless in the dark.

"A moment, please."

De Cerceau waited impatiently, keeping his gaze moving to either end of the alley.

"Affirmative. The access point in the museum is in the basement. There are a couple of cross tunnels, but I can get you there if these city schematics are accurate."

"Let's hope they are." De Cerceau waved one of the men accompanying him down into the hole, then followed, climbing down the handrails quickly.

On the ground inside the access tunnel, de Cerceau drew his machine pistol and tapped the shoulder of the man ahead of him. The man took off, trailing his flashlight cone into the darkness.

ANNJA'S PHONE RANG, pulling her attention away from the tablet PC and the information she'd been tracking concerning Janos Brankovic. She glanced at the caller ID, then realized this wasn't her usual phone and wondered how anyone would know the number.

Then she saw Roux's name in the viewscreen. She answered the call. "If you've called to tell me you and your new lady friend have discovered a quaint little bed-and-breakfast—"

"Garin is outside the museum. I think you need to be

more concerned about that than any romantic congress I might be having." Roux sounded irritated.

Standing, shouldering the phone, Annja shoved her tablet into her backpack and hurried to the nearest window that overlooked the street facing the museum. Moving slowly so she wouldn't be as likely to attract attention, she peered around the window frame.

Black SUVs flanked by brightly colored police cars sat in the street. Armed men and policemen held a cordon around the area.

"Garin called the police?" Annja couldn't believe it.

"He or Sabre Race did. I've also identified that man in the crowd, as well."

"What is Sabre doing here?"

"I assume he is with Garin. That's really not the point now. The point is how we're going to get you out of there."

"Garin's got the *police* out there. That means he has to play by the laws. He can't just take me."

"He's filed a report that you're in possession of stolen intellectual properties. The Ordizia police will take you into custody readily enough until things get sorted."

"They can't hold me."

"Holding you isn't the goal. They want your research. That's why Garin filed for intellectual property."

Annja thought of all the notes she'd uploaded to the cloud. It would take Garin time, but he could figure out as much as she had. And by the time she extricated herself from the legal situation she was currently facing, Garin and Sabre Race would be light-years ahead of them in finding the treasure.

If Garin could make heads or tails of that research. But she didn't want to risk that. Garin had been a tomb raider and opportunist for centuries. He was good at ferreting out secrets. Not only that, but he had an international firm of investigators at his beck and call.

"Annja?" Roux called.

"I'm here. Thinking."

"Maybe you should turn yourself in. Even if you get out of the museum, being hunted through the streets of this city isn't—"

"When I get out of this building—and I will—we can leave Ordizia."

"You found what you were looking for." Interest flickered in Roux's words, reminding Annja that the old man was something of a treasure seeker himself.

"Not exactly." Annja watched the activity out on the street. A clump of men in riot armor advanced toward the museum behind bulletproof shields. "What are they doing? They're acting like I'm some kind of terrorist threat."

"Garin likes his drama." Roux paused. "You don't have a lot of time, and Evita has concerns about the museum in case the situation turns ballistic."

"Okay." Annja took a deep breath and settled herself. "Ask Evita where I can hide Dr. Racz."

"Where you can hide Dr. Racz?"

"Yes. Surely in a place this big, there's somewhere he can hide for a time." Annja glanced around the museum. She could almost feel the seconds ticking off the time she had left.

"What are you going to do?"

"I'm going to give Garin and Sabre Race, *and* the local police, a reason not to look for the professor in here."

"Annja, I have lawyers. This matter can be—"

"Dealing with lawyers and court means lost time, Roux. We're close to this thing. I can feel it." Annja left the window and sprinted through the stacks, looking for Istvan Racz. "I'm not going to let him get that time. When the coast clears at the museum, get the professor and get back to the jet."

"The jet? We're leaving?"

"Yes." Annja caught a corner of a stack and wheeled around it.

"Where are we going?"

"I'll tell you when we reach the jet. Now tell me where I can hide the professor."

The muffled voices of Roux and Evita conferred for a moment. Then Roux returned to the phone. "Evita says there is a janitor's closet on the second floor. It's out of the way and most people don't find it unless they know where it is."

"That'll do. Garin's not going to waste time looking around the museum when I'm not here anymore."

"Where are you going to be?"

"Give me the directions to the janitor's closet."

Roux did, then started to repeat them.

Certain she knew where she needed to go and that she didn't have much time to make her escape, Annja broke the connection and pocketed the sat phone. She lifted her voice and yelled for Racz.

"Annja?" Racz sounded puzzled from off to her left.

Tracking the man's voice, Annja rounded a final corner and almost ran into him. The professor stepped back and nearly fell. He carried water bottles in both hands. He smiled, but that faded when she grabbed him by the elbow.

"What's wrong?" Racz asked.

"We've been followed." Annja pulled him toward the room's wide entrance. The stairway to the second floor lay just beyond.

"Followed?" The professor dragged along behind Annja. "By whom?"

"Garin and Sabre Race."

"They're here?"

"Definitely here. Outside in the street and headed this way."

Racz stopped dawdling and broke into a run.

29

Less than two minutes later, with Istvan Racz safely ensconced in a narrow janitor's closet that reeked of mildew and high-powered cleansing agents, Annja stood on the museum's roof and peered down into the street.

Garin and his men had reached the building's front doors and stood ready in an organized assault formation with guns bristling. Even when he was dressed in Kevlar, Annja easily recognized Garin. His powerful build and his handsome, devilish features made him stand out. Sabre Race was a good-looking man, as well, but where Garin was primordial, Sabre was sleek and metrosexual.

Too bad Garin could be a jerk and Sabre was a competitor.

Annja was considering calling down to get their attention, only holding back because she knew that a direct action might tip her hand, when one of the uniformed men below spotted her and pointed. She hesitated only long enough to look down at Garin and see the grimace that told her he'd seen her.

His displeasure made her want to grin in spite of the seriousness of the situation. The attraction between them was mutual, but it was something Annja never intended to follow through on, because Garin just couldn't be trusted.

She took in that look for just a moment. Then a glint of sunlight on glass on a nearby rooftop caught her attention. A warning flared inside her head as she recalled the other times she'd been on the wrong end of a sniper scope. Shoving herself backward, she felt the tug of a bullet pass through her blouse. Then the sharp crack of the rifle followed almost immediately, letting her know how close the unseen marksman was.

Turning, Annja sprinted for the other end of the building. She took advantage of cover provided by air-conditioning units dotting the rooftop. Two other shots rang out in quick succession. They dogged her tracks, slapping into the roof ahead of her and ripping through one of the big air-conditioning units behind her. The *spang* of the bullet careering away from the metal echoed around her.

Immediately, a storm of gunfire erupted from the street in front of the museum. Glancing briefly over her shoulder, Annja watched a body slide down a sloped rooftop and tumble over the edge. The corpse disappeared from view. Then metal crunched and glass shattered below and a strident car alarm blared to life.

Turning her attention to the rooftop again, Annja steadied her stride and focused on the adjacent rooftop. When she reached the edge of the building, she pushed off with her right foot and hurled herself across the empty space, knowing instantly she had misjudged the distance and wasn't going to reach the other roof. She stretched out her hands and tried not to think of the long way down.

GARIN KEPT BOTH EYES open as he followed the gunman's trajectory down the rooftop through the scope of the M4A1 assault rifle. The instant Garin had found the man in his sights, he'd opened fire.

When the corpse reached the roof's edge of the building across the street, it seemed to hang over the four-story drop for a moment. Then it plummeted onto a car parked at the side of the street. The vehicle's roof crumpled under the impact, and glass blew out of the windows.

After making sure the man wasn't getting back up, Garin lowered his weapon.

At his side, Sabre Race stared up at him. "You killed him!"

"Maybe it was the bullets or it could have been the fall," Garin agreed. "He wasn't one of yours, was he?"

"No. And what if it was?"

Garin shrugged. "He'd be just as dead. I gave orders that no one was to shoot until I gave approval."

"He wasn't shooting at us."

"He was shooting." At Annja. Garin forced himself not to think about Annja lying dead on the museum's roof. She was better than that. Still, the sniper hadn't been expected. He'd been caught off guard. She could have been taken just as easily.

"Shooting doesn't mean you kill him."

"It does today. When I give orders, I intend for them to be obeyed." Garin turned his steely gaze on Sabre. "You called me in on this thing, and I'm helping because I choose to. I got you here because I know Annja Creed and the old man she runs with. If that doesn't work for you, let me know."

"And you'll just back away?"

"No. I'm in this thing now. If you want to stay in with me, use the knowledge I have of these people, you do things my way." Garin paused. "Decide now."

Frowning, Sabre nodded. "Your way."

The quick acquiescence was surprising. One of the reasons Garin had separated company from Sabre those years ago had been the younger man's lack of cold-blooded efficiency.

"Good. Have one of your people find out who the dead man is. If that man doesn't have any ID, get photographs to my tech support." Garin took up shelter inside the arched doorway leading to the museum. There was less reason to go inside now. Annja was on the rooftop, either alive and running or dead. He tapped his comm.

"Inge, I need eyes in the air."

"What I see, you're going to see." Inge Hundertwasser spoke in a soft contralto with an Austrian accent. She was tech support for the present operation.

Inge was a black hat hacker. Garin had found the young woman outside Vienna in the Republic of Austria. She'd rifled some research-and-development files from one of his pharmacy holdings. In the beginning, he'd intended to kill her, but he'd been impressed by her skill and by her courage. Even when she'd realized Garin was there to kill her, she hadn't shown any signs of weakness. Instead of leaving her corpse in her hidden lair, Garin had hired her to run sensitive operations for him. The relationship had been mutually beneficial.

"Eyes are away," Inge announced.

One of the black SUVs parked in front of the museum opened a sunroof. Three spidery-looking aircraft with six propellers and four "feet" each took flight through the opening. All of them were less than eighteen inches across, and all of them had wireless video cameras and auditory pickups inside the Plexiglas bodies. For a moment, the drones hovered over the SUV, getting their bearings. Then they sped through the air with a quiet hiss.

Garin nodded to one of the men standing at the museum door. It was possible that Annja had returned to the building. And even if she was gone—or dead—it was possible she might have left a trail behind.

The man opened the door and a small group darted inside, taking up positions quickly with their weapons at their shoulders.

"I have eyes on her," Inge reported over the comm. "I'm boosting the signal to your phone."

Garin reached into his chest pouch and took out his smartphone. He tapped the drone app and opened the window, picking up the feeds Inge's toys were pushing. Some of his apprehension uncoiled when he saw that Annja was still alive.

He tapped the small window that gave him the best view of Annja, expanding the panel to full size. On the small screen, Annja sailed through the space between the museum and the next building, and Garin knew from the way she started falling she wasn't going to make the distance.

Desperately, Annja arched her body, not giving in, and managed to catch hold of the building's roof. She slammed into the wall and her right hand slid free, leaving her dangling by her left hand.

Cursing, Garin ran toward the back of the building, hoping that Annja could hold on long enough for him to get there.

THE UTILITY TUNNEL opened up into the museum's basement. Only weak security lights illuminated the cavernous room. The shifting of the men's boots already in the room echoed around de Cerceau as he hauled himself up from the opening.

A moment later, he stood there with a dozen men. More had joined his first group as he'd traversed the underground route. He nodded to the leader. "All right, Orayyed. We're inside the building."

"The stairs are along the east wall. They'll bring you up to the door near the main entrance."

"Understood." De Cerceau followed his team with the H&K MP5 cradled in his arms.

"The DragonTech people are breaching the entrance. One of our snipers is dead." Orayyed spoke calmly, but then, he could afford to. He wasn't on-site. No one was shooting at him.

"What happened to the sniper?" De Cerceau trotted up the steps. He'd cleared the sniper to take the shot when he'd realized Annja Creed was on the rooftop.

"DragonTech killed the sniper."

"Do they know Creed is on the roof?"

"Affirmative. They've deployed drones to track her."

"Give orders to take the drones down." De Cerceau cursed the other mercenary team's unexpected technological advantage, then saved his breath for the climb up the stairs. His men deployed across the exit, but hardly had they gotten into position when the DragonTech security people invaded the building.

De Cerceau couldn't tell who had opened fire first, but in a moment, the ensuing gunfight turned the museum's entranceway into a battlefield as the bullets flew.

CLINGING BY THE FINGERTIPS of her left hand, with the alley three floors below, Annja tried to suck in a slow breath. The impact with the wall had driven the breath from her lungs in a painful rush. Her head ached, as well, from slamming into the brick. She'd turned her head so she wouldn't smash into the barrier face-first, but the collision had nearly knocked her senseless.

Spots danced in her vision, and for a moment, she thought she was going to pass out. Instinctively, she reached up with her right hand and grabbed the edge. She hung there briefly, making sure her hold was secure. Then she took a breath that cleared some of the cobwebs from her head and she focused on pulling herself up and over onto the roof.

The climb wasn't pretty or elegant in any way. It was more like a frenzied crawl. When her hips drew even with the roof, she rolled over and lay on the backpack for a moment.

Another bullet dug into the roof's edge and sprayed her with brick chips. She rolled to her right, got her hands under her and levered herself to her feet. Sprinting for all she was worth, she ran in a zigzag across the rooftop until she spotted the edge ahead of her.

Her stomach tightened when she realized this jump was at least as far as the last, but the next building was a story lower. Bullets dogged her heels and whistled through the air around her. At the edge, she launched herself into the air with everything she had, windmilling her arms to keep her balance.

When she landed on the next roof, scarcely a foot from the edge, she threw herself forward and rolled. Movement at the corner of her eye caught her attention. Fifteen feet away, an insectoid thing floated in the air and emitted a steady, high-pitched whine.

It took her a moment to recognize the hovering drone for what it was and to realize that someone was watching her. She suspected it was Garin. The man did like his toys. Two other drones flanked the first.

She gathered herself and sprinted across the roof. With the one-story difference from the other building, the snipers weren't able to target her. Sporadic gunfire echoed behind her, sometimes buried by police sirens and bullhorn announcements.

At the far edge of the building, with her flying Peeping Toms in tow, Annja peered down and spotted a car parked in the alley between the building she was on and the next. She gripped the roof's edge and lowered her body over the side, then hung there waiting for a second.

As she expected, the lead drone floated forward and appeared just above her. Before the operator at the other end of the connection could react, she reached up with her right hand and caught one of the drone's legs. Not giving the operator a chance to power the vehicle away, if that was possible, Annja jerked the drone into the side of the building.

Propellers shattered and the Plexiglas bubble cracked. Leaving the drone no time to recover, Annja smashed it against the wall again and let the wreckage tumble to the ground. The device broke into dozens of pieces.

The other two drones hovered out of arm's reach, watching Annja with camera lenses.

Growling in frustration, Annja released her hold on the roof and dropped. She landed on her feet fifteen feet below, her knees bent to absorb the shock.

The alley door of the building opened at almost the same time and a young man in slacks, a button-up and a tie stepped out. He offered Annja an inquisitive smile.

"Is this your car?" She spoke in Spanish and smiled, hoping that Basque wasn't the only language the man was fluent in.

"Yes. That is my car."

"I need you to move it."

"Of course." The man dug in his pants pocket and retrieved a set of keys with a silver fob. "I was only stopping for a moment. To make deliveries, you see." His attention shifted to the drones floating only a few feet away.

While the man's attention was occupied, Annja snatched the keys from his hand and raced for the car.

"Hey!" the man yelled when he realized she'd taken his keys. "Hey! Thief!"

The thief part hurt a little. Annja didn't consider herself a thief. She was only going to borrow the car for a moment. Using the fob, she let herself into the sedan and slammed the door shut just as the man reached her. She locked the door as he reached for the handle. He banged at the glass and started calling her much worse names than *thief*.

"Sorry." Annja mouthed the apology through the window.

Turning her attention back to the car, she inserted the key in the ignition and started the engine. She shifted into Reverse and pinned the accelerator to the floor. The car slid back at once, putting distance between it and its owner.

She backed out into the street with the drones hovering in hot pursuit. Narrowly avoiding locking bumpers with a passing truck, she skidded out onto the street and cut the wheels sharply, aligning the car away from the police cordon farther down the street.

The drones sped out of the alley in single file. A truck racing away from the gun battle drove into the lead drone, shattering it. Braking to a screeching halt, the truck driver stared through his cracked windshield at the mechanical parts spread across the hood of his vehicle. The remaining drone immediately gained altitude, rising up behind the stalled truck.

Annja shifted her borrowed car into gear and drove down the street. Her rearview mirrors revealed one of the police vehicles had pulled away from the cordon and was now dogging her. She focused on the street ahead and drove as fast as she dared.

San Sebastián was a long way off.

30

Taking cover in the museum's alcove, Sabre Race traded shots with the men who had come up from the building's basement. At least, to his way of thinking, there was no other place for them to have appeared from. Saadiya had confirmed the likelihood of that arrival after consulting the building's blueprints. She had hacked into the building's security system and checked the video logs, noting that the men hadn't arrived through the entrances.

He tracked one of the gunmen and squeezed the trigger of his assault rifle. The short burst knocked the man to the floor and splayed him out in a loose-limbed sprawl that revealed at least one of the rounds had struck flesh, not Kevlar.

Another man went down and two of the other gunners fell back from their positions.

Crouching, Sabre slung the assault rifle over his shoulder and picked up the rectangular bulletproof shield he'd carried in. He drew one of his pistols and moved forward, intending to take advantage of their opponents' retreat. He squeezed the first pistol dry in steady blasts, concentrating on laying down suppressive fire. Then he holstered the empty pistol in his shoulder rig and drew the one holstered at his thigh. As he'd known, he wasn't alone in his approach.

Garin walked in tandem to him, somehow managing to hide his large frame behind one of the rectangular bulletproof shields, as well. He finished with one pistol and drew another. One of his shots caught an assailant in the face, knocking him back.

"Sabre," Saadiya called over the comm. "I've identified the dead man outside. He's one of de Cerceau's mercenaries."

That didn't surprise Sabre. He thought he'd spotted the mercenary leader among the men who confronted them at the entrance, but he hadn't seen him again. "Roger that. At least we know who we're up against. Do you know how de Cerceau managed to follow Annja Creed here?"

If it hadn't been for knowledge Garin had of the man Annja Creed had reached out to for assistance in leaving California, the trail would have gone cold on the hunt for the Merovingian treasure. Sabre still didn't know where the Creed woman was going if she escaped them here, and he was sure this wasn't the final destination. The treasure wouldn't be in Spain. If she and her associates got away here, Sabre hoped Garin would know where to pick up the trail again.

"Negative," Saadiya replied. "I'm skip-tracing de Cerceau's movements now, but it looks like he and his team flew straight here only minutes after you took flight."

The truth undermined Sabre's confidence a little. "Then de Cerceau knows something we don't." The man had help or insight that they didn't have in their possession.

Ahead of Sabre, Garin stepped toward the wounded man. The gunman raised his weapon and Garin shot him again. When the man relaxed back this time, there was no fight left in him. Sabre wasn't surprised at the way Garin dealt so cold-bloodedly with the situation. That was one of the things that had eventually caused Sabre to leave DragonTech.

Stepping over the dead men, Garin trailed the retreating mercenaries into the stairway from the basement. One of the gunmen fired shots that smacked into the shield in Garin's hand and caused it to jump. Without batting an eye, Garin raised his pistol and fired four shots. The action locked open as the mercenary stumbled backward.

"Reloading," Garin bellowed, stepping back against the staircase wall.

Instinctively, following training he'd received while working with Garin, Sabre stepped forward and held up his shield, covering the two of them as best he could. He swapped the hands that held his shield and pistol so he could fire around the armor.

"Like old times, isn't it?" Garin grinned as he emptied the spent magazines from his pistols and shoved fresh ones into place. The low-level lambent light hollowed the hard planes of his face.

Despite the desperate nature of their task here, Sabre returned the grin, feeling a shadow of the old excitement. "It is."

When Garin was reloaded, he held up his shield and allowed Sabre to exchange his magazines, as well. Sabre's internal clock, the one Garin had trained him to have, counted down the seconds lost while they were reequipping.

De Cerceau and his people had time to rearm and dig in. Taking the basement wasn't going to be easy.

"Saadiya." Sabre holstered one of the pistols, kept the other and picked up his shield.

"Yes."

"There's a utility tunnel under the museum. Find out where it goes."

"I'm looking at the schematics now. If they're right, and they may not be, because there has been considerable work done in this area, I see at least five different points of exfiltration for de Cerceau and his people to take."

"We don't have enough people to cover all five," Garin said. "We should have brought more troops."

Not shocked that Garin had hacked into his private team frequency, Sabre moved in step with the big man as they crept down the steps. Blood stood out on the stairs, indicating some of the men they were chasing had been wounded.

Sabre cursed the situation. They didn't have enough people to cover all the tunnels. And those possibilities would only increase if de Cerceau and his mercenaries stayed in the tunnels leading away from the museum and chose other points of escape.

"Pick two of the most likely," Sabre said, "and the one farthest away. We'll roll the dice on this one." There was no other choice.

"Roger that."

At the landing at the bottom of the steps, Garin hesitated only a moment before stepping toward the next flight of stone steps. The tunnel was dark.

Sabre drew a pen flash from his vest and switched it on. He played the high-intensity beam around the tunnel and spotted black boxes about the size of a DVD case planted on the ceiling a few steps down. Red lights pulsed to life and started cycling faster.

"Get back!" Sabre dropped his pistol, then reached forward and caught Garin's arm. He dragged the man back up the stairs. The big man tripped and went down. As they fell, Sabre lifted his shield over them.

Sabre didn't hear the explosion. This close in, he went deaf almost instantly. He kept his eyes squeezed tightly shut and lay atop Garin. He kept the shield up, trying to protect their heads. Several stone fragments struck them, and one of them was big enough and hit hard enough to numb Sabre's arm. The shield slipped from his fingers.

Pushing himself off Garin, Sabre reached into his vest pouch with his free hand and snaked out a glow stick, cracking it to life. Orange light pushed back the oppressive darkness. He held it above Garin, surveying the other man. Garin's right eye was partially swollen shut and was still swelling.

Garin said something else, but Sabre couldn't hear the words, and he had no idea what language Garin was using, so he couldn't read his lips, either. Sabre suspected it didn't matter, because the man's scowl gave away the nature of the words.

Pushing himself to his feet, Garin stood and took out a pen flash. He switched on the beam and played it over the wreckage ahead of them. Shattered rock filled the throat of the tunnel. He kept the light out of Sabre's eyes but reached over to him, pressing a finger against the younger man's cheek. When Garin drew his hand back, his finger came away wet with blood.

Garin reached into his chest pack and took out a bandage. He peeled the paper from the adhesive and affixed the large square to the side of Sabre's face. As he worked, some of the feeling returned to Sabre's face and he felt the throbbing pain. He wondered how bad the wound was.

Garin turned to the tunnel and carefully negotiated the fallen rock as he made his way down.

Face alive with pain now, Sabre pulled out a mini-flashlight and his spare pistol and trailed after Garin. Spots floated in Sabre's vision and he felt nauseous, but he followed.

When they reached the basement area, the way was blocked with more fallen rock. Evidently, de Cerceau and his men had mined the tunnel, as well, to make certain they weren't followed.

Standing in front of Garin, Sabre directed his flashlight beam toward his own face, holding it under his chin. He spoke slowly. *Where is Annja Creed?*

Garin shook his head, then spoke slowly, as well, with his own pen flash revealing his features. *Escaped.*

Can we find her again?

We will. Garin scowled at the room and headed back up the rock-strewed stairs.

31

Annja stepped through the jet's doorway and found Ian waiting. He smiled brightly at her and offered her a bottle of water. "Welcome aboard again, Ms. Creed."

"Hi, Ian. Have you heard from Roux?" Annja felt a little better aboard the jet. She'd managed to escape the last drone and get away, but she was guessing Garin would be back on her trail soon enough. Still, the adrenaline payback was taking a toll on her system, making her irritable and tired at the same time.

"Mr. Roux expects to join us in just a few minutes, actually. I talked with him a few moments ago."

"He didn't take my calls." Annja accepted the offered water and walked back into the jet. She dropped her backpack into one of the seats and tried not to feel too upset that Roux had ignored her.

"From what I gather, Mr. Roux was busy gathering Dr. Racz and making certain Dr. Elcano was squared away. Then there was some difficulty with the local police. It seems nearly all of them are interested in locating you." Ian maintained his station at the doorway. Noticing the way his jacket fit, Annja knew the man was now wearing a shoulder holster.

"Are you expecting trouble?" Annja asked as she settled into a seat.

"I am *prepared* for trouble. I would rather we had a quiet flight."

Annja raised the sliding cover from the window next to her and peered out over the airport.

A pensive look twisted Ian's features and he hesitated

before speaking. "Ms. Creed, at the risk of alarming or offending you, you might want to reconsider peering out the window at the moment. The glass is rated bulletproof, but there are bullets that can get through even the most resistant defenses."

"I don't want to alarm you," Annja said, "but if the people who are chasing us show up to kill me, I don't think they'll settle for using a rifle. They'll probably just blow up the jet with a missile."

Ian thought about that, swallowed and gave a tight nod. "Perhaps you're right. Feel free to look out the window, in that case."

Annja did, but she reached in her backpack and pulled out the tablet PC, booted it up, then connected to the jet's onboard internet. She pulled up the information about Janos Brankovic and reached for her sat phone.

EIGHTEEN MINUTES AND one phone conversation that yielded pleasant results later, Roux arrived with Racz in tow. Roux looked totally composed, as if he'd been out for an afternoon of sightseeing. The history professor looked somewhat shell-shocked as he stumbled into the jet's main cabin and flopped into a seat. He was flushed and breathing rapidly.

"Are you all right?" Annja asked.

"I'm fine. I think." Racz swallowed and looked pale. "I just feel…undone. Waiting for your friend to show up in the museum, especially after the explosions, was difficult. It was a very trying experience."

Annja had seen information about the explosions on the news releases she'd downloaded. She felt bad for Evita de Elcano. "I heard about the explosions. I'm glad you weren't hurt, and I'm glad that Garin and de Cerceau didn't find you."

"As am I." Racz gave her a wan smile and tried to look

relaxed but couldn't quite pull it off. "I don't think Evita is going to ever welcome me again."

"Evita is going to be fine." Roux walked into the cabin with a drink in each hand. He sat in a seat across from Racz and held out one of the drinks to the professor. "Drink this. It will make you feel better."

As if in a daze, Racz accepted the drink and held it in both hands. "Evita's museum is *wrecked*."

"It is, and she also just received a few million dollars in funding that will pay for the necessary repairs and help her do some additions that she has wanted to do." Roux smiled. "Trust me. All in all, she's a very happy woman at the moment. You just didn't notice in all of the confusion. Now, drink up."

Racz lifted his drink and downed it like water.

Roux raised a skeptical eyebrow and took the empty glass from the professor's hand. Without looking, he held the glass above his shoulder. Ian took the glass and Roux made a small circle with his forefinger.

"You've just had a little more excitement than you're used to," Roux commented. "You're going to be fine."

"A *little* more?" Racz shook his head. "I've never experienced anything like the past two days."

Ian returned with another drink. Roux took it and offered it to the professor, who accepted it and knocked it back, too.

"Everything is going to work out for the best. I'm sure of that." Roux handed the glass back to Ian.

"Mr. Roux," the pilot announced over the radio, "we are cleared for takeoff if you're ready."

"As soon as you can, Tamara." Roux spoke in French as he scooted back in his seat and slipped on his seat belt.

Racz struggled with his seat belt for a moment until Ian leaned in and fastened it for him.

"Thank you," the professor said.

"My pleasure." Ian nodded.

"May I have another of those drinks?"

"Of course." Ian plucked the glass from Racz's hands as the jet jerked into motion.

"Where are we going?" Annja asked as Ian gave Racz the third drink and quickly made himself scarce.

Roux shot her a look. "Don't you have a destination in mind? Dr. Racz mentioned something about a casting of the Virgin Mary. He said you seemed quite excited by the discovery. I thought surely you would know where we needed to go. I only told Tamara and Jan that we would be leaving San Sebastián."

"We need to get to Kosice, Slovakia."

Roux raised his voice and spoke again in French, which Annja had been speaking, as well, even though she hadn't thought about it. "Tamara, did you hear that?"

"I did, sir. Jan will file a new flight plan once we're airborne, which we should be in the next seven minutes."

"Thank you." Roux returned his attention to Annja. "What are you expecting to find in Kosice?"

"Father Janos Brankovic's castings of the Virgin Mary."

Roux massaged his temple with his fingertips and gave that consideration. "As I recall, no one named Brankovic had anything to do with the statue of the Virgin Mary."

"No, but Brankovic supposedly made some preliminary castings of the statue after monks reported seeing the image of the Virgin Mary in György Dózsa's ear as he lay dying. Brankovic was there at Dózsa's execution and learned the stories."

"I've never heard that."

"You were around at that time." Joan of Arc had died in 1431, forty years before Dózsa had been killed. And Roux had already been an old man by the time of Joan's death. It was still odd, after all this time, thinking about Roux as a contemporary of so much history.

Roux glanced at Racz, but the professor's head had already lolled to one side in his seat. Swooping back into the cabin, Ian took the empty glass from Racz's hands just as it started to fall.

"Would either of you like anything else?" Ian asked as he looked at Roux and Annja.

"I'm good," Annja replied.

"I'll have another." Roux handed over his glass and Ian went away. He focused back on Annja. "Garin and I were both around at that time. I wasn't in Hungary then. I was… elsewhere."

"You? Not you and Garin?"

"No." Roux shifted in his seat and scowled. "After Joan's death, we didn't get along. I blamed him for our late arrival to save her, when truly I was the one to blame, but I took it out on him because he was supposed to keep my affairs in order. We parted ways shortly after that."

The way Roux and Garin refused to talk about their pasts was a constant source of frustration. They had both seen so much that she wanted to hear about.

"The tale of the monks seeing the image of the Virgin Mary probably didn't get around much," Annja said, "but it's there in the records. What's not in most of those records is that a monk named Janos Brankovic, who was a cousin to Pal Kinizsi, was a sculptor who first attempted to make a statue to honor the Virgin Mary."

"Attempted?"

"Brankovic died from the flu the winter after Dózsa's death. However, the castings he made of the proposed statue still exist."

"And those castings are in Kosice?"

"They are. In safekeeping with Brankovic's family. While I was waiting for you, I called the family. Before we got chased out of the museum, I'd located the family in Kosice. I talked briefly with a woman named Denisa Cierny, a descendant of Brankovic's family. She's expecting to meet us tomorrow morning." Annja sipped her water and swallowed to pop her ears as the jet gained altitude. "I'm just hoping we can beat Garin and de Cerceau there."

"Do you think Garin knows about Brankovic?"

"I don't know. The research is there."

"If he knows where to find it, and I assure you that there wasn't much time. Whatever arrangement Garin fostered with the local police was stretched thin after the encounter escalated to bodies in the streets. He didn't have time to look. He and those men with him were escorted from the museum. They may have even been arrested."

Annja hoped that was the case. "What about de Cerceau?"

"I've received no word of him, other than the fact that he and his men had gotten into the museum through an underground tunnel."

"How long were they in there?"

"I don't know."

"De Cerceau may know about Brankovic."

Roux waved that away. "If he did, I'm sure he would have gone there rather than pursue you. He wants the treasure, not you."

Annja knew that was true, but she still couldn't help thinking about how the mercenary leader kept popping up.

"I found the professor where you left him," Roux said, "and I got him out of the museum without getting caught up by the local police. They turned quite antsy once gunfire and explosions became evident. I'm sure Garin is going to be caught up for some time explaining his situation there. And de Cerceau will be hard-pressed to find a way out of Spain in light of his activities. The police are actively seeking him."

"De Cerceau will find a way to follow us if he's not captured." Annja knew that was true, and she also realized that it was highly unlikely the mercenary would be caught.

"Perhaps. However, for the moment, we are in the lead."

"I still don't understand Garin's interest in all of this."

"Nor do I." Roux tapped the rim of his empty glass with a forefinger and rested his chin on his other hand. "However, I have to assume that his presence here is because of something personal."

"Why personal?"

"Because he hasn't reached out to you or me, of course. If Garin saw a way to make this mutually beneficial, he would, if for no other reason than to lessen the risk."

"Why would this be personal?"

"One of my people did research on Sabre Race. As it turns out, he was once in Garin's employ."

"Doing what?" Annja asked, though she thought she could figure that out for herself.

"Pretty much what he is doing now." Roux shifted in his seat. "He worked as a mercenary. Afterward, when Sabre Race decided to take leave of DragonTech, Garin helped the young man start his own business in Los Angeles." He paused. "Which begs the question, was Garin involved in this thing from the beginning?"

Annja shook her head. "No. Sabre Race was working for Steven Krauzer. Krauzer only wanted the elf witch's crystal back."

Roux frowned. "You do realize how deplorable that sounds when you say it, right?"

Ignoring the question, Annja concentrated on the bigger picture. "If Garin stepped in because of Sabre Race, he had to have done it after de Cerceau got the crystal. What do you think the chances are that Garin can trace us?"

"Garin has many resources, and the world is an increasingly smaller place. I don't think he will have too much of a problem locating us again. I'm sure he can trace this jet." Roux dragged his fingers through his beard. "We could get rid of this aircraft and arrange for other transportation, but if Garin learns our ultimate destination, if we dally, he'll just get ahead of us. I would rather risk him finding us than him getting ahead of us."

"I would, too." Annja lay back against her seat and tried to relax but couldn't. She set her drink aside and pulled out her tablet PC. Still, her mind wouldn't leave the problem alone. "If it should come down to us versus Sabre Race, which way do you think Garin will go?"

Roux shook his head. "I don't know." His gaze softened as he looked at Annja. "It's better to let that sort itself out. If we can find the treasure before Garin does, we won't have to worry about that."

32

Early the next morning, with the sun still streaking the eastern horizon pink, Annja pulled the rented Porsche Cayenne Turbo S to a halt in front of a large stone house that squatted on a hill outside Kosice, Slovakia. At least, she assumed the vehicle was a rental. It had been waiting for them at the airport when they'd arrived the previous night. They'd spent the night in a bed-and-breakfast where the hostess knew Roux by name.

Anticipation had threatened Annja with insomnia, and it still thrummed inside her now. She always got that way in the final stages of a hunt, and she'd become certain this was the endgame. Thankfully, after trolling some of the alt.archaeology and alt.history sites she usually kept up with, she'd fallen asleep and had stayed that way until Roux had knocked on her door.

The weather held enough of a chill that Annja could see her breath when she opened the Porsche's door and stepped out. She wore a lightweight coat and tall boots. Spring was coming to Kosice, but winter maintained a jealous grip on the countryside.

She checked the time on her sat phone and saw that it was only 7:18 a.m. local time. Denisa Cierny had confirmed that morning by telephone that she was an early riser, but Annja still felt guilty intruding so early.

"Well?" Roux closed his door on the other side of the vehicle. He carried a straight cane in his right hand that Annja knew concealed a sword. He also carried at least two pistols.

Annja looked at him.

Imperiously, Roux pointed to the door with his cane. "Aren't you going to see to the door? You're the one who's been invited."

"Get up on the wrong side of the bed?" Annja asked.

Roux harrumphed as she passed. He'd been up talking with their hostess over breakfast that morning, and Annja wondered if he'd gotten any sleep. Although he hadn't said so, she knew Roux was conflicted over Garin's involvement in the hunt.

When she'd first met them, after recovering Joan's lost sword, Garin and Roux hadn't seen each other in a long time and had still been hell-bent on killing each other. Annja knew since her arrival the enmity had taken a different turn, softened a little. Maybe it was because she was part of their lives now, or maybe it was because the sword was once more whole and back in the world, which changed things in ways they didn't yet understand.

Or maybe the sword's return had been the opportunity to rekindle some of that old master-and-student relationship. She didn't know, but she didn't like the idea of Garin and Roux once more out for each other's blood.

Annja walked to the door and used the knocker clasped in the claws of a great-eagle plaque mounted on the door. She rapped three times and the thuds echoed within the building.

Thrusting her hands into her pockets, Annja turned back to look down the long hill they'd traversed to reach the house. The narrow, winding road barely left a gray trace through the leafy trees and tall grasses. The green landscape seemed to extend in all directions, but to the west she could see the tallest spires of Kosice proper. The city was a mix of modern and old architecture. She'd never been there before and would have relished a chance to wander around.

Still slightly hungover from the previous day, Istvan Racz stood with his hands jammed in his coat pockets and his hood up. He looked pallid and his eyes burned brightly.

He'd been quiet, not talking unless someone spoke to him. Annja wondered if he was having second thoughts about continuing with her and Roux, but when the time to leave had come, the professor had gotten ready.

Roux walked over to join Annja. "Knock again."

"Give her time. It's a big house."

"She knew guests were coming. She would have been ready."

Annja realized then that Roux wasn't being impatient. He was thinking maybe Garin or de Cerceau had reached Denisa Cierny first. Annja's pulse picked up the pace as she reached for the door knocker again.

The door opened before she could touch the heavy brass. A tall woman in her later years stood before them.

"You are Annja Creed?" the woman asked in English with only the trace of an accent.

Annja smiled. "Yes. You're Mrs. Cierny?"

"Yes, but please call me Denisa." She looked over Annja's shoulder at Roux and Racz. "And these are your friends?"

Annja made the introductions.

"Please come inside," Denisa said. "I'm sure you must be tired after such a long trip, and it is still cold this time of year. Especially if you're not used to it. You said you arrived from Spain?"

"Last night, yes." Annja followed the woman into the house and felt as though she'd stepped back in time. The furniture looked like new, but it was all original from the Victorian period. The fireplace was huge and a cheery fire blazed inside, throwing out heat Annja could feel across the room. "Your house is lovely."

Denisa looked around and smiled. "My house *is* lovely. I grew up here, as did several family members before me. My grandmother left me this house, and when I'm gone, I'll leave it to one of my granddaughters who loves it as much as I do. That's the proper way to treat a house—give it to someone in the family who loves it as much as you do. Someone who will keep it. That way the love stays within these walls." She turned her gaze back on Annja. "But you didn't come here to hear about the house. Come. I'll show you the family gallery and the things we have that Father Janos Brankovic created."

STEPPING OUT OF the house through a door off the kitchen, Denisa walked through an elegantly appointed garden to a building under tall trees. Only a few cold-weather plants and flowers were in bloom. The splotches of bright yellows and whites stood out against the dark green. A stone fence ten feet high encircled the grounds.

The gallery was a two-story squared-off building made of stone that looked as if it had been quarried from the same place as the stones that made up the main house. Here and there, pieces of mortar were missing, but it seemed to be in fine condition. The windows were smaller and had iron bars over them.

"Even with the walls, or perhaps because of the mystery those barriers created, we've had trouble with people breaking in over the years. Mostly they were young people who were curious and wanted to take a closer look, but there were others who attempted to take things." Denisa produced a heavy iron key from a sweater pocket and thrust it into the large iron lock in the hardwood door. "My grandfather chased a few would-be thieves from the grounds when I was just a girl. Those remain vivid memories for me. I thought it was all very exciting." She nodded toward the house. "I visited often. That was my room. Up there."

After the lock clicked, she turned the knob and followed the door inside. Old musk and the smell of paint hung heavy in the still air inside the building. Annja slipped a pen flash from her backpack.

"You won't need that." Turning to her right, Denisa

punched a short code into a cutting-edge alarm system and reached for a light switch. When she flicked the switch, bright light filled the building. "When I inherited the house, the first thing I did was get an electronic security system and install electricity. My grandfather liked to keep things as they were, but I chose to modernize and provide a constant environment. A few of the art pieces were ruined over the years from mold and a leaking roof. Finding those things always made my grandmother sad. I promised myself that would not happen while I lived."

Staring at the huge collection of paintings, statues and pottery, Annja felt sad at those losses, too. She recognized items that had to be hundreds of years old, judging from the craftsmanship and subject matter. She couldn't imagine the treasures that had been destroyed.

Denisa strode forward, brushing by Racz.

Annja stepped in behind the woman and followed her through a vast collection of art. Large murals covered the walls. Other pieces hung on freestanding walls. Cabinets housed pottery and carvings and objects Annja couldn't quite grasp.

A small room occupied the back of the first floor. Denisa paused to open the door and reach inside to flip on a light.

"This room was built to house Father Brankovic's work." Denisa stepped inside and Annja followed.

Almost fifteen feet to a side, the space was filled with old statues and castings of various sizes. Some of the pottery pieces had been fired and stained with colorful bisques. Deep reds, emeralds and blues drew the eye to shapes of ships, people and creatures.

Denise turned a hand toward the room. "Please feel free to help yourselves. Just do be careful. All of these things are irreplaceable."

Drawn by the beauty around her, Annja wandered the aisles and stared at the pieces. "We're actually most interested in the castings Father Brankovic did of the Virgin Mary. Are you familiar with those?"

"Of course. They are among Father Brankovic's first works." Denisa walked to the far end of the room and opened a cabinet mounted on the wall.

When the doors were open, six castings of the Virgin Mary with her head covered and dressed in robes were revealed. She looked fragile and innocent and so calm. The castings ran from one foot tall to three feet. All of the poses were similar, and they were all rendered from material so dark that they looked almost black.

"Since you came here looking for these," Denisa said, "I'm sure you've heard the legend of how Father Brankovic came to create these."

Annja nodded. "During the execution of György Dózsa, monks attending his death claimed to have seen the Virgin Mary in his ear."

"Strange to think something like that happened, isn't it? Yet there are several other stories that tell of appearances by the Virgin Mary."

"They're called Marian appearances. Usually she's only seen by one or two people, and the appearance is named after the town where the sighting took place. The Roman Catholic Church gets involved at that point because they have to verify the sighting through the Holy Office."

"The Congregation for the Doctrine of the Faith," Denisa said. "It was established to protect Catholic doctrine. When Father Brankovic heard the story of the monks seeing the Virgin Mary in Dózsa's ear, he made notes of their description and made these castings. Unfortunately, he died before the church ruled on the authenticity of the appearance. The task of creating the statue of the Virgin Mary passed to another artist. I have read his journals. He was so hopeful he would get to make the statue."

"Any of these would have been beautiful."

"I always thought so."

"May I see the journals?"

"Of course." Denisa led Annja to a large desk area that sat below a shelf containing several thick books. She looked at the spines, made a selection and brought the book down to the desk. "Those entries should be in this volume. Father Brankovic was very creative. In addition to the sculptures and pottery you see here, which is only a small amount of the things he made, he also sketched and wrote constantly. He made these books himself."

Reverently, Annja opened the book and looked through the pages. Frustration chafed at her when she saw they were written in Slovak, not Latin as she'd hoped. Annja didn't read any of the Slav languages well enough to get through the entries more than to establish dates.

"You don't read Slovak, do you?" Denisa asked.

"No." Annja hated feeling helpless. She glanced at Roux, who nodded, indicating that he did. She wasn't surprised. Give me five hundred years and I'd know a lot of languages, too, she thought.

"Then allow me." Denisa switched on a desk lamp over the pages and began reading in a strong voice.

33

"'I did not expect to like György Dózsa when I met him,'" Denisa read, trailing an immaculate finger down the lines of neat script without actually touching the page. "'From all accounts I had of the man, he was a dangerous and blood-thirsty criminal, a man who had raised up a rebellion among peasants who struck out at their masters.

"'However, I have been a man of God for twenty-three years and I have come to know that people are often viewed differently by their peers. Jealousies often preside and take over an historian's quill in the throes of writing what will become truth. I have read histories that were merely airy words and a waste of paper.

"'General Dózsa was a fit warrior in his middle years, a man of fierce temperament and resounding courage. I could expect nothing else. Pope Leo X had chosen the general because of his resolve and keen tactician's mind. If he had been properly outfitted and had gotten to march his troops against the Ottoman Turks, I have no doubts that he would have given a good accounting of himself. The Christian Crusade against our enemies would have advanced.

"'Instead, the general rotted in his cell and awaited the ugly end that he met on that fiery iron throne. I listened to his screams of horror at seeing his brother and his men slain before him, all the while begging his captors to spare the lives of those soldiers. I prayed for General Dózsa's soul, and that his torture might make a quick end of him. Alas, that was not to be so. The general lingered for a long time.

The scent of his charred flesh filled my nostrils and still I cannot cleanse my mind of that memory.

"'After General Dózsa died and his body was being prepared, I was surprised when the young monks claimed to see the Virgin Mary in his ear. I agonized over such a thing, that they might see then when I—who had spent time with General Dózsa for days beforehand—was not so blessed.

"'One more curious incident happened after General Dózsa's death. Two men rode into town the next day and asked after the general. They found themselves in trouble with the noblemen quickly, and were swiftly jailed. I visited them, as I do to all unfortunates that God chooses to send before me.

"'Neither of those men were talkative, but I gathered they were fighting men themselves. One was in his advanced years, but the other was much younger, a dark taciturn man whom I believed to be of Frankish origins who spoke only to the older man.

"'The older man asked me about General Dózsa and told me that he himself had served King Matthias Corvinus of Hungary as a member of the Black Legion. He said that King Corvinus had, on his deathbed, given him a task to find the lost treasure of the Merovingian kings, and now that General Dózsa was dead, the trail they had been following had also expired. He told me that they had learned of a captain who guarded the king's great library and was himself an indefatigable reader. That tale had brought them seeking General Dózsa.

"'I had to struggle to keep calm, because I knew of the story. General Dózsa had entrusted it to me, telling me that one of the Black Legion captains had read of the tale of the lost treasure in a book in King Corvinus's library before it was scattered. King Corvinus had only late in his life discovered the tale and had intended to follow up on the possibility that such a treasure existed.

"'When General Dózsa had told me the story and given me the possible location of the treasure, I must admit that I had at first thought it was just a tale a man told to make himself appear more important than he is. That was, however, at odds with the man I believed the general to be. He was important. He was just a man undone by the vagaries of fate. So I know of the Merovingian treasure.

"'I have, in recent days, wondered why I did not tell those men what I knew of the treasure. I have examined myself for weaknesses and failings, and I have asked myself if I was giving in to greed. Now I believe I was merely keeping General Dózsa's secret because he had entrusted it to me, and I should not just hand it out to anyone. I was being careful.

"'So I left the jail that night and kept my secret. Rather, I kept the general's secret. On the morrow, I decided to talk further with the prisoners and rethink my decision. I thought maybe I was being too cautious and that I was being given a sign to give up my uneasy burden.

"'That assessment was taken out of my hands, though, because when I returned to the jail, the two men were gone. Like desperate thieves, they had stolen their freedom from the iron bars and taken their leave. Four guards lay dead in their wake and orders were given for them to be hunted down and killed.

"'I could not follow them, for I knew not where they were bound, nor did I wish to suffer their unkind fates. I never learned their names.'"

"THE OLDER MAN," Istvan Racz spoke up, interrupting Denisa's reading, "was Vilmos Racz, one of my ancestors. He's the one who handed down the stories of the Merovingian treasures in my family."

The professor seemed hypnotized and didn't look well. Perspiration dotted his cheeks and his eyes looked too bright.

"Are you all right?" Annja asked.

"I'm fine." Racz turned away. "Fatigue is catching up with me, I suppose. These past few days…" He shook his head. "And now this." He looked at her. "Do you realize how close we are to finding that treasure? After all these years. But it's still just out of reach. It's maddening."

Racz walked away and sat in a chair, putting his hands together to support his chin as he worked on breathing.

Annja returned her attention to Denisa. "Is there any further mention of the Merovingian treasure?"

Denisa stared at her. "Do you think it actually exists?"

Before Annja could respond, Racz spoke up in a stern voice. "Of course it's real. My family has spent centuries looking for it. And to know…to know that Vilmos was so very close to finding it…" The professor left the rest of his thought unspoken, or perhaps he couldn't think that far.

For a moment, silence filled the room.

"There is more, but it's all confusing." Denisa turned a page to reveal an inked illustration of two men sitting on the floor of what had to be a jail cell. One of them looked to be in his sixties, worn and lean with a scraggly beard. The other was young, bearded and too familiar looking in worn clothing, but Brankovic had managed to capture that rebellious gleam in his eye.

"Wait." Annja stayed the woman's hand. "Are these the two men Brankovic talked to that night in the jail?"

"Yes. There are a lot of drawings he did from memory. I have seen some of the places he traveled to. Buildings still stand in a few of those places, and you can see how skilled he was."

"Oh, yeah." Annja waved Roux over to join her and pointed to the picture. "I think we know why Garin is so heavily invested in the outcome of this hunt."

Roux stood silent for a moment, taking in the image, then nodded. "That would explain it."

Dark and taciturn, defiance gleaming in his gaze, Garin Braden looked out from the manuscript page.

Temesvár
Kingdom of Hungary
July 1514

WAKING INSTANTLY AT Vilmos Racz's touch on his shoulder, Garin opened his eyes and saw only darkness around him. He shifted his gaze and picked up the wan light of a torch in a sconce hanging on the wall down the passageway from the cell where he and his friend were being held.

"Are you with me?" Vilmos asked. He crouched only a few feet away, and the torchlight flickered along his profile.

The years since the time they'd served in the Black Legion under Matthias Corvinus had been hard on Vilmos. He'd aged and been reduced to a much frailer version of himself. Seeing him as he now was, it was difficult to believe he'd once been a feared commander of warriors, a man to be reckoned with when he had a sword in hand.

Now he was old and vulnerable. But he was still driven.

"Of course, my friend." During the twenty years they'd served together and searched for the Merovingian treasure, Garin hadn't aged. On occasion Vilmos had mentioned this, remarking on Garin's good fortune to have his health for so long.

Garin had merely acknowledged the compliment but hadn't commented on it. He'd liked serving with Vilmos. Being in the Black Legion, fighting and traveling around the Kingdom of Hungary, had suited him. After he'd separated from Roux, he'd been lost, wandering from place to place and living however he could. He'd gathered fortunes only to see them slip between his fingers because he hadn't been disciplined.

Vilmos had seen greatness in him, the old man said, and

he'd worked hard to bring that greatness out of Garin. He'd taught him to be a good warrior, then a good leader and commander and to properly manage his financial affairs. Now, even after the disbanding of the Black Legion and the death of Matthias Corvinus, there were lands and a fortune that awaited him.

He owed it all to Vilmos Racz. And Vilmos had also taught Garin to pay his debts. But maybe some of that had come from riding with Roux for so long, too. Both of the old men were similar in that aspect.

"Where are we going from here?" Garin had no doubt about getting out of the jail. He and Vilmos had broken out of other places much more competently built and guarded. With General Dózsa dead, with the threat of the rebellion only a ghost of what it had been, security was lax. He'd briefly considered killing the priest who had visited earlier and using his robes as a means of disguising himself and getting Vilmos out of jail.

Vilmos hadn't wanted to kill the priest, so they'd waited.

"The Merovingian treasure is out there somewhere, Garin." Vilmos flashed a smile that almost erased a decade from his face. "I mean to honor King Corvinus's wish to find it."

"And then what?"

Vilmos smiled even more broadly. "Keep it, of course. Do you think me a fool?"

Garin laughed quietly at that. "We already have fortunes. Perhaps it's time to rest and settle down to enjoy the fruits of our labors."

"Is that what you want to do? Settle down?"

Thinking of the risks they were about to run during their jailbreak, of the adrenaline that would soon be coursing through his veins, Garin laughed again, but this time he laughed at himself.

"No. I don't want to settle down."

"Neither do I, and I want this treasure. Promise me this as my friend and as a warrior who served faithfully under me... promise me that as long as I or one of my sons still walks this earth, you will help find this treasure."

In that moment only a few hours before dawn, alive with the prospect of a violent death that would end his seemingly immortal life, Garin thought of everything Vilmos Racz meant to him. They had shed blood together and escaped death together, faced what could have been insurmountable odds at times and had enjoyed all that life had to offer when the times were good.

Garin had never had that with anyone else. He'd never found anyone he could trust so much. He had never found anyone who cared so much for him. Vilmos had treated him like a true son, not an adopted serf.

"I promise," Garin answered. With everything they had shared, there could be no other answer.

"Good." Vilmos grinned at him there in the darkness and unshed tears glistened in his eyes. "Now, let's leave this place before our captors decide to have a couple more executions in the morning." He pulled the picklock he carried from his hair and set to work on the lock.

"WHAT ARE WE waiting for?"

Sabre Race's voice drew Garin's thoughts back to the present. They sat in an SUV two miles from the house Annja Creed and Roux had headed to once they'd reached Kosice. When he'd learned where the jet was headed, Garin had called in a favor from associates who worked within the city to watch over Annja and Roux.

He shifted in the seat, remembering the hard floor of the jail cell. It was surprising what would stay with a man even after so many lifetimes. There were exotic meals, strange cities and romantic interludes that he knew he'd forgotten because he had learned he couldn't remember everything.

Yet he recalled that jail cell, that night, Vilmos and that promise with ease.

On those occasions that he thought of Vilmos Racz, as he did now, Garin couldn't help but miss the man. He'd been one of the first people Garin had lost in the inevitable forward march of time.

Vilmos had died only a few months later, struck down by a cruel knife blow from a jealous man. Vilmos had only been kind to the young woman the man had been interested in.

Garin had paid for Vilmos's burial, tracked down and slain the man who had killed him, and then returned to his friend's widow and told her of her husband's death. For a time, he had lived among Vilmos's family and helped out. But in the end, he'd had no other recourse than to leave. His agelessness and his own wandering nature pushed and dragged him back out into the world.

"We could go get her," Sabre went on. "Out there, she has no place to run."

"Don't underestimate Annja Creed." Garin chuckled, thinking of the times he had done exactly that. "Don't underestimate the old man, either. Right now we could be watching them and he could have a small army sitting right on top of us. After everything that happened in Ordizia, he's not going to leave himself open to attack. No, he knows we're out here. Or close by."

"Then what are we going to do?"

"We're going to be patient." Garin thought of Vilmos and him trading stories while lying in the jail cell and waiting for night to come. They'd done similar things dozens of times in the years they'd fought together. "It's something an old friend taught me to do. Try it." He folded his arms across his chest. "For right now, we're going to let Annja Creed do what she does best."

"What's that?"

"Find the answers we need." Garin smiled in anticipation.

34

"Have you found anything?"

Worn, tired and frustrated, Annja turned from Father Brankovic's dark-hued third casting of the Virgin Mary to glare at Roux. "Don't you think if I'd found something by now I'd tell you?"

Roux ignored her tone and short temper. "Actually, I thought perhaps you'd gone to sleep."

"With my eyes open?"

Roux shrugged. "It's been known to happen."

"I wasn't asleep." Annja turned back to the casting. After studying the casting for hours, she remained unenlightened.

Denisa Cierny proved to be a gracious host and insisted on preparing meals even though Roux offered to have a caterer deliver. After a short time in the kitchen, she returned with steaming bowls of thick stew, slabs of homemade bread and strong tea.

Denisa tried to remain on hand to find journal entries and translate Slovak. She had a good memory of the journals and was ready, willing and able to lend a hand. Father Janos Brankovic's later entries provided more hints and details about the man's search for the Merovingian treasure, but they didn't give away the location of where it might be.

Brankovic, Annja surmised, had to have been as frustrated as she currently felt. She touched the casting again, running her fingers along the surfaces. The Virgin Mary, as the artist always envisioned her, stood innocent and still, and it was the second smallest casting, no more than a foot and a half tall.

Annja glared at the statue, willing it to speak and share whatever secrets it might possess.

The only things Annja had noticed that were different about the third casting were the slight risings and the ridge line along the statue's back. She had taken a rubbing of those bumps and the ridge and raised them on the paper in a series of dark splotches that didn't quite make sense.

If she squinted at it just right, she thought the bumps made a map of sorts. But there was no way knowing what that map might reference.

She ran her fingers over the statue again, feeling the bumps and the ridge. At first she'd thought they might be irregularities, which had stood out against everything she'd seen in Brankovic's work. The man had been meticulous. If something was on a piece, then it was supposed to be there.

The stone felt cold and hard beneath her fingertips, almost like marble. Then she realized the truth about it.

She sat up straight on the chair she'd borrowed, heart thumping as she considered what she was thinking.

"This isn't a casting," she said quietly.

Roux, Racz and Denisa shifted their attention to her.

"What did you say?" Roux had been leafing through one of Brankovic's journals.

"I said, this isn't a casting." Annja ran her hands over the statue again. "The other figures of the Virgin Mary are true castings, made of plaster from molds Brankovic had made." She smiled. "This is a true statue, carved from a block of stone."

Roux joined her, bringing the journal with him. He placed it on the table and examined the statue more closely. "Is this marble?"

"No." Annja grinned more broadly as things started to come together in her head. "Although it's often confused with marble. This is limestone. Tournai limestone to be exact. The Romans had it quarried and shaped into all kinds of things, including baptismal fountains. They called it Tournai marble, but it's not marble."

"I don't see how that helps us."

"Brankovic didn't just choose his materials by some random whim. Everything he did was by design. Look through the journal that talks about the castings he did of the Virgin Mary. It only mentions *five* castings."

"But there are clearly six." Denisa stood on Annja's other side.

"Of course there are six. They were created to disguise this one. Because, if I'm right, it holds the location of the Merovingian treasure."

"You think the statue is a map?" Racz's voice was hoarse. He'd been looking worse for the wear over the past few hours.

"The statue *is* a map." Annja picked up the rubbing she'd done and held it up so the light shone through the paper and made the dots and the ridge stand out more. "Those dots are geographical reference points. And this—" she tapped one of the dots on the lower right side "—isn't a dot at all." She squinted at it, trying to make it out, then gave up and referenced the statue.

Using her digital camera, she took a picture of the statue's back, then used the built-in editing software to raise the contrast so the dot she was talking about stood out more sharply.

It wasn't just a dot like the other raised areas. The image clearly showed separations that put her in mind of a—

"That," Racz declared in a shaking voice, "is a key. Most likely, it is the Key of Shadows."

Annja turned to face the professor. "What is the Key of Shadows?"

Racz licked his lips and ran a hand through his hair. "According to the stories that were handed down by my ancestors, Childeric III knew that Pepin the Short was working to wrest the throne away from him. The Merovingian kings had been relegated to figureheads, more or less, and the actual power was used by the mayors of the cities. In order to keep Pepin from getting everything if that day came, Childeric set aside part of his treasure, seed money for himself or his family to attempt to retake the throne."

"We're looking for a key?" Roux asked.

"No." Racz shook his head and pointed at the statue of the Virgin Mary. "That is the Key of Shadows. It contains a map of where the treasure is hidden."

"This statue is like the key on a map," Annja said, understanding.

"It *is* the map key. But that's not going to do us any good if we don't know where to look. We have to know what area it references." Racz cursed and walked away. "Do you realize how close I am to finding that treasure?"

We, Annja automatically corrected, but she didn't say anything aloud, because her mind was already turning over other information she had. "This is Tournai marble."

"You said it was limestone," Racz pointed out.

"It is limestone, actually sediment left over from the Carboniferous Period, or the Tournaisian, depending on a geologist's preference. That was when amphibians and what eventually became insects dominated the world. There were very few land creatures, and even those remains are spotty. The lack of fossil records is called Romer's gap. Most geologists and archaeologists believe there was some kind of extinction event that took place."

"We're not talking about *dinosaurs*." Racz trembled. "We're talking about a king's fortune."

"What I was getting at," Annja replied, ignoring the almost-open hostility, "is that at the time, there was only one place people went to get this kind of stone. The city of Tournai—they called it Tornacum—was a small way station for Roman soldiers and merchants on the road from Cologne to Boulogne. They traveled along the coast and crossed the river Scheldt." She pointed at a rumpled layer of the Virgin Mary's robes. "I think this is the coastline, and this—" she touched the twisting ridge down the statue's back "—is the Scheldt."

"The river?" Racz's eyes narrowed. "You think that's the river?"

"I do."

"You can't match that to a map."

"Actually, I think I can." Annja turned to Denisa. "Could I see the journal that has the entries regarding Brankovic's journey to Tournai after Dózsa's death?"

"Roux has it there." Denisa pointed to the volume in the old man's hands.

Carefully, Roux placed the book on the worktable next to the statue of the Virgin Mary. "I just saw a map." He flipped through the pages until he came to a full page of topography.

Annja's gaze slid along the coastline, matching it to the one she imagined in her head. Everything fit, including the line that represented the Scheldt. She drew in a breath. "Brankovic made the map on this statue's back from this document."

She reached for the rubbing she'd done and matched it up to the geographical features on the map. Symbol by symbol, she matched up the dots to mountains, lakes and small towns.

Only one dot remained unaccounted for, and it was the one that looked slightly different from the others. Going back to the picture she'd taken of the statue's back, Annja flicked her fingertips across the screen and blew up the image.

There, revealed under magnification, was a symbol that looked like a circle with three spokes that crossed it like a wagon wheel.

"Brankovic was serious about his details."

"That is an IX monogram," Racz whispered.

"It is." Excitement coursed through Annja. "It's formed

of the Greek letter *I*, which stood for *IHCOYC*, Jesus in that language, and *X*, which stood for *XPICTOC*, Christ, again in that language. The Merovingian kings were all Christian." She looked back at the statue, which stood silent and serene. "Unless I'm wrong, and I don't think I am, that's where we'll find Childeric's treasure."

"Then we should get under way." Roux folded the journal under his arm and turned to Denisa. "Dear lady, I have to ask that you allow us to take this volume with us for a short time. I promise that no harm will come to it, but we can't leave it here to fall into the hands of the men who are following us."

Denisa hesitated. Then she looked at Annja.

"We'll bring it back when we're finished," Annja said. She hoped that the woman would go along with Roux's request because the old man was capable of simply taking the book. He'd already gone out of his way by asking permission.

Some of the worry left Denisa's face, but not all of it. She probably sensed the same conclusion. "For you. I will let you take Father Brankovic's journal for a time. It will give you an excuse to come back for another visit."

Annja smiled. "I will."

"Well, then," Roux said, "let's go."

LEAVING DIDN'T TURN out that easy. According to the young woman Roux talked to on his sat phone, the house was surrounded by Garin and his people, as well as de Cerceau and his men.

Standing at the window in the large living room, feeling the welcome heat of the fire soaking into her back, Annja glared into the darkness that covered the landscape. She hadn't realized until that moment how much time they had spent at Denisa Cierny's home.

And now that they knew the possible location of the Merovingian treasure, they were cut off from escape.

Roux sat by the fire in a wingback chair and talked to Denisa as though they were old friends. Annja knew he was working to allay her fears about parting with Brankovic's journal, but she also believed Roux had developed a fondness for the independence Denisa obviously showed.

"What are we supposed to do?" Racz swayed nervously back and forth beside Annja.

"Wait."

"Those men might get tired of waiting and decide to come after us."

"If they do, we'll deal with it. For now, this is in Roux's hands."

"What is he going to do?"

"He's already done it." Annja gazed up into the dark sky and spotted a sleek shark shape sliding through the low-lying clouds. A moment later, the helicopter's spinning rotor became audible, thundering inside the house.

"THEY'RE COMING." ANNJA WATCHED from the cockpit of the helicopter rising from the front yard of Denisa's estate as vehicle headlights raced toward the home. There were at least a dozen of them speeding along the twisting roads. Sparks jumped from the sides of the vehicles and she recognized them as gunfire.

"It won't matter," Roux replied from the backseat. "They won't arrive in time."

The ground fell away as the pilot powered up the rotor to gain altitude. One of the vehicles suddenly blossomed into a fireball and careened into the forest a quarter mile away from Denisa's home. Annja hoped it wasn't Garin, then hoped he'd lost their trail this time but knew that probably wasn't the case. The man was nothing if not tenacious.

"The forest will catch on fire." Denisa looked out one of

the windows in the back of the helicopter. Roux had convinced her to join them in departing the grounds, though she had done so reluctantly. "My house could be destroyed."

"Your house will be fine," Roux assured her. "The proper legal authorities have been summoned, and the fire department has also been notified. They'll have everything in hand soon enough."

Annja hoped so. She didn't like thinking about Denisa losing her home. She put that out of her mind because she didn't have any control over that. Instead, she turned her attention to the image on her phone, hoping that she had figured out everything and that something yet remained of whatever the Merovingians might have left.

35

The Lille-Lesquin Airport in France lay only seventeen miles from Tournai, Belgium, which was just across the border. Roux's private jet arrived at the airport just after 3:00 a.m. after the flight from Kosice. Even though Roux managed to make most of the arrangements before they touched down, it still took time to gear up and to put Denisa Cierny into a safe house under the protection of security specialists.

The woman had looked exhausted when Annja had last seen her, but she'd been filled with excitement over the outcome of the hunt, as well. Roux had spent the flight showing her how to play Texas Hold'em, and she'd turned out to be surprisingly good. Roux had staked her $1,000, and she was up another $6,000 by the time they got to Lille, France.

Annja also suspected Roux was playing to occupy Denisa's attention and probably throwing the game, as well, but she hadn't paid much attention, because she'd been busy combing through the facts she had learned about the Merovingian dynasty.

Denisa's house was fine, which Annja was glad to learn, but someone had gotten inside before the police had arrived on the scene. There were also dead bodies strewed along the roadside leading up to the estate. Roux left instructions with Denisa's bodyguard to keep the news from their unexpected guest for as long as possible. Those details would be better dealt with, Roux said, when more things were settled.

Bleary-eyed but somewhat rejuvenated by a hot cup of tea, Annja snatched the keys from the college-age clerk who had delivered a rented steel-gray Range Rover Autobiography.

"I'm driving," Annja declared. She was tired of being a passenger, and the eagerness to get to the hunt filled her.

"Of course you are." Roux didn't look happy, but he seemed unwilling to invest in an argument. He hoisted up the basket that contained the breakfast they were going to eat on the road and clambered into the passenger seat.

Without a word, looking gaunt and antsy, Racz took a seat in the rear of the vehicle. Annja already had her foot on the accelerator and was headed for the airport's exit gates before the professor had locked himself into the seat.

AN HOUR LATER on a service road that followed the river Scheldt, satisfied she'd accurately followed the directions she'd ciphered out from the map and the statue, Annja pulled onto a dust-covered side road. They'd made the trip in relative silence, each of them occupied with his or her own thoughts. Annja knew she was on the verge of collapsing from adrenaline overdrive. She'd snatched a fitful nap while on the plane, and she was currently running on empty.

Six miles later, Roux pointed to a side road that was almost concealed by thick tree growth. "Pull over there. I have to speak to a man so that we can get permission to drive onto the property."

Racz leaned forward and surveyed the forested hills that lay before them. "Who owns this place?"

"Me, actually," Roux replied. "At least, I will as soon as the mortgage companies open this morning and the documents are made legal."

"You bought these lands?" Racz sounded incredulous.

"I did. It seemed simpler than trying to figure out who owned the treasure once we find it. If we own the land, we own the treasure."

"You don't even know that the treasure is here."

Roux shook his head. "I don't *know*, that's true. But I have faith in Annja. If she says it's here, it's here. She's never been wrong before."

Where Tournai proper lay in a basin alongside the Scheldt, the surrounding lands formed part of the upper rim. The incline rose a few hundred feet above the city miles away. Rough forested areas that looked relatively unchanged over the past few centuries stood on either side of the dirt road. Here and there, huge shelves of black rock thrust through the uneven landscape.

Annja checked her rearview mirrors often, but other than a dust cloud that followed them in perpetual pursuit, she saw nothing. Still, the vague feeling that Garin was out there somewhere wouldn't leave her thoughts. He hadn't been detained in Kosice, and he hadn't been among the dead.

"Here." Roux pointed ahead to where a dark red sedan sat parked in front of a gate marked Private Property in French, English and German.

Annja pulled the SUV to a stop a few feet from the red car. As she did, a man in dark business attire got out of the vehicle with a slim, expensive briefcase in hand. The man smiled and waved.

"Good morning, Jean-Luc," Roux said in French. He stepped down from the SUV and walked over to shake hands with the man.

"Good morning, Mr. Dowd. I trust your flight went well."

"It did indeed. Thank you. I assume the offer to your corporation was met with approval."

Jean-Luc smiled and Annja got the distinct impression the man thought he was getting the better of Roux. "The offer did indeed meet their expectations, but the board of directors was surprised at what you intend to do with the place." He pulled out a sheaf of documents.

Roux smiled magnanimously. "What? Don't people routinely buy castles in ruins with the hope of restoring them to their former glory?"

Jean-Luc laughed. "I've never heard of it."

"Well, then, later you can tell people you were the first to do this. One of my side corporations produces reality television. We believe there's a market for a show based on revitalizing a castle."

"Really?"

"Otherwise you wouldn't be getting my money," Roux assured the man. "Shows have been made about so many other things. Cakes, renovations of bathrooms, inaccurate histories of villains and supernatural creatures."

Annja guessed the latter was a pointed barb at *Chasing History's Monsters* and chose to ignore it, but she would remember it. She and Roux would have a more in-depth conversation at a later date.

"Well, I wish you well on the project, and I'm certain you'll have a hit on your hands before you know it," Jean-Luc said. Though he smiled, the expression lacked any real confidence.

"You have the documents prepared for my signature?" Roux waved toward the briefcase.

"I do indeed." Jean-Luc placed the briefcase on the front of the car and snapped the locks open. He reached inside the case and took out a tablet PC. "Electronic documents, just as you asked." He powered the device on.

"Splendid." Roux took the stylus the man offered and scrawled his name across several digital pages. When he was finished, he handed the tablet and stylus back to the real estate agent. "I believe that's everything."

Jean-Luc checked through the pages and nodded. He took another moment to upload the files through the internet service in his vehicle, then handed over a key that he said was to the gate. He shook Roux's hand once more before climbing back into his car and driving away.

"Well," Roux said, pulling on his sunglasses, "let's go see what I've paid for, shall we?"

He walked over to the gate and used the key to open the industrial-grade padlock. Once the way was unlocked, he swung the gate open wide on rusty, shrieking hinges. Annja liked the sound. It meant no one had been this way in a long time.

After Annja drove the SUV through the gate, she waited for Roux to lock the barrier and return to the vehicle. She drove south, using the vehicle's GPS and following the topographical map she'd put on her sat phone.

Only a few minutes later, still grinding steadily upward, Annja caught her first glimpses of the ruined castle sitting at the top of the hill. Staggered piles of cut stone lay partially claimed by trees and brush. Two of the walls remained standing, but both looked as if they'd taken severe beatings over the past centuries.

Seeing the state of disrepair, Annja felt all hope she'd held on to that there would be something to discover fade.

"There!" Racz pointed, leaning forward against the seat restraint. "I see it!"

Less than a hundred yards from the broken-down castle, Annja stopped the SUV because finding a path through the trees was becoming problematic. The underbrush was thick and could mask ditches or stumps that would disable the vehicle. She switched off the engine and got out, walking to the back of the vehicle, where Roux was already sorting through the equipment they'd brought. He handed her a headset, which surprised her. Normally, he didn't go this high-tech.

Roux looked at her, noticed her disbelief and shrugged. "We're out here alone, and Garin has been nipping at our heels. I thought it best if we claimed any edge we might have. Staying in touch when we might have to separate seems like a good idea."

Annja wrapped the headset into place and checked the

connection while Roux handed another headset to Racz. She had to help the professor put his headset on because he wasn't familiar with it.

"Did you find out anything from Jean-Luc about the castle while you were negotiating the purchase of this place?" Annja strapped a SIG Sauer P226 to her hip and tied down the holster. She opened her backpack and added extra magazines for the pistol and for the AK-47 assault rifle that Roux pushed toward her. She was familiar with both weapons and hated the need for them. The potential presence of Garin and de Cerceau necessitated carrying them, though.

"Not anything that we didn't already know." Roux strapped on two P226 pistols, one at his hip and another in a shoulder rig. He ended up looking like a very lethal senior soldier of fortune. Instead of an AK-47, he carried a Dragunov SVDS sniper rifle with a folding stock. "The castle was established under Childeric I to provide a garrison for guards to protect trade along the river outside town. It was supposed to replace the Roman soldiers when they started pulling back as a result of the Germanic migrations and invasions. Merchants lived there, as well, and it was a small town outside Tournai proper. Over the years, the fortress fell into ruins as the city's defenses built up."

"The merchants living there probably got tired of paying taxes to the king," Annja said. "When the city fortifications built up enough, they probably wanted to take advantage of that."

"What about me?" Racz asked.

While shoving grenades into his thigh pockets, Roux turned to the professor. "What about you?"

"Don't I get a gun?"

"Do you know how to use one?"

"Yes." Racz matched Roux's silent stare for a moment. "I've been around them a few times."

"Then the answer," Roux said gruffly, "is no, you're not

getting a gun. It's going to be dark in there, and I don't relish the thought of being shot in the back by someone who is supposed to be helping me. I don't make it a practice to arm amateurs when there's a chance I'll be shot by them."

Racz's voice rose. "You can't just let me go in there unarmed."

"If we're lucky, we'll be in and out of this place before anyone knows it."

"And if we're not lucky?"

"Then I suggest you run away from any such person. Very fast."

"If you thought we were going to be lucky, you wouldn't have brought all those weapons."

"You're right. I wouldn't have." Roux rummaged in the back of the SUV for a moment, then came out with a five-cell flashlight that was almost as long as Annja's forearm. He handed it to Racz. "Here. If you have to, hit your opponents. I recommend using the big end."

For a moment, Annja thought Racz was going to throw the flashlight to the ground in disgust. Then the professor breathed out and took a firm grip on the handle.

"All right." He looked out at the castle. "Can we get started?"

In answer, Roux slammed the cargo door and locked the vehicle with the key fob, and they headed out on their trek to the castle.

As THE SUN rose higher in the sky, the day grew hotter. Annja had stripped off the lightweight canvas jacket she'd worn against the morning chill and tied it around her waist.

She didn't know what she was looking for or even if it might be there. Whatever Childeric III had hidden could have been stolen away years ago. Pepin the Short could have found the treasure or someone could have chanced upon it later.

It might even have been taken away by the soldiers who had been stationed there. Soldiers got bored, and bored soldiers either got drunk or went looking in places they weren't supposed to be looking.

"Annja," Roux called over the headset she wore. His voice was quiet and focused, and the intensity spiked her anticipation. "Have you found anything?"

"If I had, I would be calling you." Annja didn't bother to filter the frustration she was feeling. "So what have you found?"

Roux laughed softly. "Come to me. I want to show you something. Slowly and carefully. I don't want you to scare them."

"'Them'?"

"Come see."

Heart beating a little faster, Annja headed in Roux's direction. They'd split up and headed in different paths around the fallen fortress. Racz followed her, still carrying the flashlight.

On the other side of the castle ruins, Roux sat hunkered down in tall brush. Only the top of his gray head showed above the leafy foliage. He spotted her and waved her down.

"Stay low. I can show you this without them, but I'd rather you see it for yourself."

Curious, Annja crouched and circled wide to reach Roux. When she got to his side, he pointed at a tumbled mess of rock buried mostly in the ground.

"What?" she asked. Then movement caught her attention near the bottom of the rock pile.

Two slender, furry bodies dashed from the shelf of rock and frolicked in a patch of sunlight in the tall grass. Given how small the creatures were, Annja thought at first they were squirrels. Then she noticed the creatures' longer necks, larger ears and elongated plump bodies. Darting and dodging, they played and scampered in mock combat.

"Weasels?" Racz cursed in disbelief. "You're looking at weasels?"

At his tone, the young animals forgot their play fighting and scurried back in among the rocks.

Roux stood and approached the rocks. "Not weasels. Martens. They're indigenous to Belgium, but with the population density in this country, you seldom see wildlife like this."

"Why would you be so interested in those things? We need to be looking for a way in."

"Martens, like a lot of mammals, want warm, dry places to sleep," Annja said. "They don't live in the trees, so there has to be a den around here."

"We're looking for a den?"

"Yes," Roux replied crossly. "These creatures were heavily hunted in Europe by fur trappers for many years. They're also considered pests when they live in town because they crawl up into parked cars. They like to gnaw on things and end up doing a lot of damage to those vehicles."

"You're worried they may damage the car?"

Roux knelt and picked up a scrap of cloth from the ground. The remnant wasn't much bigger than Annja's palm and consisted mostly of gnawed edges and faded colors. He displayed the cloth to Racz. "No, I think they might know how to get into the castle."

He held up the scrap, and though the image was only a memory of what it had been, Annja could see the outlines of an armored knight.

"Unless I miss my guess, that's part of a Flemish tapestry," Roux said.

"Tournai was known for its tapestries." Annja held the moldy cloth and looked at it more closely. "The weavers there were part of the Flemish Hansa of London." She picked at the tapestry for a moment, then looked around, searching for more. "This hasn't been lying outside for long. Otherwise it would have disintegrated by now. Judging from the condition, it's probably only been out here a few weeks."

Roux nodded. "That means those little furry fiends brought it from within." He leaned down, unclipped a flashlight from his vest and shone it into the hole under the rock. "There's a tunnel." He gazed around at the uneven ground. "Looks like this part of the castle has emerged due to soil erosion. The structure was definitely underground at one point." He returned his attention to the hole in the ground. "We're going to need a shovel to get to it."

Dropping to the ground beside Roux, Annja peered into the space. It was almost big enough for her to crawl into, and it definitely led to a larger area.

Farther back, four sets of eyes gleamed a demonic red. Annja hoped they weren't a sign of things to come.

36

Covered in a slick coating of mud because the ground was still wet from recent rains, muscles burning because she'd done most of the work with the shovel, Annja went forward through the tunnel on knees and elbows. She had a miner's lamp strapped around her head that lit the way. Carefully, she continued to crawl, dragging her backpack at her side.

The tunnel stank of age and earth, but it was relatively dry because the opening angled up from where it emerged under the fallen stones. As Annja crept along, she tried not to think that it might all shift and fall on her, either crushing her instantly or trapping her inside the empty space.

The farther she crawled, though, the more excited she became. She'd found other bits of tapestry, which gave her more hope that she was headed toward something. Judging from what she could make out of the tapestry portions, they weren't all from the same piece. All of the fragments had gone into her backpack for later examination.

Given the angle of the tunnel, she guessed that she was crawling into the hill and would end up underneath where the castle had once stood. Her breath puffed out and pushed up little dust clouds. Perspiration soaked her blouse.

A dozen feet farther on, the tunnel widened enough that she could stand. After she did, she added her miniflashlight's beam to the light put out by her lamp.

The lights skated across the remnants of a small room. Stone walls encrusted with tree roots that stabbed through the crumbling mortar stood on three sides. A dark doorway lay in shadows under a snarled gob of roots that partially covered the opening.

In spite of her excitement to see what lay beyond the door, Annja played her miniflashlight's beam across the floor. A thick layer of damp earth mostly covered the stone floor, but patches of the cut rock showed through in places. The soil erosion hadn't always flowed down the hill.

Several small animal tracks stood revealed in the earth, showing where the martens and other larger mammals had walked.

The tracks disappeared into the doorway, definitely indicating more space lay beyond.

"Well, that's a bit of good news." After coming to a stop beside Annja, Roux aimed his flashlight at the tracks in the mud. "Nothing human has been this way in a long time." He pointed his beam at the doorway and drew one of his pistols, flicking off the safety.

"Why do you have the gun?" Racz stood behind them.

"In case whatever made those tracks is still with us." His voice echoed slightly in the room.

Racz didn't say anything, but his flashlight shifted as he gripped the handle more tightly.

"Shall we?" Roux asked Annja.

Taking out her own pistol, Annja crossed the room to the doorway. As she entered the passageway, the light from her headlamp and miniflashlight chased the darkness back, revealing huge sections of hammock webs that hung from the ceiling. Large spiders moved jerkily through the strands.

Rather than disturb the spiders, Annja squatted and duck-walked under them. The spiders continued moving only inches above her head. She had to ignore the crawling, itching feeling in her hair, telling herself that it was just her imagination. Then Roux swiped a hand across her hair and a large spider slapped against the wall and dropped to the floor before scurrying under rock debris that crunched underfoot.

Mouth dry, hair still itchy, Annja kept moving forward.

Eleven steps farther on, she came to a three-way inter-section. She shone her flashlight over the other two tunnels. She went to the right, a habit she'd learned when exploring unknown places. In case she got lost, she had a way of fig-uring out how to get back to her starting point. She took a piece of yellow chalk from her backpack and marked the wall, tagging it with the direction indicated by the compass she carried.

The new passageway curved slightly, making it hard to see what was coming ahead. Twenty-seven steps later, the flashlight lit up the bottom of a stone staircase that led up fifteen feet to a doorway partially filled with fallen rocks.

Staying close to the wall, Annja picked her way over the rocks that covered the steps. She paused at the doorway and cast her light over the large room ahead.

Rocks filled three-quarters of the room, blocking off all exits that surely existed except one to Annja's left. The re-mains of several campsites at the bottom of the rocks left her feeling dismayed. Charred wood sat in clumps, surrounded by crushed beer cans and cigarette butts. Soft-drink bottles lay on their sides.

"We're not the first ones to come this far," Roux said. "It looks like some of the local young people found a way in at some point."

Annja made no comment and pressed on, crossing the floor to the doorway and going through. The next room was larger and held more campsites, and it was empty of fallen rocks, though the ceiling bulged conspicuously above them. Cracks showed through the mortar, and pieces of the ceiling seemed on the verge of crashing into the room.

"You aren't disappointed that this place isn't pristine, are you?" Roux asked.

"A little," Annja replied.

"It's nothing to be concerned about. Many of the greatest

finds in history were discovered in places explorers thought they knew."

"I know. Archaeologists are still finding tombs in Egypt." She moved into the next passageway and followed it, realizing they were going deeper into the broken remains of the castle. The soft scrape of their footsteps and the occasional crunch of a rock underfoot echoed, letting her know considerable empty space existed before her.

A wide door opened to a huge room on her right. She aimed the flashlight inside and saw more campsites across the floor. Piles of rubble had been scooted out of the way to make room for transient visitors.

The walls on either side of the room contained ragged cracks. Rocks had broken loose and lay spilled inside the room nearly six feet from the original wall.

But on the other side of the room, the wall was solid. Covered by grime and spiderwebs, chipped by debris, the wall featured a ten-foot-by-twenty-foot section of dark stone that had been chipped out of what looked like black marble. Dust coated it in a gray patina, giving it a faded and worn appearance.

Beneath the dust and debris, a woman stood more to the right of the section.

Drawn by the woman's beauty, wanting to see more of what lay beneath the dust, Annja crossed the room. She stopped and wiped dust from the woman's face. The figure, like the rest of the scene, had been carved of stone, rendering the image in bas-relief, and fitted so precisely together that it was difficult to see the seams. Most of the small lines disappeared even more once the dust was removed.

"It's the Virgin Mary." Roux stood beside Annja, playing his light over the sections her dusting revealed.

"I know." Annja holstered her pistol, slid her backpack off and positioned her miniflashlight on a rock so the beam shone onto the wall. She worked with both hands and used her jacket to knock dust from the stone, steadily revealing what lay beneath.

Within a few minutes, with Roux working beside her, the image was revealed. It was, as Annja had thought, the Virgin Mary. The nimbus around her head gave her away immediately. She stood in front of a mounted knight on a battlefield. Plate armor covered the warrior from his shoulders to his knees, leaving his head bare. The armor and the broadsword placed the time at around the ninth or tenth century. The knight's head was bare, turned so that he was calling to the troops who stood ready behind him.

"Do you recognize the knight?" Roux asked. The confidence in his voice betrayed the fact that he believed he knew who it was.

"Childeric III," Annja said. The profile was the same as the one that had been struck on coins during the king's reign. "This castle was built under Childeric I's rule, over two hundred years before Childeric III became king."

"Childeric I was a lothario," Roux said. "After he'd seduced the wives of many of his nobles, he was exiled from the country for eight years. It wasn't until he helped defeat the Goths that he was once again recognized as king of the Franks."

"Why did Childeric III have this wall built?" Annja studied the scene, taking in the wide swath of warriors. "Designing this, even if it was done here, took a long time. Probably years."

"The castle would have stayed in the family." Roux reached out to touch a spot where a piece of the stone mural had either fallen out over time or been knocked out.

Other bare places stood out as well, revealing the stone wall behind the mural. Tool marks scarred several of those places, showing where someone had dug into the mural, either to see what lay behind it or to take souvenirs. The campers who had littered the area might have claimed some of those stones as keepsakes for bragging rights to prove they'd been to the castle ruins.

"Childeric III didn't do this on a whim." Annja stepped back from the wall, taking it all in again. "He had a reason. And the stone is Tournai marble. The same as the statue Janos Brankovic made."

"You think the choices are connected?"

"They have to be." Annja considered the string of information that had brought them here. "The manuscript Julio Gris left mentioned the treasure, and it was a message hidden within a message."

"As was Brankovic's Virgin Mary. Also a message in a message."

Annja touched the cool surface of the stone.

"The Virgin Mary was carved here first. Then it was turned into a statue by Brankovic." Annja paused. "No, that's not true. The monks saw the Virgin Mary in Dózsa's ear as he lay dying." Excitement coursed through her. "What if they didn't see the Virgin Mary?"

"Then the Catholic Church would have a problem on its hands. They verified the story was true." The light reflected from the mural lifted Roux's sardonic smile from the shadows. "But if we follow your logic, perhaps they were two monks whose faith wasn't just in God."

"They were listening to the ravings of a dying man who was holding on to a secret." Annja searched the mural and ran her hands across it more slowly. "Maybe they were caught trying to get information out of Dózsa."

"And they covered that up with the story of the Virgin Mary. Half truth, half lie."

"It could be that Dózsa told them some story about the Virgin Mary that put the suggestion in their minds so that they saw her in his ear."

"God does work in mysterious ways."

Annja combed through the stories that she had heard

while at Denisa Cierny's home. "There was something Racz said. Something about the Key of Shadows."

"He said the statue was the key."

"Or maybe there's more than one key."

Distant voices reached Annja's ears, and from the hollow way they carried, she knew they hadn't come from outside the castle. She turned to face Roux. "Did you hear that?"

Roux nodded. "We're not the only ones in here." He drew his pistol and picked up his light as he glanced back. "Where is Racz?"

Annja pointed her flashlight behind them. Istvan Racz was nowhere to be seen.

37

Clad in bulletproof armor and carrying a machine pistol, Garin Braden moved silently through the forest. He peered through the surrounding foliage and looked for the people who satellite telemetry indicated were ahead of him. He knew they were somewhere in the forest because his team had found their vehicles—and the men who guarded them—a quarter mile back. They'd parked that far away so the engine sounds wouldn't carry to Annja and Roux.

"Look sharp," Inge whispered in his ear. "You're only forty meters or so from the unfriendlies. Don't want to give away the element of surprise, now, do you?"

"Not hardly." Garin put his back to a tree and peered at the jumble of rock ahead of him. He let the machine pistol dangle from its shoulder strap and took a pair of microbinoculars from his chest pack. He pulled them to his eyes and scanned the fallen castle.

Three men in combat gear and camouflage uniforms stood near a pile of broken rock about seventy yards from the main body of the castle's remains.

"I count three guards," Garin said.

"Roger that," Sabre Race replied. "Confirm three guards."

"Inge?" Garin prompted.

"Same," she answered coolly. "Confirm three guards. *Outside.* They won't be guarding an empty tunnel."

"Do you know if they are de Cerceau's men?" Garin couldn't think of anyone else who would be there.

"I've matched one of them to the men you crossed paths with in Kosice."

"If they're not part of de Cerceau's crowd, the other two should pick their friends better." Garin put his binoculars away. "Snipers."

"Ready, sir," a male voice and a female voice replied.

Turning to peer around the tree, Garin pulled the machine pistol into his hands. "Take them down."

A second later, two of the men dropped bonelessly as suppressed rounds punched through their faces. After seeing what had happened to his mates, the third man tried to run and tried to search for where the attack was coming from at the same time. A bullet caught him in midstride, whipped him around and punched his body to the ground.

Garin led the move forward, flanked by Sabre on his right. When he closed on the dead men, he spotted the tunnel behind one of the bodies. Reaching down, he fisted the uniform and yanked the corpse clear of the opening.

He dropped to his hands and knees beside the opening, took up the machine pistol and peeked around the edge. Darkness filled the tunnel after only a few feet inside, but thirty or forty yards distant, a light gleamed.

Garin rolled away from the tunnel mouth and looked at the man photographing the three dead men on the ground. The man stepped back and tapped on the camera quickly, then put it away.

Holding his position, Garin opened the comm. "We're sending pictures."

"I've got them," Inge replied.

"Are they all de Cerceau's people?"

"Affirmative. Two of them have outstanding warrants in Bern."

"How did de Cerceau beat us here? We followed Roux's jet as quickly as we could."

"De Cerceau had to have known where Roux and Creed were going before we did. That's the only explanation I have. No one could have gotten you here faster than I did."

That answer didn't sit well with Garin. He believed Inge's assessment of her abilities. Even with the police attempting to stonewall him in Kosice, he and his people had gotten free in short order.

Sabre knelt beside him. Concern chiseled the young man's face. "Those are de Cerceau's men?"

Garin nodded.

"How did they get here so quickly?"

"They're working with someone inside," Garin said.

Sabre grimaced. "My brother's doing, no doubt."

Memory of the two brothers as boys touched Garin's mind fleetingly. Istvan had been the older brother, supposedly the one who would take up the family legacy of looking for the Merovingian treasure, but the stories had captured Sabre's dreams. Of the two, Sabre had always been closer to the grandfather.

"Okay, get your men ready," Garin said. "We're going in, and they're going to know immediately that we're there."

WEARING NIGHT-VISION GOGGLES, de Cerceau stepped through the darkness carefully and followed the chalk marks on the wall to the stone stairwell built into the wall. He paused at the foot of the steps when he spotted the soft glow of artificial light through the doorway at the top.

A shadow blotted out the brightness for a moment as it passed through, then started down the steps. The person walked carefully in the darkness, feeling for each step and keeping one hand on the wall.

De Cerceau lifted his rifle, keeping his sights on the man. So far there had been no unexpected encounters. Following Annja Creed and her companions had been easy.

Now there was the excitement of this tumbled-down wreck to sort out.

"Stop where you are," de Cerceau ordered in a low voice.

The shadow stopped moving immediately and raised its arms. "It's me," a man's voice replied. "I brought you here."

"You're SEEKER4318?"

"I am."

"Prove it."

The man quickly recited the Swiss bank account de Cerceau used to funnel the man's payments through. Slowly, the man lowered his arms, gaining confidence from his declaration. "You work for me."

De Cerceau let that pass. Officially, he *was* still working for the man, but as soon as the treasure proved itself real, all bets were off. He lowered the rifle and signaled to his men to do the same.

"Where is Creed?"

"Deeper inside the castle. Only a short distance away. You have to be quiet. They're armed."

The fact that the old man and the woman were armed didn't worry de Cerceau. They were only two people, and he'd brought a lot of men with him. The mercenaries stood behind him in the tunnel.

"Is the treasure there?"

"I believe so. We haven't found it yet, but it has to be here."

"Take us there," de Cerceau said. "It won't matter if they're armed."

"I want Annja Creed alive," the man said. "I'll need her to find the treasure."

De Cerceau agreed. Arguing now would only make problems. Killing them all later wouldn't be difficult. And he planned on doing that anyway to tie up loose ends.

"I want a weapon. They wouldn't give me one."

De Cerceau nodded at the man closest to his employer. The mercenary handed over one of his pistols.

The man took the gun and made a show of checking the

action and making sure a round was chambered. Then he turned and walked back up the steps. "Follow me."

Three steps behind, de Cerceau trailed him up the stairs.

HOLDING HER PISTOL in one hand and her miniflashlight in the other, Annja eased forward and stopped when she heard a foot scuff on the other side of the entrance she faced. Hiding was no use. The light had already announced her presence.

"Don't shoot," Istvan Racz said. "It's me."

"Come through the door slowly," Roux ordered. He kept his pistol centered on the door.

A moment later, Racz stepped out of the darkness into the beams of light. He held his hands up above his head and shut his eyes against the brightness.

"Where did you go?" Roux demanded.

"I had to relieve myself."

Roux grumbled and lowered his weapon. "The next time, tell someone before you wander off."

"Sure." Racz gave a little embarrassed shrug and lowered his hands. Then, more quickly than Annja expected, the man's hands reappeared holding a pistol.

Annja barely had time to recognize the threat before Racz fired three shots from less than ten feet away. All three bullets struck Roux with meaty slaps.

Not believing what she was seeing, not comprehending that three bloody holes now stood out on Roux's chest, Annja moved, reaching the old man as he toppled. She caught him, tried to hold on to him, but she couldn't keep him from going down. She went with him, cradling him as much as she could.

Behind Racz, Kevlar-clad men stepped into the room.

Lying on his back in Annja's arms, Roux exhaled once and was still. His open eyes stared up at nothing.

"Roux!" Annja stripped off her shirt, leaving herself clad only in an undershirt, and worked frantically to stanch the wounds. Grief threatened to overwhelm her, but she forced herself to move. The blood was still pouring out of him. *"Roux!"*

Just as she was about to start CPR, knowing that she would risk losing the old man to blood loss while she worked on him, a calloused hand wrapped around Annja's upper arm and yanked her to her feet.

"Get up," de Cerceau ordered as he put his pistol under Annja's chin.

Annja considered her chances of fighting back. Her hand stretched out and she felt the sword hilt in the Otherwhere.

De Cerceau grinned. "Try it and I'll leave your brains scattered all over your grandpa's corpse."

Seeing all the men grouped behind de Cerceau and Racz, knowing she'd never make it out of the room, Annja stood still as de Cerceau relieved her of her pistol and rifle.

"All right," the mercenary leader said. "Let's go find that treasure."

38

"Roux!"

Annja's voice, filled with pain and incredulity, froze Garin in his tracks as the echoes of three shots faded into the cavernous depths of the castle.

"Roux!"

The agony in Annja's cry tore at Garin. There was no way the old man could be dead. For years they'd risked their lives doing things other men would never have dared. And for some of those years they had tried to kill each other. Unsuccessfully, obviously. He'd come to believe it wasn't possible.

"Garin." Sabre stood at his side staring at him.

He nodded. Annja needed help. He forced himself to concentrate on that.

Garin went more quickly now, almost at a run as he sped around corners and spotted the chalk marking on the wall. He followed it to carved stone steps, then went up. At the doorway, he moved more carefully, then went through two rooms before he spotted the pool of liquid on the stone floor.

Kneeling, Garin took off a glove and touched his fingers to the pool. It was still warm and oily. He wiped his hand on his pants and replaced the glove.

Whoever had killed Roux wasn't going to live to see the outside world again.

None of them were.

"YOU KNOW WHERE the treasure is," Racz yelled at Annja.

She stood before him, defiant even though she faced a roomful of mercenaries. The old man's blood stained her undershirt; she could see it in the combined light of all the lanterns de Cerceau's men had produced. The beams reflected from the surfaces of the Tournai marble mural on the wall.

"We didn't find any treasure." Annja spoke in a cold voice, but pain showed in her eyes.

She was angry with him. Racz knew that and accepted it. Being angry after he'd killed her friend was a natural thing. But her anger wasn't going to prevent him from getting the treasure.

"The treasure is *here*." Racz made himself speak in a normal voice, but he felt that it was on the edge of cracking in his frustration. "I know it's here. We followed all the clues. We found those manuscripts. We found the statue Brankovic did of the Virgin Mary." He pointed the pistol in his hand toward the mural of dark stone. "We found *this*. It's here."

"Where?" Annja demanded. "Where is the treasure? Because I don't see it."

She looked past Racz at de Cerceau. "I hope you got your money up front, because there's nothing here to get."

"That's not true." Racz pointed the pistol at her.

"If you pull that trigger," de Cerceau stated quietly, "you'd better know where that treasure is."

"What?" Racz turned to face the big man. "What did you say to me?"

Bathed in the lantern light, de Cerceau's face was hard and unforgiving. "I didn't come all this way just for the money you were paying. I came for the treasure."

"The treasure is mine." For an insane moment, Racz almost turned the gun on de Cerceau. The only thing that kept him from doing that was the knowledge that he would be dead before he could pull the trigger.

De Cerceau glared at him. "You'd better hope you find that treasure."

Racz turned back to Annja. "She'll tell me. One way or

another, she'll tell me. Women try to keep secrets from you, but I know how to get those secrets out of them." He tucked the pistol into his waistband and took a folding knife from his pocket. "A scalpel would do the job better, but I can still get those secrets with this."

Light splintered from the razor-sharp knife's edge as Racz stepped toward Annja.

"Now you'll tell me," Racz said in a voice as tight as tungsten steel. "You'll tell me what the Key of Shadows holds secret."

Annja took a step back toward the mural. Her gaze was focused on the blade in Racz's hand, but her mind was sifting through facts and images. The Key of Shadows. The Virgin Mary had been at the center of all of this.

A thought struck her and she held up a hand. "Wait. I think I know what it means."

Racz held back and his eagerness played out on his face. "Tell me."

Drawn to the mural, Annja stared at the image of Mary, following her outlines until she spotted the almost-invisible penumbra that lay to Mary's side. Part of it touched on Childeric III's sword pommel, and there the stonework was darkest.

With a steady hand, Annja reached for the stone and felt along its edges. It stood out higher than the other stones around it. With the dark canvas of the black Tournai marble, the slight difference wasn't noticeable.

But she could feel the difference.

She pushed on the stone, but nothing happened. Leaning closer, she saw that the fittings around the stone were wider, more gapped, than they were elsewhere on the mural. There was room around the stone to slip her fingertips in and maybe to move it.

Room to *twist* it.

Like a key.

Before she knew what she was doing, Annja twisted the stone to the right. It took some doing, but it turned.

Something inside the wall grated. The stone floor vibrated, and a four-foot section of stone at the base of the barrier recessed and slid up into the wall, leaving a square opening filled with darkness.

Slowly, Annja leaned down and peered inside. She shone her miniflashlight inside. The bright light bounced off the stacks of gold that filled crates in the underground room beneath the wall.

"The treasure." Racz started to say something else, but his words were cut off by a sudden explosion of gunfire that filled the room with thunder.

Mercenaries at the back of the pack were mowed down. Others scattered throughout the room to take up positions to return fire.

Annja knew instantly that the gunfire was from Garin and his people. No one else would have been able to find the castle. He'd been there the whole time at their heels. She only wished he'd gotten there in time to save Roux.

"Into the treasure room!" de Cerceau roared. "Take cover there." Following his own advice, he grabbed Annja and shoved her through the entrance.

They fell through the opening and landed ten feet below. Annja got the worst of it when she was pinned by the big man's bulk. Recovering quickly, still searching for her breath as she and de Cerceau scrambled to their feet, she reached for one of the mercenary leader's pistols.

He backhanded her, knocking her sprawling across the spacious room. She tripped and tumbled through the crates of treasure, knocking a stack of gold ingots loose. The bulky chunks of gold clunked to the stone floor in the spinning shadows cast by the moving lights from above.

Snarling curses, de Cerceau aimed at her and fired three times in rapid succession.

Annja was already in motion, and she was in the darkness outside the glowing pool of light cast by the lantern de Cerceau had dropped when they'd plunged through the hidden door.

Bullets thudded into the gold and the crates.

Crouched, taking cover as other mercenaries tumbled into the room, Annja reached into the Otherwhere and pulled the sword into the room with her. The weapon felt steady and sure in her hand as she rounded a crate. She remembered the way Roux looked when she'd last seen him, and there was no mercy in her heart.

She slashed the first mercenary she came to, burying the sword in the space between his shoulder and neck. The blade cleaved down into his chest. The pistol he'd been trying to bring to bear slid from his hand as he died.

Moving swiftly, following the sword, Annja caught the pistol in the air before it hit the floor. She turned, immediately facing another mercenary, and lifted the pistol into the man's face. Annja squeezed the trigger, then moved on.

She darted around one of the four thick stone columns that supported the stone ceiling. Quivers ran through the floor, and she wondered if all of the noise from the weapons in that room and the room above would collapse the building.

That was only a small thought in a whirlwind of others, lost as she concentrated on tactics and position and tried not to think about Roux.

She left the cover of one column and raced to the next. Other mercenaries had retreated into the room. She swung the blade one-handed and disemboweled a man racing toward her. As the man tripped and went down, she fired the pistol three times into the two men who followed the first, putting them down with shots to the face.

On the move again, making a circle in the room, Annja

ducked as one of the mercenaries came up firing. Bullets zipped over her head. She twisted and turned, getting strength and momentum behind her, and threw the sword at the shooter ten feet away.

The sword sailed true, piercing the body armor and the man. Shocked, the dying man went back and down, releasing his weapon and grabbing the sword. Another mercenary reached for the sword, but Annja called it back to her and his gloved hands closed on air.

He looked at her, and she placed a bullet between his eyes as the sword reappeared in her hand. After the bullet left the gun, the pistol's action locked back empty.

Annja tossed the pistol away and stripped another from a dead man who toppled through the hidden entrance to the room where all hell had broken loose. Before she could move, an arm snaked around her neck and pulled her backward.

"I'm still going to open you up, Ms. Creed," Racz growled into her ear. "I'm going to find out all your secrets." His knife flashed toward her face.

Annja pulled the sword up and blocked Racz's arm, cutting into his flesh. Surprised, he squawked in pain but tightened his hold and tried to stab her with the knife anyway. She brought up her captured pistol and fired blindly over her shoulder, guessing where Racz's head was.

Cursing, Racz released her then and pulled his knife back. Stepping from the man's embrace, Annja spun and swung the sword backhanded in a swing parallel to the floor. The keen edge caught Racz under the chin and plowed through his neck. His eyes blazed with hatred and his mouth was pulled back in a sneer when his head toppled from his shoulders.

"Kill her!" de Cerceau roared from the shadows.

Annja leaped over Racz's falling body as bullets slammed

into his flesh and blood. She ran forward, trying to see through the web of darkness.

A mercenary stood before her and took aim with his rifle. She fired the pistol, never breaking stride, but the bullets didn't find their mark or the body armor deflected them. She dropped into a baseball slide, skidding across the dust-covered floor, and collided with the man, taking his legs out from under him. He fell face-first but managed to release his rifle and catch himself before his head hit the ground.

Reaching over him from the side, Annja hooked her forearm at the base of his skull and smashed his face into the stone floor. He shivered, then went still. Annja rolled to her feet as a fresh fusillade of bullets tore into the unconscious mercenary.

Grenades exploded in the room above. The noise seemed barely audible over the din in the room. Dead men and shrapnel toppled into the room.

A mercenary spun around one of the columns ahead and leveled his assault rifle. Annja dodged left, ducking behind the column he was using for cover. Bullets ricocheted off the wall to her side. Keeping close to the column, she hurried around to her right, trying to reach the man before he could adjust.

The mercenary spun quickly once he'd figured out what Annja was doing. He came around firing, muzzle flashes cracking the darkness again and again.

Annja swung the sword and knocked the man off balance. The blade didn't cut into the body armor, but the blow was hard enough to pin him up against the column. Scared, maybe surprised to still be alive, the mercenary tried to raise his rifle. Pointing the pistol from almost point-blank range, Annja fired and the man's struggles ceased.

Breathing heavily, not certain where anyone was anymore, Annja held her position as the dead man fell to the floor. Gunfire in the outer room had become sporadic. She moved forward, senses alert.

A shadow separated from the wall underneath the hidden opening. The lack of light and the haze of gun smoke trapped in the room made it difficult to see.

Lifting her pistol, Annja took aim.

"Annja, behind you." Roux's voice sounded weak and thready. He fired his pistol twice and the muzzle flashes revealed the blood staining his shirt.

Spinning, still stunned by Roux's appearance after she'd thought him dead, Annja spotted de Cerceau staggering back, driven by Roux's bullets. Then the dull click of Roux's weapon firing dry barely made it through the ringing in Annja's ears.

With a large grin, de Cerceau raised his weapon. "You people are dead."

Annja fired her pistol dry, aiming at center mass even though de Cerceau's armor would prevent penetration, while she ran at him. When the action blew back and locked, she dropped the pistol and called the sword into both hands. Staring down the barrel of the assault rifle as it swung in her direction, Annja whipped the sword down.

The keen edge cut through the assault rifle and de Cerceau's hands, leaving him staring fearfully at the bloody mangle at the ends of his arms. Before he could speak, Annja brought the sword down again, cleaving the mercenary leader from crown to chin. She kicked the body backward, freeing her sword.

Panting, the stink of cordite burning in her nose, Annja looked around at the room full of treasure and dead men.

"It's just us, I think." Roux fumbled with his weapon and slid a fresh magazine into place.

Not believing what she was seeing, Annja walked toward him. "You're not—"

"Dead?" He frowned in mock annoyance, but his features

were pale and bloodless. "That wasn't the first time I've ever had cause to fake my death." He ran a hand over his chest, smearing blood over his shirt. "But that was far closer than I've been in a long, long time." He wobbled unsteadily.

Annja let go of the sword back into the Otherwhere and wrapped her arms around the old man, helping support his weight. She knew he needed treatment. Tears slid down her cheeks and she let them come.

"Is he still alive?" Garin, his face spattered with blood, leaned in from the hidden door and aimed a flashlight at Roux and Annja. Sabre Race joined him at the door.

"Yes, but we need a medic."

"We have one." Garin spoke briefly to Sabre, and then both men climbed through the door and lowered themselves into the room. Garin's first order of business was Roux. He bent and easily cradled the old man in his arms. Then his gaze wandered around the room. "We're splitting this, right?"

"You're going to have to talk to Roux. He owns the castle."

Garin grinned. "Of course he does."

EPILOGUE

Six days later, still in Tournai, Annja stood on a sixth-floor hotel balcony overlooking the river Scheldt. The wind blew through her hair, chilling her, but not enough to make her don a jacket.

The announcement of the find at the old castle had been in all the media, which had drawn a lot of attention. Annja's messaging service was filled with calls and emails. It was going to take a while to get everything sorted out, but she was looking forward to the work and to the papers she'd be able to write about the Merovingian kings when she'd gone through the documents Childeric III had left among the treasures.

"Have you ordered breakfast yet?" Dressed in a robe, Roux walked cautiously out to the balcony. His hair and beard were rumpled, but his voice sounded strong.

"I did. It should be here soon."

Roux pulled out one of the chairs ranged around the small patio table. He sat gingerly, his face going white with the pain he was dealing with.

He'd undergone surgery to remove the bullets, and the doctors had been amazed at his vitality. As soon as he'd regained consciousness and a little strength, he'd arranged for private medical care in the hotel. Annja hadn't fought him. She knew how stubborn he could be, and she wasn't about to argue with someone who could take three bullets to the chest and walk away from it.

She turned and rested a hip against the balcony railing, studying him.

"Are you going to loiter all day?" Roux reached for one of the newspapers on the table and opened it. "You haven't spent any time in Tournai. A city that is *filled* with history, and you're not bothering to go see any of it."

"Actually, I have."

"When?"

"After you had your pain meds. They put you out for hours and you snore unbearably."

"I don't snore."

"You do." Actually, he didn't, but Annja didn't like Roux feeling he was too perfect.

"Well, if I snore, I should be allowed. It's probably the damage from being shot."

"If you say so."

"Has Garin been here?"

Annja smiled at the neediness in Roux's voice. During the surgeries, Garin hadn't left the hospital. He'd even flown in specialists to follow up on Roux's recovery, though Roux didn't know that.

Garin had also spent part of the first few days dealing with Sabre Race. Even as evil and twisted as his brother had turned out to be, Sabre had lost family and that loss had hit the young man hard. Garin helped him through some of it, and worked out the legal issues so Sabre could return home.

She wasn't sure, but she believed Garin had given Sabre some of his share of the treasure.

Despite her gentle but insistent questioning, Garin hadn't talked much about his time with Sabre Race or the man's ancestors. Whatever Garin had experienced back in those days of the Black Legion, he was hanging on to it.

For now. Annja hoped to get the story one day.

"Garin's been here *every* day," she told Roux.

"I haven't seen him."

"You sleep a lot. He already knew you snored. He said it's the worst he's ever heard."

"Garin will lie to you." Roux turned the page, allowing Annja to see the photographs of the castle ruins above the fold. He wouldn't say so, but he didn't mind preening over the success of their quest. "Has he been back out to the treasure room?"

"He has."

"And you've made certain one of my people has been with him every time?"

"I have."

"Because he'll rob you blind if he thinks he can get away with it."

"Roux, he carried you out of the castle."

"You could have carried me out of the castle."

"He wouldn't let me."

"Maybe you could have insisted a little more strongly."

Annja thought about arguing that point, but Garin pushed the breakfast cart out onto the balcony. The covered dishes gleamed in the morning light.

"I saw the waitstaff outside your door and thought I'd bring it." Garin parked the cart by the table and sat, then helped himself to a plate. "I figured I'd join you for breakfast. Annja said you were up and around."

"Did you pay for that meal?" Roux asked.

"Of course not. I signed off on your room number." Garin didn't hesitate about piling his plate high.

Roux appeared on the point of arguing, but Annja crossed to the table and sat. "There's enough to go around," she said, and started preparing a plate for Roux.

"That's what I keep telling the old skinflint about the treasure we found in the castle, too." Garin glared at Roux.

"You would never have found that treasure if it hadn't been for—"

"Me, actually," Annja said. "I'm the one who figured out where the treasure was. And I say there's enough to share."

She looked meaningfully at Garin. "Even after the tax people get through with it."

Garin nodded sullenly. He had wanted to "disappear" the treasure before any of the authorities got a chance to make an accounting of it.

"Neither of you *needs* a treasure." Annja fixed a plate for herself. "You both have treasures enough to last you several lifetimes. Money isn't an issue. You both just love the hunt."

Neither of them disagreed with her.

"That said, during my little sojourns away from the apartment, I happened across a legend in one of those books Childeric III had saved in his vault." Annja buttered a piece of toast and knew without looking that she had the full attention of both men. "I thought maybe we could discuss whether it was worth following up on a legend concerning Saint Eligius. I trust you've heard of him?"

"He's the patron saint of goldsmiths," Garin said. "Of course I've heard of him."

"Well," Annja said, "Childeric III came by an interesting story about Saint Eligius that involves a mystical caduceus and a misplaced temple dedicated to the Greek god Hermes. I thought we'd talk about that."

As they ate and talked, it struck Annja she was a far cry from that orphan child who had grown up in New Orleans. She was a woman with a bright, interesting future.

And a family she could rely on.

* * * * *

COMING SOON FROM

GOLD EAGLE

Available December 1, 2015

GOLD EAGLE EXECUTIONER®
FINAL ASSAULT – *Don Pendleton*
When the world's first self-sustaining ship is hijacked and put up for auction, terror groups from around the world are scrambling to make an offer. Mack Bolan must rescue the hostages and destroy the high-tech floating fortress before it's too late.

GOLD EAGLE SUPERBOLAN™
WAR EVERLASTING – *Don Pendleton*
On a desolate ring of islands, Mack Bolan discovers that a reactive volcano isn't the only force about to blow. A Russian mercenary and his group of fanatics are working to destroy America's network of military bases and kill unsuspecting soldiers.

GOLD EAGLE STONY MAN®
EXIT STRATEGY – *Don Pendleton*
One reporter is killed by a black ops group and a second is held captive in Mexico's most dangerous prison. But when Phoenix Force goes in to rescue the journalist, Able Team learns that corruption has infiltrated US law enforcement, threatening both sides of the border.

UPCOMING TITLES FROM

KILL SQUAD
Available March 2016
Nine million dollars goes missing from a Vegas casino, and an accountant threatens to spill to the Feds. But with the mob on his back, the moneyman skips town. Bolan must race across the country to secure the fugitive before the guy's bosses shut him up—forever.

DEATH GAME
Available June 2016
Two American scientists are kidnapped just as North Korea makes a play for Cold War–era ballistic missiles. Determined to save the scientists and prevent a world war, Bolan learns he's not the only one with his sights set on retrieving the missiles…

TERRORIST DISPATCH
Available September 2016
Atrocities continue in the Ukraine and the adjoining Crimean Peninsula, annexed by Russia in March 2014. With no end in sight, a plan is hatched to force American involvement by sending Ukrainian militants to strike Washington, DC, killing civilians and seizing the Lincoln Memorial as protest against their homeland's threat from Russia. Can Bolan bring the war home to the plotters' doorstep?

COMBAT MACHINES
Available December 2016
What began in a Romanian orphanage twenty years earlier, when a man walked away with ten children and disappeared, leads Mack Bolan and a team of Interpol agents to fend off a group of "invisible" assassins carving their way across Europe…toward the USA.

THE EXECUTIONER

DON PENDLETON'S

"An American patriot and Special Forces veteran determined to extinguish threats against both the United States and the innocents of the world."

The Executioner® is a series of short action-thrillers featuring Mack Bolan, a one-man protection force who does what legal elements cannot do in the face of grave threats to national and international security.

Available *every month* wherever Gold Eagle® books and ebooks are sold.

SPECIAL EXCERPT FROM

Check out this sneak preview of
FINAL ASSAULT
by Don Pendleton!

"We need a new plan," he said, looking toward the building where the majority of the fire was coming from.

"The plan is fine," Spence snapped. "It was fine until you had to start making changes. I shouldn't even be here! I'm not a goddamn field agent!"

Bolan didn't waste his breath arguing. Instead, he looked up. The sun was starting to rise. Once they lost the dark, they'd also lose the only real protection they had. The militants would realize they were facing only two men, and they'd swarm them. Bolan and Spence had to take the fight to the enemy.

Bolan popped a smoke canister free from his harness and pulled the pin. He lobbed the grenade over the wall and immediately grabbed for another. "Get ready to move," he said as he sent the second spinning along the narrow street. Colored smoke started spitting into the night air.

"Move where?" Spence demanded.

"Where do you think?" Bolan asked, pointing toward the building. "You said we needed to bring a gift, right? Well, how about we give them the best gift of all—dead enemies."

"Enemy of my enemy is my friend, huh, Cooper?" Spence said in a tone that might have been admiration. He grinned. "I can dig it."

"Then on your feet," Bolan said, freeing a third smoke grenade from his combat harness. He hurled it toward the building as he vaulted over the wall. Smoke flooded the street, caught in the grip of the sea breeze. He and Spence moved forward quickly, firing as they went. They took up positions on either side of the doorway. The smoke was blowing toward them and into the open building. The gunfire had slackened, and Bolan could hear coughing and cursing within.

He caught Spence's attention with a sharp wave. Spence nodded, and Bolan swung back from the door and drove his boot into it. Old hinges, ill-treated by time and the environment, popped loose of the wooden frame with a squeal, and the door toppled inward. Bolan was moving forward even as it fell, his weapon spitting fire. He raked the room beyond, pivoting smoothly, his UMP held at waist height. The gunmen screamed and died.

Bolan stalked forward like Death personified, his gun roaring.

Don't miss
FINAL ASSAULT by Don Pendleton,
available December 2015 wherever
Gold Eagle® books and ebooks are sold.

DON PENDLETON'S MACK BOLAN

"Sanctioned by the Oval Office, Mack Bolan's mandate is to defuse threats against Americans and to protect the innocent and powerless anywhere in the world."

This longer format series features Mack Bolan and presents action/adventure storylines with an epic sweep that includes subplots. Bolan is supported by the Stony Man Farm teams, and can elicit assistance from allies that he encounters while on mission.

Available wherever Gold Eagle® books and ebooks are sold.

GOLD EAGLE®